SPLENDOR IN THE GLASS

TAMAR MYERS

SPLENDOR IN THE GLASS

A DEN OF ANTIQUITY MYSTERY

AVON BOOKS
An Imprint of HarperCollinsPublishers

MF

This is a work of fiction. Names, characters, places, and incidents are products of the author's imagination or are used fictitiously and are not to be construed as real. Any resemblance to actual events, locales, organizations, or persons, living or dead, is entirely coincidental.

AVON BOOKS
An Imprint of HarperCollins*Publishers*
10 East 53rd Street
New York, New York 10022-5299

44404176

In memory of my father-in-law,
Charles E. Myers

Acknowledgments

While some of the glass pieces in this book are figments of my imagination, others are described and pictured in *Lalique,* by Jessica Hodge, published by Thunder Bay Press.

SPLENDOR IN
THE GLASS

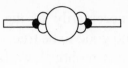

1

I left Charlotte, North Carolina, to become an S.O.B. I now live south of Broad in the beautiful, historic city of Charleston, South Carolina. My new hometown boasts so many churches that it is fondly referred to as the Holy City, and it is no secret that God lives here—south of Broad, of course. Just blocks from my house is the Battery, where the Ashley and Cooper rivers meet to form the Atlantic Ocean. Everywhere I turn I see historic buildings and lush semitropical gardens. There is no need for me to ever travel again. After all, I am *here*.

My business is here, as well. The Den of Antiquity, which was a successful antique store up in Charlotte, now has a sister store on prestigious King Street, slightly north of Broad. I never dreamed sales would be this good. I can barely keep up with demand, and find myself in need of a shop assistant.

My two best friends, Rob Goldburg and Bob Steuben, are also antique dealers from Charlotte. They moved here a month after I did, and bought a shop on King Street adjacent to mine. They have the same problem— more business than they can handle. We are not complaining, mind you. We all knew we were moving to heaven, but not necessarily to the land of silk and money. It seems too good to be true.

In fact, the last six months have been a virtual fairy tale. It began when I married the man of my dreams, Greg Washburn. He was an investigator with the Charlotte police force, but retired from that position to pursue his lifelong dream of becoming a shrimp boat captain here in the Charleston area. Judging by the perpetual grin on Greg's handsome face, he is deliriously happy.

Even my mother, Mozella Wiggins, is happy. She adores Greg and loves Charleston. This is fortunate because Mama lives with us now at Number 7 Squiggle Lane, and, trust me, a miserable mama is not someone with whom you want to spend time. In addition to Greg and me, my petite progenitress has her new church—Grace Episcopal on Wentworth Street—to keep her spirits up. Within days of moving here, Mama had her membership transferred and had volunteered for every committee. I see less of her now that we live together than I ever did before.

Last, but not least, my cat, Dmitri, approves of our new address. How could he not? Half of the second story piazza is warm and sunny, while the other half offers him a bird's-eye view of—well, birds. The mockingbird nest in the magnolia is just out of reach. Mama and papa birds seem to know this, and while they keep up a steady stream of chatter whenever my ten-pound bundle of joy is outside, they have yet to dive-bomb him. On his part, Dmitri has never been happier.

In addition to wealth and happiness, we all have our health, which, according to that old Geritol commercial, means we have just about everything. I won't contest that. I, too, should be walking around with a goofy grin on my face. And I am happy, I'm just not delirious.

Alas, I realize that much as I love my adopted city, I can never be considered a real Charlestonian. Even if I live to be a hundred—which means I would have lived here over fifty years. My children's children, assuming they were born here, would be natives of Charleston, but they would not be real Charlestonians. Three hundred years from now their descendants might lay claim to that title. *Might*.

Don't get me wrong. Not everyone in Charleston—even those fortunate enough to live south of Broad—can claim colonial antecedents. In recent years numerous natives have moved to the cheaper 'burbs, making way for an influx of the wealthy. What began as a trickle became a flood as property taxes soared in keeping with rising real estate values. Today the historic district south of Broad contains the fifth highest concentration of wealth in the nation.

Like me, these new citizens of Charleston—many of them retired doctors and lawyers—only become real Charlestonians when they travel, and then only to folks who don't know better. They may lead happy and productive lives, and quite likely rub shoulders with the real McCoy at the theater, or in restaurants, but they will forever be outsiders. And no doubt, like me, many of them gaze longingly into ancient windows, wishing with all their hearts that they were inside. *Truly* inside. Imagine my great joy, then, when I received an embossed invitation to tea from Mrs. Amelia Shadbark, Charleston's most distinguished citizen.

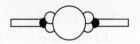

2

"It's pronounced '*Shay*-bark,'" I said.

My friend C. J., who was visiting from Charlotte the day the missive arrived, wrinkled her button nose. "Why, that's just silly, Abby. What happened to the D?"

"This is Charleston, dear. It doesn't have to make sense to us. The family has pronounced it that way for three hundred years. That's all that matters."

C. J.—her friends lovingly refer to her as Calamity Jane—fingered the heavy paper as if it were the Holy Grail. Still, I held my breath. More often than not, C. J. lives up to her name.

"Abby, who will mind your shop while you're away?"

"I'll close early, dear."

"But won't you lose some business?"

"Undoubtedly. But this tea is my entrée into Charleston society. It's a once-in-a-lifetime opportunity."

She nodded. "Abby, it says here that you can bring a guest. Who is it going to be? Your mama?"

"Mama's at a church retreat in the mountains. She doesn't get back from Kanuga until the following day."

C. J.'s eyes glittered. "Then who are you going to take?"

It was time to tread carefully. While I wouldn't hurt my pal for all the tea in Mrs. Shadbark's larder, I certainly didn't want C. J. coming with me. The girl is—how shall I put this delicately—a sandwich short of a picnic. No, make that a cucumber sandwich shy of high tea.

"I thought I might take Greg," I said. It was a lie, pure and simple. Greg doesn't give a fig about high society. Shrimp are what floats his boat.

C. J. may play with a partial deck, but she's not stupid. Not by a long stretch. In fact, her IQ puts her up there in a league with Marilyn vos Savant. You know, that genius who has a column in *Parade Magazine*.

"Abby, it says here it's a ladies' tea. Greg's not—I mean, he isn't a cross-dresser, is he?"

I had to laugh. My studmuffin is six feet tall and has shoulders like a linebacker. While he looks good in a barbecuing apron, frilly frocks are not his forte.

"No, dear, Greg's not into dresses."

"So then who are you going to take?"

I sighed. "You, of course."

C. J. squealed. "Ooh, Abby, you really mean it?"

"On one condition."

"Anything, Abby!"

"The condition is you promise not to tell Mrs. Shadbark any of your Shelby stories."

C. J. is a big-boned gal, almost five feet ten. She wears her emotions on her size fourteen sleeves. At the moment, she looked about to cry.

"What's wrong with my Shelby stories?" Shelby, North Carolina, by the way, is where Jane Cox was born and raised. Although she lives in Charlotte now, Shelby is always on her mind.

"Because—well, you must admit, some of them are pretty farfetched."

C. J. shook her head, the shoulder-length dishwater blond hair whipping across her face. I knew what was coming.

"But they're not, Abby. They're all true. You should go to Shelby sometime and see for yourself."

"I've been to Shelby, dear. It isn't remotely the way you describe it."

"Have you been to Buckingham Palace?"

"Buckingham Palace is not in Shelby, dear."

C. J. laughed. "Ooh, silly, I know that. But my Granny Ledbetter from Shelby has been to the palace. She was invited to tea."

"You don't say."

"Ooh, but I do. Granny was in London then, you see, and she was able to get all the right stuff."

"You mean like a fancy hat? One with oodles of silk flowers?"

"No, shoes. You see, it was summer, and all Granny had with her were her flip-flops. Anyway, Granny said the Queen was very nice. Asked her if she wanted milk or lemon in her tea. Because Granny didn't want to offend Her Majesty by declining one or the other, she said both. Well, wouldn't you know, the second the Queen squeezed lemon into Granny's milk tea, it curdled. Turned thick and lumpy right there in the cup. Granny was grossed out, but not Her Majesty. She tasted the stuff, said it was good, and gave it her royal stamp of approval. And that's how cottage cheese was invented. Only at first it was called palace cheese. The name got changed later on account of palace cheese sounded too expensive for the average citizen."

"C. J.," I said patiently. "I doubt if Queen Elizabeth II squeezes lemons. Besides, cottage cheese was invented long before she was born."

"Ooh, it wasn't her, Abby, it was Queen Victoria."

I nodded. Some of C. J.'s stories make Granny Ledbetter out to be older than God. Within that context, it was possible the two women had met.

"C. J.—sweetie—this is the kind of story you have to promise not to tell Mrs. Amelia Shadbark."

"But it wasn't a Shelby story, Abby."

"Nevertheless, you've got to promise me you won't say anything, but 'hello,' 'how are you,' 'yes please,' 'thank you,' and 'good-bye.' "

C. J.'s lower lip extended as if hydraulically operated. "What if she asks me questions those words don't cover?"

"Then answer them, but keep your answers short and simple. I'm warning you, though. If you so much as mention Granny Ledbetter, or Shelby—or your cousin Alvin, for that matter—I will never invite you along with me again."

C. J. was on the edge of her seat. "But if I promise to behave, you'll take me along this time, right?"

"Yes."

"Ooh, Abby, you're the best!" C. J. threw her arms around me. She smelled of lemons and sour milk.

We cleaned up mighty well, if I do say so myself. C. J. had shed her uniform of jeans and a man's T-shirt

for a pale yellow linen suit and an ivory shell with a
scalloped neckline. The hem of the linen skirt swept
her ankles, in what Mama and I called "the Episcopal
length," due to its popularity among the women at
church. C. J., who is about as coordinated as an orang-
utan on steroids, wisely chose to wear flats. They
weren't the most expensive shoes I've seen, but at least
they were made of leather—brown leather—and there
were no holes in the soles. Except for pearl stud ear-
rings, she wore no jewelry. In short, my not-so-short
friend looked smashing.

I'm sure I looked smashing as well in my periwinkle-
blue, polyester-silk blend dress with the princess seams
and square neckline. My hemline stopped just above
my knees because, you see, I stand only four feet nine
inches in my stocking feet. I have to be extremely careful about my choices, lest I look like a little girl playing dress-up. Or worse yet, like a little girl dressed to
suit her age. Long skirts are definitely out, as is anything too fussy. Heels are a must.

"Ooh, Abby," C. J. said when she'd had a good gan-
der. "You can't wear that."

"And just why not?"

"It's polyester."

"It's a polyester-silk *blend*." I sniffed. "It's forty-five
percent silk—I checked—which is almost half, so it's
perfectly acceptable."

"But it doesn't wrinkle."

"That's a plus, dear."

"Not with the rich, Abby. They love wrinkled
clothes and chunky jewelry. Helps to detract from all
the wrinkles they get lying about in the sun."

"Now you're just being ridiculous."

"Nuh-unh. They especially love linen. The 'Linen Ladies,' that's what Granny calls them." She flinched when she realized she'd uttered the G word.

"Well, that's too bad. I can't stand the wrinkles."

C. J. clucked. "Don't blame me, Abby, if you're not accepted into society."

"I won't."

I whisked her out the door before she had time to notice that the left leg of my pantyhose had a run just below the knee.

Because it was summertime and the living was easy, we decided to walk to tea. It was only three blocks, after all, and as long as we did the Charleston walk— maintained a moderate pace and kept to the shade—we would arrive none the worse for wear. That was the plan. However, by the time we reached the Shadbark mansion, C. J.'s outfit was so wrinkled she looked like she was wearing a pair of Chinese shar-pei dogs, instead of a suit. Wisely, I said nothing.

The massive Shadbark residence, like many Charleston buildings, was set up almost against the sidewalk. A set of double wrought iron stairs flanked the front, converging on a small front landing. Tradition has it that in more modest times, men used the left stair, women the right. The intent was to preserve the modesty of the ladies, whose ankles would surely be exposed by the act of hoisting their hoop skirts high enough to allow them to climb. Ah, the scandal!

By mutual agreement, C. J. took the gentlemen's stairs, and I took the ladies', but it was she who won the paper, scissors, rock game and got to ring the bell.

The heavy oak door opened almost immediately. I

had expected a butler, but was not disappointed when I saw the uniformed maid.

"Yeth?" It was more of a demand on her part than a question.

I smiled graciously. "We're here to have tea with Mrs. Shadbark." I accidentally pronounced the D.

"Zat's Shay-bark!" she barked. The maid turned to C.J. "Und you musht be Mrs. Vashburn."

C.J. beamed. "Ooh, I've always wanted to marry a stud like Greg. But Granny says I've got to save myself for Cousin Alvin—"

I may have tiny feet, but my shoes are pointed. C.J. yelped like a whelp.

"I'm Abigail Wiggins Timberlake Washburn," I said evenly. "I actually prefer Timberlake for professional reasons."

The maid was an amazon of a woman, even larger than C.J. Dark-eyed and deeply tanned, her looks belied her strange, but vaguely Teutonic accent. Her sun-streaked blond hair looked like it hadn't seen a comb in decades. A vertical scar, the size and shape of a sardine, dissected her left cheek.

"Zee closhe," she muttered in disgust. "Polyeshter."

"Forty-five percent silk," I wailed. "May we come in?"

"Yah." She didn't step aside, merely turned so that poor C.J. had to squeeze past an enormous bosom. There are advantages to being small, and I managed to slipped through underneath.

But once we were inside, Brunhilde, as I thought of her, took the lead. "Zeeth vay. Und no touching zee shtuff."

Our mouths hung open as Brunhilde led us through

rooms that smelled like lemon Pledge and lavender. Sideboards, servers, and settees, not a piece was younger than this country. I had to will my eyes to remain in their sockets.

"Ooh, Abby," C.J. moaned, "I think we've died and gone to heaven."

"I'm inclined to agree. If she serves us anything chocolate, then we'll know it's true."

"Vait here!" We'd reached a set of closed doors, which Brunhilde opened just wide enough to admit her bulky body, and then closed hard behind her. I could feel the vibration through my feet.

We were in a wide, dimly lit hallway, and it took a few seconds for our eyes to adjust. Because C.J. is younger, hers adjusted first.

"Ooh, Abby!" she squealed. "Do you see what I see?"

I turned and gasped. Just inches from me, lined up on a Louis XV marquetry commode, were three glass vases. The center vase was the tallest—approximately nine inches high—and had a frosted background, upon which perched life-size opalescent parakeets molded in high relief. To the left of this magnificent piece reposed a spherical vase in brilliant cherry red, which had a fish motif. To the right stood a translucent footed spherical vase in pale peppermint green.

"Lalique," I whispered in awe. "René Lalique, the French jeweler and glassmaker who contributed greatly to the Art Nouveau movement."

"I know who he was," C.J. said. If she sounded a bit miffed, she had a right to be. The big galoot might be missing a bulb or two in her chandelier, but her business acumen is sharper than mine. Not many twenty-five-year-olds can own and operate a highly successful antique store.

"Sorry, dear, I was just excited and—"

The richly paneled doors open and Brunhilde stood there in all her imposing glory. "Zeeth vay," she ordered.

We followed her meekly into a large, brightly lit room. Again, my eyes had to adjust. But when they did, it was not for long. My head swam, and the room began to spin. I could feel myself crumple, like a soufflé when the oven door has been slammed. At least I didn't have far to fall.

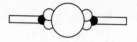

3

C.J. caught me. "Oopsy, Abby." She swooped me up and set me back on my feet in one smooth move.

I struggled to remain upright. Glass cabinets with backlighting lined all four walls. Arranged tastefully, with just enough space between pieces, were several dozen exquisite works of art, all of which appeared, at first glance, to be the creation of René Lalique.

"C. J., tell me I'm dreaming!"

"You're not, Abby. I see it, too."

"Then it *is* heaven."

C.J. sniffed the air. "Ooh, Abby, I don't smell chocolate."

"Forget the chocolate!" I cried. "Look at all that Lalique!"

C. J. has a one-track mind. Unfortunately, it's off the track half the time.

"Abby, I'm pretty sure this isn't heaven. Maybe my nose is stopped up and I can't smell the chocolate, but I sure don't see any ducks."

"Ducks?"

"Well, I had this little duck named Sparky, you see. Granny Ledbetter gave him to me for Easter, the year I

13

turned eight. Abby, he was the cutest little thing you ever saw. I played with him all time. Even put him in the tub with me when I bathed—only I had to be careful not to get the water too hot. Then one day—my birthday—I couldn't find Sparky anywhere. That night at supper Granny served duck a l'orange."

"How awful."

Her big head nodded vigorously. I wasn't supposed to know, of course, but I did. Right away. You see, Sparky had a crooked wing, on account of one time I got the water too hot and he banged his wing getting out of the tub real fast. Anyway, that was the piece Granny served me. Course I cried for days and days, until Granny told me that ducks—and even some chickens—that get eaten go to heaven."

"You believe that?"

"Well, not *all* ducks—there are some bad ones, you know. And definitely not chickens. But I know Sparky is there. So we aren't."

"Heaven was just a metaphor, dear. This is Mrs. Amelia Shadbark's private museum."

"You're absolutely right," a strange voice said.

I whirled, as did C. J. She has hands the size of Ping-Pong paddles, and one of them hit me square in the back. I shot forward like a Ping-Pong ball. If it were not for the spike heels of my petite pumps, which I dug into the thick carpet like crampons, I would have confronted our hostess head-on. Literally.

"Sorry," I gasped, as I struggled to right myself.

The woman smiled. Her face had more wrinkles than a dried peach, so it took a few seconds to arrange them all in the appropriate pattern. I had a feeling, however, that the grande dame's contour lines were due to advanced age, rather than the sun. Or maybe both.

Whatever the reason, she was a class act. Her snow-white hair was pulled into a chignon, from which not a single strand escaped. Her pale blue dress was textured silk, possibly from Thailand. And around her throat hung a single strand of opera-length pearls, tied once into a knot with a five-inch loop. Matching pearl drops dangled from drooping earlobes. Each pearl, in my estimate, was worth a small fortune.

"I'm Abigail Timberlake," I gasped.

She extended a withered hand. It felt as light and dry as one of Mama's homemade biscuits.

"Amelia Shadbark," she said, still smiling. "Please call me Amelia."

"Then you must call me Abby. And this is Jane Cox," I said, introducing my young friend by her correct name. "She's my assistant."

"Ooh, Abby, really?"

"Later," I whispered from one corner of my mouth. I returned Amelia's smile.

"I just can't get over your collection. It's mind-boggling."

"I'll take that as a compliment, child."

At that moment the massive Brunhilde materialized out of thin air. Amelia didn't seem to notice.

"Please, have a seat," she said.

I hadn't even noticed the furniture. Sure enough, in the middle of the room was a suite of three chairs and a coffee table. They were Danish Modern in style, built of blond wood, and all but blended into the beige carpet. They certainly did not detract from the fabulous glass collection. At any rate, I slipped quickly into the nearest chair. In the game of musical chairs I was always the first one out, even when I played it with my children. Brunhilde was not going to beat me at this game.

I need not have worried. C. J. sat at right angles to me, Amelia across. Thank heavens Brunhilde was not invited to sit.

"Bring the tea things now," Amelia ordered.

Brunhilde glared at us—me in particular—but she did as she was told.

Amelia waited until the maid was gone before speaking again. But the second the door closed, the craggy face came to life.

"I hope you will forgive me, Abby, but I've invited you here under false pretenses."

I stiffened. The last time those words were directed to me was when my college math professor tried to kiss me. He was a tall man, and I was sitting down. I managed to head butt him in the—well, let's just say, if he ever becomes President, there'll be no need to worry about a scandal in the Oval Office.

"Oh dear," Amelia said, "I hope I haven't offended you. "It's just that in addition to tea, I have a business proposition I'd like to discuss."

My heart pounded. "Please, go on."

Amelia glanced at the door. "I hope you don't mind if I talk fast. I'm afraid Brunhilde is fond of eavesdropping, although getting the tea things should keep her busy for a while." She giggled. "I hid the Earl Grey."

"I can't believe my ears!"

"You must think me awful."

"Not at all. What I can't believe is that your maid's name is Brunhilde."

"Oh, but it is. Brunhilde Salazar. She's Brazilian of German descent."

"That certainly explains the accent."

C.J., bless her heart, could not stand to be left out of the conversation. "I had a Brazilian cousin," she said. "Carmen used to put a bowl of fruit on her head and—"

"Not now, dear," I said gently. I turned to Amelia. "You said you had to make this fast. What's your proposition?"

"Well, honey, believe it or not, I'm seventy-six years old."

"Get out of town!" I said. I wouldn't have pegged her for a day under ninety.

Amelia smiled so wide, I feared her face would shatter. "Oh, but I am. Celebrated that birthday just last week. Anyway, I decided it's finally time to take it a little slower. Downsize a little bit, too. So I've made up my mind I'm moving into Bishop Gadsden."

"I beg your pardon? Did you say you were moving in with a bishop?" That seemed a little eccentric, even by Charleston standards. Unless, of course, said bishop was a relative, and the relationship platonic.

Amelia laughed. "Abby, you're such a mess."

Being called a mess where I come from, in the Up-country, is a bit of a compliment. It means one is a cut-up, a "card," entertaining—you get the picture. I wasn't quite sure, however, if the term meant the same here in the Lowcountry. The Lowcountry, inciden-tally—and it is all one word—is the name applied to the coastal strip of South Carolina, particularly the area around Charleston. The name is really a geo-graphical description, as the highest point in

Charleston County is less than thirty feet above sea level.

"You think I'm funny?" I asked.

"You're a stitch. Of course I'm not moving *in* with a bishop—although I've known a few over the years who might have been able to tempt me. Anyway, I'm moving *into* the Bishop Gadsden Episcopal Retirement Community here in Charleston. They have a nice cottage reserved for me—they ought to, after all the money I've donated to them over the years."

I waved my arms around my head. "You're giving all this up?"

She sighed. "I've enjoyed my life, but there comes a point when one wants to simplify. To strip down to the essentials, so to speak. This may be hard for someone your age to understand, but I no longer want the responsibility of *things*."

"What will you do with your things?" C. J. asked in a little-girl voice. She was on the edge of her Danish Modern chair.

"C. J., how impertinent!" I snapped.

Amelia laughed again. "It's all right, dear. I don't mind the question. In fact, Abby, that's why I invited you here. I want you to help me dispose of some of these things. Particularly this collection."

It's a good thing I wasn't sitting on the edge of my chair, or I would have fallen off. Thanks to my short legs, I'd been forced to settle well back into the safety zone.

"Please, go on," I said in a little-girl voice of my own.

Amelia nodded. "Yes, I better move this conversation along. Brunhilde may have found the tea by now.

So, as I was saying, Abby, I'd like you to broker this collection for me." She paused. "That is, if you're willing."

"Of course she is!" C. J. practically shouted.

Amelia ignored the girl. "Are you interested, Abby?"

I shivered. It was like having Mel Gibson proposition me, naked, a rose between his teeth, a bottle of Hershey's syrup in one hand, whipped cream in the other. In that case, however, I'd have to say no. I am, after all, wed to Greg, whom I love dearly. But I wouldn't be breaking moral or religious laws by brokering the fabulous Lalique collection.

"Why me, if you don't mind my asking? I mean, I've only been in town a few months."

"That's precisely why I've chosen you," she said. "I know most of the dealers on King Street. Been to their christenings, watched them grow up. It wouldn't feel right, picking one over the others."

"I see. Well, just how much of the collection do you want to part with?"

"Virtually all you see here. I've saved out several pieces—you may have seen them in the hall—that I plan to take with me."

I caught my breath. "Well, I'd certainly like to try selling some of the pieces in my shop. But the bulk I'd like to turn over to Sotheby's. Frankly, you'd probably get a better price that way, since there'd be a larger pool of potential buyers. You wouldn't be paying me a commission on those pieces, of course. Just the ones I sell personally. I charge twenty percent of the selling price, which I think you'll find is really quite reasonable."

She nodded. "So you'll make the arrangements? With Sotheby's, I mean?"

"Absolutely."

"Then we have a deal."

That very second the door to the little museum flew open and in stumbled Brunhilde Salazar. Balanced atop her head was, not a bowl of fruit, but a huge silver tray. The woman staggered in our direction, but much to my amazement she managed to plunk the heavy object on the coffee table without losing a single item. A few drops of milk may have been spilled, but that was all.

"Thank you, Brunhilde," Amelia said graciously. "That will be all."

"But I muth pour zee tea, yah?"

"I'll pour," Amelia said firmly.

Brunhilde scowled. "But zeeth is my yob, no?"

Amelia sighed softly. "Very well, Brunhilde. You may pour."

The maid grunted her satisfaction. First she served Amelia, who took her tea with milk and sugar, in the proper English fashion. Then she served C.J., who took her tea with lemon and sugar, and more sugar, in the popular Shelby fashion. At last the formidable woman turned to me. "Meelk or limon?" she snarled. It was clearly a challenge.

"Milk and sugar," I said confidently.

Brunhilde glared. "Vell, eef you vant it zat vay." Then she proceeded to fill my cup so full that it was a miracle she was able to get it to me without spilling. However, the mere act of transferring it from her hand to mine caused a tidal wave of steaming liquid to surge over the edge and into my lap.

I yelped and leaped to my feet. In the process I dropped the cup. Fortunately the beverage missed Brunhilde and me, but it drenched the carpet.

"Zee vaht you haff done!" she roared.

"Ooh, Abby, that has got to hurt." C.J. sounded sympathetic, but she hadn't moved a muscle.

"Abby, honey, are you all right?" Amelia was surprisingly spry for a woman her age. Before I knew it her biscuit dry hands were patting my wet loins with cloth napkins.

"I'm fine," I assured her. The hot beverage stung, but I wasn't seriously burned. Merely mortified.

"Zee carpet, senora," Brunhilde said stubbornly. "Vaht about zeeth lovely carpet?"

"Forget the silly old carpet, Brunhilde. My guest may have been burned."

"But I'm not," I wailed. I looked around in vain for a crack in the floor into which I could crawl. For someone my size that's sometimes a real option. Only not with wall to wall carpet.

"Your beautiful dress," Amelia said. "I hope it's not been ruined."

"Eeth yooth polyeshter, señora."

"Brunhilde, that will be enough." Amelia was too much of a lady to speak sharply to her servants, but she didn't have to. There was a crispness in her tone that sent Ms. Salazar slinking from the room.

When the maid was gone, and I was dabbed reasonably dry, Amelia Shadbark herself served me tea. She also served me scones with butter and peach preserves, dainty little sandwiches with the crusts removed, and chocolate cake.

Then, as C.J. stood up to say our good-byes, the

grande dame gave me a present. Just the gift wrapping would have knocked my socks off, had I been wearing any. As it was, my pantyhose slipped southward several inches.

"A little extra something for your trouble," Amelia said, working her wrinkles into a smile. "But wait until you get home before you open this."

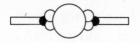

4

"Oh, Abby, what is it?" C.J. was jumping up and down like a little girl on Christmas morning.

I unwrapped the gift carefully—that is to say, about as fast as the leaves change color here in Charleston. I wasn't trying to agitate C.J., mind you; it was simply habit. Mama made my brother Toy and me fold our wrapping paper. On subsequent gift-giving occasions Mama would steam iron the paper under the protective surface of a thick towel. In the Wiggins household, even plain wrapping paper stood a good chance of outlasting the gift.

"Ooh, Abby, can't you go any faster?"

The poor girl was about to bust a gut, which believe you me, is far messier than spilling milk tea on a beige carpet. I ripped the paper off like it grew on trees. Inside was a white box six inches square. Inside that was tissue paper, and since Mama saved, but never ironed, tissue, that came out in a flash. I reached in and gently removed the most beautiful perfume bottle I had ever seen.

"Oooooh!" C.J.'s voice rose like a fire engine siren. I stared at the treasure. Only René Lalique would think to make a flask in the shape of a peacock. The head was the stopper, and the broad tail, which was not fully expanded, the bottle's base. The colors ranged from the simple green of the peacock's crest, and the iridescent blue of his head and neck, to a rainbow of shimmering hues.

"I think his eyes are emeralds," I said.

"What did you say, Abby? You're croaking like a frog."

"I think his eyes are emeralds."

This time she heard me. "They look like emeralds. Too bad it's not a real Lalique."

"Of course it is." I turned the bottle over. "There, you see? The signature is as plain as the ticks on a hairless dog."

"But Abby, you have a cat—"

"It's just an expression. René Lalique began his career as a jeweler. Have you ever been to the Gulbenkian Museum, C. J.?"

"Where's that?"

"Portugal."

C. J. hung her massive head. "I've never been out of the Carolinas."

"You haven't missed much, dear. Anyway, I had the privilege of visiting a friend in Lisbon—oh, about five years ago, before I met you—and she took me to the Gulbenkian. There's a whole section devoted to jewelry and small decorative items by Lalique. I think I remember—"

I stopped in midsentence because the love of my life, Greg Washburn, had just entered the room. I was surprised to see him home so early. The shrimping season in South Carolina lasts from June to December, but it was only the tenth of August. To my knowledge shrimp were still quite plentiful. On a good fishing day I didn't expect to see Greg until seven or eight in the evening.

"Is something wrong, dear?"

Greg shook his handsome head. He has thick dark hair and sapphire-blue eyes. The sun the past few months had turned him cigar-brown. I was tempted to run over and kiss him, but I knew better. Boy, did I know better! His nets haul up a lot more than just shrimp. After a day catching, and sorting, the sea's bounty, my dearly beloved smells like a sushi bar in the Sahara Desert. One to which the electricity has been off for a week.

This smell, which lingers even after my love showers, is one that I hope to eventually get used to. For our cat, Dmitri, it is heaven. The second Greg returns from a fishing trip, our ten-pound puddytat is wrapped around his legs like kelp on a buoy rope. Today was no exception.

Greg picked up the ten-pound lug and cradled him like a baby. "Nothing's wrong," he said, trying to sound cheerful. "We just decided to follow the tide in and call it a day." The "we" Greg was referring to were his cousins Bo and Skeeter, partners in the venture.

"How many pounds was your catch?"

"Two hundred."

C.J.'s eyes widened. "Wow! That's some big shrimp!"

Greg laughed. "That's actually thousands of shrimp. But it's not as much as it sounds. Old-timers tell me they used to catch two *thousand* pounds on a good day."

C.J. wrinkled her nose. Her lips were pulled back like those of a snarling dog.

"Y'all sure do eat a lot of shrimp down here, don't you?"

"Yes," I said. "As a matter of fact, that's what I'm planning to serve for supper."

The big gal struggled to keep her nose from disappearing altogether. "Sounds wonderful, Abby."

I knew she was lying through her exposed teeth, so I was stringing her along. There was, in fact, a nice pork tenderloin in the refrigerator, just waiting to be popped into the oven.

"Good," I said, "because I'm serving shrimp cocktail, followed by shrimp bisque, then shrimp Creole. And for dessert, homemade shrimp ice cream."

C.J. turned seafoam-green about the gills. "Ooh, Abby, I'm sure your shrimp ice cream is delicious, but if it's all the same to you, I'd just as soon pass. I ate too much of that at Granny's last Thanksgiving and—well, it kind of left a bad taste in my mouth."

I chuckled. "Good one, dear."

"Abby, I'm serious."

"Give me a break, C.J."

My friend would not give up. "But it's true, Abby. I made it myself on Granny's crank-style freezer. It went really well with the pumpkin and shrimp pie Cousin Alvin brought."

I changed the subject by showing Greg—at a distance—the exquisite perfume bottle Amelia Shadbark had given me. He was suitably impressed.

We spent a pleasant evening, the four of us. After Greg showered, we three humans devoured the tenderloin, along with several side dishes, while Dmitri made short shrift of a can of gourmet cat food. Afterward Greg dozed in front of the television, remote in hand, Dmitri in his lap, while C. J. and I played a quick game of Scrabble. We weren't in a hurry, by any means—it's just that C. J. trounced me. I wouldn't be surprised if she knew every word in the official Scrabble dictionary, and how to spell it, forward and backward.

I finally gave up, woke Greg so we could go to bed, and said good night to C. J.

"Abby," she said, as we stood in the hall, "you're not going to do those silly tricks again tonight, are you?"

"What tricks?"

"You know, knocking on my door, and then hiding when I answer it. Ooh, and jangling all those keys. That was a good one! Where did you get so many?"

"C. J., I haven't got a clue what you're talking about."

The girl yawned so wide a circus tiger could have stuck his head in her mouth. No doubt about it, another benefit of being short was that I couldn't see the remains of her supper.

"Have it your way, Abby. I'll pretend it's a ghost, if that's what you want."

"Ghost?"

"Abby, everyone knows that a lot of these old houses are supposed to be haunted."

"Well—some people claim they are."

C. J. shivered. "Yeah, but is *this* house haunted?"

"I don't know." I really didn't. I'd purposely not asked our real estate agent if there were any ghosts associated with this place. My imagination is far too active as it is.

My guest was suddenly wide awake. "I mean, because if it is, I can't stay."

"C. J.!"

"I'm not kidding, Abby. I know most ghosts are
harmless—maybe they all are, just being spirits and
such—but they scare me. So, if that wasn't you last
night, making all that noise, then I've got to go."

"Where?"

"To a motel, I guess."

"C. J., it's the height of tourist season. You might not
find a room this time of the night, and even if you do, it
will cost you a small fortune."

"That's true, Abby. So quit teasing me, and admit it
was you."

"But it wasn't—"

The color drained from her face. "Then I'm outta
here."

I grabbed a gangly arm. "Don't be ridiculous, C. J. If
you want, I'll sleep in there with you. Or you can have
Mama's room until she gets back."

C. J. wrenched free of my grip. "Have you ever slept
in your mama's room?"

"No."

"Then you don't know if it's haunted, do you?"

"No, but we can call her—no, wait a minute. She's
staying in one of the cabins at Kanuga. They don't
have phones."

"Bye-bye, Abby."

"Then stay in our room," I cried.

"With you and Greg?" Thank heavens she sounded
skeptical, and not hopeful.

"I'm sure Greg's gone back to sleep by now. You

and I can drag your mattress across the hall. We'll find room for it at the foot of our bed."

"Okay," she said reluctantly. "But if I scream, you have to promise to come to my rescue."

"I will," I promised.

There was, alas, no one to come to my rescue. Greg slept like a hibernating grizzly—one experiencing horrendous nightmares. Although sound asleep, he thrashed about and moaned continuously. It was worse than sex.

Meanwhile Dmitri, attracted to our bed by the lingering smell of fish, sought refuge on my side. Being a lap cat, Dmitri prefers to sleep on top of me, or, since we've been married, on top of Greg. He prefers Greg, I am convinced, because of the extra surface area. Tonight was no exception. But every few minutes the ten-pound oaf would abandon his bigger buddy and clamber aboard my small frame. As soon as Greg settled, Dmitri hopped off me again.

I might even have been able to sleep through all this, were it not for C. J. The girl has a deviated septum, and it was certainly deviant tonight. You've never heard such snores. There are tugboats in Charleston Harbor with softer, more melodic horns than C. J.'s schnoz. One thing is for sure; if the girl had slept that soundly, and loudly, the night before, there was no way she could have heard jangling keys. Or even a loud rap on the door.

At four A.M. the alarm went off and Greg got up for work. If he thought it unusual to find a five-foot-ten-inch blond sleeping at the foot of his bed, he kept it to himself. With Greg gone, Dmitri finally settled down enough to enable me to drift off to sleep. C. J.'s tugboat snores hadn't abated, but I pretended to be sprawled on a deck chair of a cruise ship, a book in one hand, a stiff drink in the other. That seemed to do the trick, because I gradually incorporated those images into a dream. My dream, however, offered no explanation for the large tomcat on my chest.

I slept for about four hours. I'm sure I would have slept until noon, had I not been rudely awakened by someone shaking me.

"Not now, dear," I muttered. "I have a headache."

"Wake up, Abby. It's important."

"Some other time, Greg. C. J.'s in the room with us."

"But Abby, it's me—C. J.!"

I opened one eye. "It is you. Do me a favor, dear. Make yourself some breakfast and chill out in another room. There's cable TV, of course, and plenty of books. I'll join you in, say, four hours?"

"Sorry, Abby, but no can do."

"Of course you can. There's cereal and milk, if you don't feel like cooking. Even a package or two of instant grits—but they're hidden behind that five-pound bag of sugar on the spice shelf." Mama would disown me if she ever found out I used the instant product. In my defense, let me explain that I use it only when she's out of town, and then it's usually when I'm running late.

"Abby, I already had breakfast. And so did the detectives."

"That's nice, dear. Then—" I opened the other eye, pushed a reluctant Dmitri off my chest, and sat up. "What did you say?"

"I said I cooked breakfast for Investigators Scrubb and Bright. At first I thought they were missionaries, on account they dressed so neatly, and there were two of them. I told them I already belonged to a church, thank you very much, which really isn't true, Abby, because Granny's church back in Shelby burned to the ground, and since it was the only one of its denomination, I haven't belonged anywhere for a long time." She paused to breathe. "Then they said they weren't missionaries, but detectives, and asked to speak to you personally. I told them you were sleeping in, and that I wasn't going to wake you. So then they told me why they were here, and I agreed to wake you—but only after I made them breakfast. I wanted to buy you a little time, you see. Anyway, now they say they've waited long enough, and if you're not out there in three minutes, they're going to get a warrant." She wagged a long, thick finger at me. "Abby, you really should buy a better brand of bacon. What you've got in there now is far too lean. I had no choice but to serve it crisp."

Bless C. J.'s oversize heart. Her ramblings had given me enough time to wake sufficiently to think. I still wasn't operating on all cylinders, but mine is a small engine, after all.

"What on earth could a pair of detectives want with me?"

"They want to ask you about Mrs. Shadbark's death."

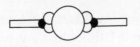

5

It's amazing how fast the human body can move when the pressure is on. I dressed, washed my face, brushed my teeth, and combed my hair—all in just under three minutes. It may have not been the perfect toilette, but I was certainly presentable. Gathering my wits about me took only a few seconds more, so it was three minutes exactly when I opened my bedroom door. The fact that C. J. had wasted precious time babbling was not my fault.

I have, alas, been involved in other crime investigations. Therefore, even though I was dying to know—if you'll excuse the pun—what had happened to Mrs. Shadbark since our tea, I knew it was vitally important for me to act unconcerned until officially presented with the facts. To my credit, I appeared positively nonchalant as I breezed into the drawing room to greet my visitors.

The detectives rose to their feet when they saw me, so I knew they were native Southerners. Either that or they'd been just plain well brought up. Or both. At any rate, they didn't look in the least perturbed.

One was tall, middle-aged, balding, and with a slight paunch. "Good morning, Mrs. Timberlake," he said, extending his hand.

I shook it. "Actually, that's Mrs. Washburn. It used to be Timberlake, but now I use that only for professional reasons. Please, just call me Abby."

"Sergeant Magnol Bright," he said.

I raised a shapely eyebrow. "Magnol—now that's an interesting name."

Sergeant Bright sighed. "Mama was fond of flowers. I have a twin brother named Azal. If we'd been girls, we would have been Magnolia and Azalea."

"Good thing your mama didn't like asters," the second detective said.

I smiled. "And you are?"

"Sergeant Peter Scrubb."

It would be hard not to like Sergeant Scrubb. As hard to not like looking at him. He was, in my opinion, a dead ringer for the actor Ben Affleck.

"Good morning Sergeant. What can I do for y'all?"

"Psst, Abby," C. J. said from behind me.

I ignored her. "My friend said you wanted to speak with me."

"Yes," Sergeant Scrubb said. "We—"

"Psst!"

"C. J., not now!"

"But Abby, your blouse is inside out."

I glanced down. No wonder the dang thing had been so hard to button. Well, at least my slacks were zipped.

"That's all the rage in Milan, dear." I smiled at the cute cop. "You were saying?"

"Do you mind if we sit? This may take a while."

I waved to a pair of chairs. "By all means."

They waited until C. J. and I sat, and then followed suit. Magnol spoke first.

"I apologize for the intrusion, Abby. I know how bad migraines can be. It's just that—"

"Migraines?" I know it's not nice to interrupt, but sometimes a girl just has to.

"Severe migraines," C. J. hissed. "She has them all the time."

"I do not!"

"She's having one now, and doesn't even know it. That's how severe they are."

I glared at the big gal. "Don't you need to wash dishes or something?" I turned to the men. "Good help is so hard to find these days."

C. J. hopped to her feet with the ease of a gymnast. "Well, there's no need to be rude. If you want me, Abby, I'll be visiting the Rob-Bobs."

By comparison, I struggled to my size fours. "Sorry, C. J. That was unkind of me."

That big heart is pure gold. "That's okay, Abby. But I was planning to visit them anyway. I haven't seen their new Charleston shop yet."

"Then give them my love," I said.

Both men stood. Sergeant Bright looked inquiringly at his partner, who seemed to be the one in charge.

"Just a minute," Sergeant Scrubb said. "I'm going to need a contact number."

"She's staying here for the next few days," I said. "Or do you mean the Rob-Bob's?"

"Where is the Rob-Bob's, ma'am?"

"It's not a where," I said, "it's a who. They're a pair of mutual friends; Rob Goldburg and Bob Steuben. They just moved here from Charlotte, and have opened a shop on King Street called The Finer Things."

The men exchanged glances. "They know anything about glass?" Sergeant Scrubb asked.

"Fine glassware, yes."

"They're experts on just about everything," C.J. said loyally.

"Mind if I come with you?" Sergeant Bright asked C.J.

C.J. nodded. "I walk kinda fast, though. You might not be able to keep up."

The older man laughed. "You're on."

I poured myself a cup of C.J.'s coffee—which was much better than mine, by the way—and settled into a William and Mary period wing armchair. The pale yellow fabric, emboldened by larger-than-life blue flowers, is my new favorite look. Sergeant Scrubb, his cup refilled, sat in a matching chair opposite. He seemed surprisingly comfortable with my frou-frou.

"Shall we begin?" he asked.

"Fire away!"

"I beg your pardon?"

"Well, haven't you been grilling C.J. all morning?" I caught myself. "I mean, she cooked you breakfast. You had to talk about something."

"Actually, we had a very nice conversation. But I must say, Miss Cox has an interesting way of putting things."

"Well, that's one way to put it. Did she tell you any Shelby stories?"

He chuckled and ran long, strong fingers through dark hair. "One or two." He cleared his throat. "Miss—Mrs.—"

"Abby," I reminded him.

"Yes, Abby. I understand you and Miss Cox attended a tea at the home of Mrs. Amelia Shadbark yesterday afternoon."

"That's correct," I said.

"And, judging by your reaction—or lack thereof—when you walked into this room, you already knew about Mrs. Shadbark's death."

"C. J. told me. That's the first I'd heard of it, I swear."

He nodded. "Suppose you tell me about your relationship with the diseased."

"There was no relationship. I'd only met her that once—for tea."

"Was she the friend of a friend?"

"I don't have any friends—well, except for the Rob-Bobs, and C. J., who is only visiting. We've just moved here, you see, and it's hard to meet people when you're working full-time—something my husband, Greg, and I both do. Making friends is like dating. It takes time and effort."

Sergeant Scrubb found that comment interesting enough to jot down in the little brown notebook he held in his right hand. He used a pencil stub so short that from where I sat it looked like he was writing with his fingers.

"Then why do you think it is she invited you to tea?"

I smiled. "Oh, that's easy. She wanted me to broker her Lalique."

"Ah, yes, the trinket collection Miss Cox mentioned."

"Trinkets? *Trinkets?* I'll have you know that René Lalique was the finest glassmaker of the Art Nouveau period. Maybe of all time." I hopped off my chair with anger-fueled agility. "Look at this," I said, snatching the peacock perfume bottle from its place of honor on the coffee table. "Does this look like a trinket to you?"

He looked closely, but didn't touch. "It's kind of pretty, I guess. If you go in for that sort of thing."

"Pretty? It's exquisite! You should have seen all the fabulous pieces Amelia had."

His eyes flickered. "Amelia?"

"She asked us to call her that!" I wailed. "I didn't know her until yesterday, I really didn't."

The stubby pencil got a good workout. "Miss—uh, Abby—"

"You see! I asked you to call me Abby, and you just did."

He smiled. "Touché. So, Abby, please describe your tea yesterday."

I carefully set the peacock down and returned to my chair. "Well, C.J. and I got there at four o'clock, which was right on time. I had to close my shop early, of course. Anyway, this very stern housekeeper, maid, whatever—Brunhilde, her name was—answered the door. Hey, if you're looking for a suspect, I suggest you try her."

"Suspect?"

For such a small person, I have a huge mouth. If I was a python, I'd be able to swallow myself. I gave my wayward mug a gentle, corrective, slap.

"Well, I mean if there's been any kind of foul play," I said.

He said nothing.

"Well, *has* there been?"

"Abby, I'm not at liberty to discuss this case."

"Then what are we doing now?"

He smiled again. "I'm afraid this is when you talk, and I listen."

"Gotcha. In that case, maybe I should call my lawyer."

The smile shrank until it disappeared altogether. "I wouldn't advise that, ma'am."

"Ma'am? What happened to Abby?"

"I'm afraid this isn't a game, ma'am."

"Indeed it's not. That's why I think it would be a good idea to have an attorney present." I reached for the phone on the mahogany end table next to my chair. "Unless, of course, you specifically forbid me."

He waved at the phone. "By all means, call. But I think you should know that—seeing as how there haven't been any charges—calling an attorney now could look suspicious."

"To whom?"

Again, he said nothing.

"Okay," I wailed, "I'll finish my story. It's just that all those notes you're taking make me nervous—not that I have any reason to be, of course."

The smile returned and he balanced the little book on his crossed knee. The pencil disappeared, no doubt hidden by his huge hand.

"Please continue, Abby."

I took a deep breath. "So anyway, this Brunhilde person led us through the house and made us wait in a room that was literally a museum. There were glass cabinets along all the walls, and they held the largest, and finest, collection of Lalique I've ever see—outside of the Gulbenkian."

The pencil materialized. "Gull—gull—what?"

"Gulbenkian." I sounded the word slowly, but I had no idea how to spell it. "It's a fine arts museum in Portugal. Anyway, Amel—I mean, Mrs. Shadbark, has a little sitting area in that room, and that's where we had tea. Brunhilde, incidentally, prepared it."

"Did she pour as well?"

My, how well-bred Charleston detectives were. Tea pouring is, after all, a ritual, and not something a guest does for herself.

"Yes, Brunhilde poured. And with an attitude, I might add."

"Attitude?"

"Sergeant Scrubb, that woman could stare down Attila the Hun at a hundred paces."

He made note of that. "What did she serve to eat?"

"Scones with butter and peach preserves. They were m-m-good!"

"Anything else?"

"Wait a minute! Mrs. Shadbark wasn't poisoned, was she?"

"Abby, please just answer the question."

I sighed. I knew where he was going with that.

"Okay, I'll tell you, but you have to believe me when I say I ate one of everything. Let's see . . . there were cucumber sandwiches, of course. Watercress sandwiches. Salmon and cream cheese sandwiches—oh, and chocolate cake. But that, I didn't really eat. Just one bite. It had the worst icing I've ever tasted. Didn't taste like chocolate at all. C.J.'s an icing freak, but she didn't like it either." I quit yapping long enough to swallow some bad manners. "I'm sure Mrs. Shadbark meant well by the cake."

"That it then?"

"Well, there was milk and sugar for the tea, as well as lemon."

He nodded. "What did Miss Cox eat?"

"She ate everything as well. In fact, she had seconds of everything. Three scones even. It was only that horrible cake—" My petite paw found my maw.

Scrubb's stub got a good workout. "What about Mrs. Shadbark?"

"She had a scone—no, make that just half a scone, but a fairly large piece of cake. And tea with milk and two sugars. Nothing else. I remember because—"

He closed the little book and slipped it into the breast pocket of his suit. The pencil magically disappeared again.

"Thank you, Abby, you've been very helpful."

"I have?"

He stood, fixing his Ben Affleck gaze on me. "Miss Cox said you were married." There was definitely a question there.

"Very," I said, looking him straight in the eyes.

"Your husband's a lucky man."

"I'm a lucky woman."

He looked away first. "I'm going to need your work number. In case I have any more questions."

For what's it worth, Magdalena Yoder, a friend of mine up in Pennsylvania, claims that a woman's hunch is worth two facts from a man. Well, I had two hunches: one, that I'd be hearing from Sergeant Scrubb again soon, and two, it wouldn't necessarily be about business. At least the business of Amelia Shadbark's untimely demise.

I hope you understand then why I lied.

6

"You *what*?" Bob Steuben boomed. The man has a deep bass voice that must originate in his toes. That's the only way I can explain how such a slight build produces such a rich sound.

After ushering Sergeant Scrubb out my front door, I'd gone straight to my shop, the Den of Antiquity. I hadn't even bothered to turn my blouse right side out. Bob had seen the cluster of folks waiting for me on the walk, and had hurried over to help with sales. Apparently he and Rob had gotten into a tiff—something I hoped to hear more of—and he was glad to be of service. But in this business customers come and go in waves, and we were currently experiencing calm seas at low tide. I'd taken advantage of the lull to fill my friend in on the last eighteen hours.

I hung my head in shame. "I lied to him. I transposed the last two digits."

"For shame." Bob sounded more amused than disapproving. "It's not like he won't find you. One doesn't have to be a detective to call information."

"I know," I wailed. "But since I knew what he was up to, I didn't want to make it easy. I think he gets the message."

"What? That you're playing hard to get? Abby, me-thinks you flatter yourself. Not every handsome man that comes along has the hots for you. Could it be that you have the hots for him?"

There are times when I can feel myself blush. This was one of them.

"Bob, you know that I wouldn't be interested in anyone except for my own, dear hubby."

"Yes, if only I could say the same about Rob."

I'd been dusting a bronze statue and I let the feather duster fall. "What do you mean?"

Bob scooped up the duster and handed it to me. "Abby, this has to stay between you and me."

"It will."

"You swear?"

"Cross my heart and hope to die, stick a needle in my eye."

"Ouch, Abby, I always hated that saying."

"Bob, just say it, will you?"

"Well, I always thought Rob and I didn't keep anything from each other, but lately he's been acting very secretive."

"How so?"

"For one thing, he insists on collecting the mail."

"That's it?"

"And he screens our e-mail before I get a chance. And last night he was on the phone to someone, and when I walked into the room he hung up immediately. Didn't even say good-bye. When I find out who this person is, believe me, he's going to be one sorry guy."

"How do you know it's a male?"

Bob rolled his eyes. "*Please.* I said he was acting strange—not crazy."

"Right. But I think you're jumping to conclusions. In fact, this sounds like something I saw on a TV show once. Turns out the person sneaking around was just getting his GED."

Bob's laugh rattled the panes in shop windows. "Robert Goldburg has a master's degree in art history."

I gave the bronze a good thrashing with the duster. "Whatever. My point is, it's undoubtedly something innocent, and you're going to feel like a fool when he tells you."

"I'll settle for that."

The strap of sleigh bells suspended on a hook on the front door of my shop jangled. I looked over to see two middle-aged women in shorts and T-shirts. They were obviously tourists—which is not a put-down, mind you. Tourists have at least enough money to travel. In some cases a whole lot more.

I smiled and said hello, but then turned my attention back to Bob. Experience has taught me that while most shoppers like to be acknowledged, they prefer not to be followed around the shop like I was a vulture, and they were starving antelope about to drop dead on the Serengeti Plains. Besides, 168 King Street is not a large shop, and is very well organized, if I do say so myself. Unlike most shops, I've elected to display my wares by century, and each item is clearly marked. In addition to the date, the identifying card, which is tied to the piece with ribbon, contains as much information about the provenance as I can ferret out of the original owner. If no information is available, I offer my educated guess, and mark it as such. By the way, I price goods to allow for a ten percent discount, should the customer ask. In rare instances, I can come down as much as twenty percent. It never hurts to ask, but strangely, most folks don't.

"So," Bob said, when it appeared as if the customers were managing on their own, "tell me more about this fabulous Lalique collection. Couldn't you just die?"

I smiled weakly. "Sadly, someone did. But Bob, it was incredible. She had tableware, vases, scent bottles, jewelry, decorative furnishings, even lighting fixtures."

Bob dabbed the corners of his mouth with a silk handkerchief. He was on the verge of having a religious experience by proxy.

"What was your favorite piece?"

"That's hard to say. I mean, I love the peacock perfume bottle, because it's mine. But there was this rectangular box that I think is the most beautiful thing I've ever seen. It was clear glass, but frosted and stained a pale green. The four sides of the box had a stylized relief of fern leaves. On the satin-sheen lid were two nudes, their heads thrown back, their arms stretched forward, their hands locking. They were the handle."

Bob moaned behind the cloth.

"I just can't believe she's dead," I said. I whirled. Someone had tapped me on the back.

"Miss, I need your help." The speaker was wearing a yellow cotton T-shirt with a splattering of orange-brown stains, and a pair of lavender spandex shorts. Although she had plenty of curves, they were not arranged in an hourglass pattern.

I looked at the Ming dynasty, Cheng-te period porcelain box she held. The emperor during this reign was a fourteen-year-old pleasure-seeker who preferred traveling around China incognito to governing. Control of the government was turned over to Muhammadan eunuchs. Their influence shows up on the Arabic inscriptions that decorate many artifacts of this area. This particular box had a white glaze with blue scrollwork, which translated read: "The fool judges first, and asks questions later."

"That's a very rare piece," I said. "The best I can do is come down ten percent."

"That's not what I want to know," the shopper snapped. "Does this box come in other colors?"

It was a good thing Bob had his mouth covered. I'm sure he was grinning like a Cheshire cat.

"No, ma'am," I said with a straight face.

"How about a larger size, then. And I need two of them, one for my daughter's coffee table, and one for mine."

"Ma'am, this is the only one I have."

"How do you know? You haven't checked the stock-room yet."

Bob chortled, sounding for all the world like a quartet of bullfrogs. The customer, thank heavens, didn't seem to notice.

"I know I don't have more because I bought this piece at an estate sale up in Charlotte. It was the only one of its kind."

The woman in dirty yellow and lavender spandex was joined by a friend. The friend was wearing a green, one-size-fits-all dress that didn't live up to its label.

"Mildred, what's taking so long?" the friend asked.

"She's being difficult," Mildred said.

"I am not!"

"Let's just leave," the friend said.

"But I want this," Mildred said, waving the porcelain box about as if it were a Glo Light stick.

"Whatever for?" The friend grabbed Mildred's arm. "Come on, I've seen better ones at Pottery Barn."

"Bigger sizes?"

"All sizes. Connie got herself one so big she uses it for a coffee table."

Mildred thrust the Cheng-te box at me. Lucky for her I managed to get a good grip.

"But this one is only twelve dollars," she said. "The ones at Pottery Barn have got to cost more."

"This one is twelve hundred dollars!" I shrieked. "Those are zeroes!"

"She's nuts," Mildred's friend said.

Bob Steuben roared with laughter.

I let Bob laugh as long as I could possibly stand it. Then I gently put the business end of the feather duster to his mouth. He pushed it aside and spit.

"Well, Abby, you have to admit that was funny."

"About as funny as graffiti. Twelve dollars indeed!"

The door opened and a party of four entered. They were casually dressed as well, but none of them were wearing shorts. I smiled my approval. This is Charleston, after all. A three-hundred-year-old city deserves at least a modicum of respect.

After greeting them I turned to Bob. "You know, I really should get a helper. Don't get me wrong, I love having the shop, but the thrill for me is in acquiring the merchandise, not selling it. You sure I can't tempt you to hang out here on a permanent basis?"

It was a joke, of course, since Bob is full partners

with Rob in more ways then one. He certainly didn't need a job working as my flunky.

"You know, Abby, sometimes I think you're psychic."

"You sure you don't mean psy*cho*?"

"Hey, none of us is perfect. But you see that guy there? The one in the khaki pants and blue knit shirt?"

"Yes, what about him?"

"He's not with the others. He's here to get a job."

"Cute."

"No, I mean it. He stopped by our shop this morning looking for a job as sales clerk. We didn't need him, of course, but I told him you might. He came straight over here, but you weren't in yet. I told him to keep trying. I hope you don't mind."

"Well, uh, does he have any experience?"

"Why don't you ask him yourself," Bob said. "While I wait on the others."

Experts claim that we are biologically programmed to dislike nearly twenty percent of the people we meet. For my friend Magdalena Yoder up in Pennsylvania, the figure is more like eighty percent. It stands to reason, at least in my cotton-picking little brain, that by the same token we are inclined to find a similar proportion of people highly desirable. And I don't necessarily mean in a sexual way.

Trust me, there was nothing sexual about Homer Johnson. He was pale and doughy, with enormous jowls that spilled over the collar of the blue knit shirt. His head was as bald as a Goodyear tire, and he was wearing the first pair of square glasses I'd seen in years. But I liked him. I can't explain why; I just did.

"Mr. Johnson," I said, "what experience do you have?"

"Ma'am, I'm sixty-eight years old. You name it, I've experienced it."

I couldn't help but smile. "What I meant was, what experience do you have working with antiques?"

"Ma'am, my wife is seventy. Just thirty more years and she meets federal specifications."

"I'll tell her you said that. But seriously, have you ever worked in an antique store?"

"No, ma'am. I was a haberdasher up in Knoxville. Owned my own shop—Genuine Gents—for forty-five years. Was sick only thirty-nine days." He ambled over to inspect a collection of glass paperweights I keep locked in a display case. "Them is right pretty," he said.

"Indeed, they are. Did you say you were sick for thirty-nine days?"

"Yes, ma'am, but that's thirty-nine days altogether. That averages to less than one sick day per year."

"You're quite right. Well, at least you have experience working with the public."

"And I can work a cash register—even one of those newfangled computerized ones. But more importantly, I can add and subtract."

"That is certainly a plus. What brings you to Charleston, Mr. Johnson?"

"Winter."

I nodded. A lot of retirees pick the Charleston area because of its mild climate.

"I'm not fond of winter either, Mr. Johnson. Give me a nice hot summer day anytime."

He grinned and the jowls quivered. "Winter is our

daughter's name. She moved down here last year to take a job at the College of Charleston. She's a professor."

"How nice for you. And for her! My mother lives with my husband and me, but my children are away at college. Kids can be a pain at times, but I miss mine terribly."

I'm not sure he heard me. He was staring at a Tiffany-style lampshade.

"Excuse me, ma'am," he said with a slight bow, "but that ain't real, is it?"

"In fact, it's not. How did you know?"

"My wife's mama's aunt had a real one of those. The glass was—well, prettier."

"Prettier in which way?"

"Sorry, ma'am, I spoke out of turn. It's just that when you're in the haberdashery business, you get to know quality."

I smiled. The man wasn't eloquent, but he did have a discerning eye.

"Mr. Johnson, I'll certainly keep your name on file—"

"Just a minute, please," he said. Then he hurried over to where two Linen Ladies had been mulling over a sabre-leg classical sofa for the past five minutes. At least. They'd taken turns sitting on it, inspecting the fabric closely (it was original 1825 fabric over horsehair, and in remarkable condition), and were now standing with arms akimbo, just staring at the piece. This was, of course, all a bit silly, since my asking price was only twenty-five hundred dollars, and this pair was wearing enough money on their respective persons to send some deserving person to a private college for a year.

I held my breath. What did a haberdasher from Tennessee know about Linen Ladies? Tourists in spandex shorts, maybe, but not our local Linen Ladies. And these women were definitely local. I'd seen their faces in the society column several times. One of them, I think, went to Mama's church.

Although I couldn't hear what Mr. Johnson first said, the next thing I knew all three of them were laughing. I sneaked closer, keeping a pair of highboys to my right as my cover.

"And it's really comfortable for napping, too," Mr. Johnson said.

The ladies roared.

I stopped dead in my size-fours. Something bizarre had just happened. On the way home from work I would check a few of the charming Charleston gardens for signs of giant pods. It appeared as if the body snatchers had mounted another successful invasion.

"I don't suppose you could give me a discount," the principal buyer said, her voice dripping honey. After all, the rich don't stay that way by parting with their money.

Homer Johnson bowed slightly, his jowls flapping forward like fleshy wings. A few feathers, a lot less weight, and he might achieve liftoff.

"Ma'am," he said, "for you I'd cross the Cooper River—under water. But I'm afraid I have this piece marked as low as I can get it, and not have my mama call me a fool."

The Linen Ladies laughed. "Not even just an eensy-teensy bit?" one purred.

He sighed dramatically. "Ma'am, it's a steal at this price. In fact, I wish I still had room in my parlor for a piece this size. You see"—Homer Johnson glanced around conspiratorially—"this sofa is of particular interest."

"What do you mean?" they asked in tandem.

"I think I remember seeing one just like this at the Smithsonian last year."

I *think* I remember. Brilliant. And who knows? Perhaps he had.

"Then I definitely want it." The buyer reached into a purse that cost almost as much as the sofa and withdrew her wallet. "Which other pieces do you find particularly interesting?" she asked.

Homer Johnson was hired.

No doubt about it, the man was a gifted salesman. And wouldn't surprise me to learn he'd been potty-trained before the age of one. All you had to do was to show Homer—as he asked me to call him—something one time, and he had it down pat. As for my "newfangled" cash register, he found it easier to work with than did I. If only all the senior citizens in my life caught on as fast as Homer Johnson.

"Abigail Louise Timberlake!" Mama cried at the top of her lungs the second she entered the shop. She hadn't even looked to see if I was with a customer. Thankfully, I wasn't.

"Mama! What are you doing here? You're supposed to be up at Kanuga."

My petite progenitress patted her pale pink pearls. They were a present from Daddy the year he died, and Mama has never willingly taken them off. I suspect she even showers in them, although you can be sure I've never peeked. That the pearls have any nacre left—and indeed they do—ranks, in my opinion, up there with some of the holy mysteries of the church.

In fact, I'm surprised there is anything left of the beads. When Mama gets even mildly agitated she pats the pearls. She does this even when she's happy. When she becomes annoyed she rotates the necklace, between right thumb and forefinger, slowly at first, her speed increasing as her blood pressure rises. Sometimes she gets so worked up the pearls become a blur.

"How can you expect me to lollygag around in the mountains with a group of church people I hardly know, while you're down here ruining our lives?"

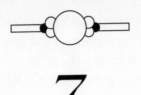

7

"Say what?"

"You heard me, Abby. That's all anyone could talk about—Mrs. Amelia Shadbark. I must have heard that name a million times. Now she's dead, and I didn't even get a chance to meet her."

"Mama, who told you she was dead?"

"Sudie May heard it from Lilly Beth who heard it from Margaret Anne who—"

"Never mind, Mama, I get the picture."

"Abby, did you know Mrs. Shadbark was the grande dame of Charleston society?"

"Well, I—"

"Abby, she was our entrée!"

"Then who was the appetizer?" I asked wickedly.

The pearls began their first rotation. "Abby, I'm being serious. You were invited to tea at Charleston's finest, and you didn't take me!"

"That's because you were up at church camp hobnobbing with Charleston's second finest. Besides, as it turned out, it was only a business tea. You would have been bored. That's why I took C.J."

Mama gasped. "You took C.J.?"

Alas, the rumor mill was not nearly as reliable as I'd expected. The information pipe had gotten plugged somewhere between Charleston on the coast and Kanuga in the mountains. In this case it appeared as if missing information was going to be more of an issue than wrong information.

"Like I said, it was business. And anyway, Mama, she behaved herself very well." I refrained from adding, "unlike some people I know."

"C. J. might have behaved herself," Mama said, giving the pearls a complete spin. "But did you?"

"Of course!" I stared at her. Boy, was I wrong. The pearls were spinning so fast my head was following suit. "Mama, what have you heard?"

"Nothing."

"Spit it out, Mama!"

"Abby, do you know your blouse is inside out?"

"It's the newest fad, Mama. But that's not what the ladies at Kanuga were gossiping about. I want you to tell me what they said. Tell me *now*."

"Well, dear, if you insist."

"I do."

"I'm afraid it isn't pretty, dear."

Rumors seldom are. I braced myself against an eighteenth-century secretary.

"Go ahead. I can take it."

"Very well." The pearls were a streak of pink. "It's been suggested that you might have—uh, contributed to Mrs. Shadbark's death?"

"What?"

"You know, poisoned her. Although, frankly dear, now that I know C. J. was there, this sheds a whole new light on things. Not that she would do it on purpose, of course, but you know how she is. We don't call her Calamity Jane for nothing."

I looked around weakly for a place to sit. Fortunately there was a genuine Turkish ottoman within collapsing distance.

"Mama, you didn't honestly think I did it, did you?"

"Of course not, dear. But you try convincing the others."

"Forget the others," I cried. "You know I didn't do it. That should be all that matters."

"Of course, like I said, there is C. J.—"

"What about C. J.? Are you telling me you suspect her?"

"Well, you've got to admit she's a pecan or two shy of a pie."

"She's also one of your dearest friends."

Mama blinked, and the pearls flopped to a stop. It was the truth. The fact is, Mama has more in common with C. J. than she has with me. Ever since Daddy died, my dear mother's elevator hasn't quite made it to the top floor. And although Daddy's unfortunate demise— killed by a dive-bombing seagull with a walnut-size brain tumor—happened in the seventies, Mama has been mysteriously locked in the fifties. She wears dresses that nip in at the waist, and with full-circle skirts puffed by layers of crinolines. Her living room furniture is "blond" and her lime-green drapes hang from scalloped wooden cornices. On a recent survey she listed Mamie Eisenhower as the woman she most admired, and *Lawrence Welk* as her favorite television show.

"Abby," she said, "I get your point. C. J. wouldn't harm a fly."

"Exactly. In fact, she once told me about the time she glued the wings back on a fly that had been hurt."

"Where is she now?"

"She looked in on the Rob-Bobs this morning—at the Finer Things—and then went off to take a carriage tour of the historic district, and to do some shopping." I glanced at my Rolex. "She should be home by now."

"Our house?"

"Yes, Mama. She doesn't return to Charlotte until the day after tomorrow."

Mama nodded, pleased at the information. "Then I'm making shepherd's pie for supper. That's her favorite, you know."

"Yes, but if I recall correctly, C. J. said that's because up in Shelby they put a real shepherd *in* the pie."

Mama giggled. "Oh, Abby, you're terrible."

I hoisted my petite patootie off the ottoman. "Well, Mama, I'll see you at supper then."

At five feet even, Mama is three inches taller than I, but her voluminous skirts take up as much room as a linebacker. When I tried to pass, she neatly blocked me.

"Not so fast, Abby. Who's that lean, mean, sex machine over there?"

My head swiveled like Linda Blair's. "Where?"

"Over there, sitting behind your desk."

"That's Homer Johnson, my new assistant. And I'd hardly call him lean."

"Is he married?"

"Yes, he is."

"You sure? He's not wearing a ring."

This from a woman who practically has to hold her

hymnbook with her toes in order to read it. Ever since she broke her last pair of bejeweled, batwing frames, back in the eighties, Mama has refused to wear glasses.

"I'm sure, Mama. He has a daughter named Winter—"

Mama wrinkled her nose. "Maybe so, Abby, but I smell single."

"Whatever, Mama." The woman has always claimed she can smell trouble coming. But smelling marital status, now that was new.

"So, are you going to introduce me, or what?"

"Or what, Mama."

I wasn't being rude, mind you, but merely stalling the inevitable. Within minutes Mama had worked up the nerve to introduce herself to Homer Johnson, bless his heart, and I was superfluous. Mama seemed to have forgotten me—forgotten supper even—and Homer seemed quite content with all the attention. Perhaps he really wasn't married.

Every time the shop bells rang, however, Homer immediately excused himself and scurried to wait on the customer. The magic I'd seen him work earlier was repeated time and time again, and my business boomed like never before.

Given the fact that I appeared to be unneeded by my new employee, and unseen by the woman from whose loins I sprang (practically fully grown, to hear Mama tell it), I decided to steal a few minutes and do a little investigating of my own. It's not that I didn't trust the Charleston Police Department, but I had more at stake in finding Amelia Shadbark's killer than did they. They merely had their professional reputations on the block. I, on the other hand, had my social reputation, not to mention Mama's. Failure to clear my name from any and all suspicion could mean that my descendants would be blacklisted in the Holy City for generations to come. The names Wiggins, Timberlake, and even Washburn would join the likes of Sherman, Grant, and a host of nefarious carpetbaggers.

So, while Homer was occupied unloading a rice planter bed that had been taking up far too much room, and Mama was busy "reapplying" her face, I ducked out of the shop. Fortunately I'd driven to work that morning, so it took me only a few minutes to reach the Shadbark mansion. I may have a smaller cranium than most women, but that doesn't make me stupid. My intent was not to visit the scene of the crime; I knew from past experience it would be closed to me. My intent was to find Gladys Kravitz.

You see, it had occurred to me that every neighborhood has its version of that *Bewitched* character. Maybe not as extreme as that meddling woman, but someone who pries and spies, nonetheless. Such folks are not only tolerated, but often subtly encouraged. They function as human watchdogs for the community. Sure, we all feel free to complain about them "sticking their big noses where they don't belong," but in the end we feel safer for having them around. We may even pass on to them our own observations—in an offhand manner, of course—and let them do the broadcasting.

But even if I couldn't locate the Gladys Kravitz who lived on Amelia's street, I was certain to find someone who would talk. Tragedy—and murder ranks at the top of that list—generates in even the most taciturn of folks the need to talk. Recall, if you will, the last time an ambulance or fire truck was spotted parked on your street. Were not your neighbors, yourself included, gathered in little clumps to both observe and discuss the matter? "I didn't know she had a heart condition." "He always bragged about his gun collection." That kind of thing. This need to discuss tragedy has a half-life of several days, and it had been only a matter of hours since the detectives had been to my house. Besides, the news had not made it into the morning's issue of the *Post and Courier*. There was still plenty to speculate about.

Although I expected to find someone to talk to, I certainly didn't expect to hit the jackpot. Especially not without trying.

"Ma'am!" I heard the woman call.

I was standing on the sidewalk opposite the Shadbark residence. Actually, I was hiding behind a palmetto trunk, trying to decide which of the houses flanking the mansion was my best prospect. The call came from behind me.

In order to save face, I pretended not to hear.

"Ma'am! There's nobody there at the moment. Not likely to be for a while, now that it's all taped up."

I turned reluctantly. You could have fried an egg on my face. The woman was seated on a third-story balcony, or piazza, as they say in Charleston. Because her house, like many on the peninsula, was set right up against the sidewalk, she was perched practically above me. Who knew what-all she had observed.

"I'm not a rubbernecker—honestly. It's just that I knew Mrs. Shadbark."

She took a sip from a tall glass. "Yes, I know."

"You do?"

"You were over there yesterday. Four o'clock on the nose. You and a tall blond girl. Is she your daughter?"

"C. J.?" I couldn't help but laugh. Neither my daughter, Susan, nor my son, Charlie, looks anything like me. My ex-husband Buford was a good ten inches taller, and was bigger boned proportionately. But I would have had to sleep with a Nordic King Kong to produce offspring like C. J.

"I take it she wasn't your daughter." She waved her glass. "Hey, I'm having a little late-afternoon libation. I'd be happy if you joined me. With two, it's an official cocktail party."

She didn't need to twist my arm. "Sounds wonderful. My name is Abigail Timberlake, by the way."

"Evangeline LaPointe," she said. "I'll be right down to let you in."

Ms. LaPointe was, at least by my standards, an extremely tall woman with a prominent proboscis and short, almost wiry, strawberry-blond hair. The color wasn't natural, and it had been recently applied, so it gave me no clue as to her age. But there was tightness about the eyes that suggested she night be a woman in her sixties trying to pass for a decade younger.

She met me at the wrought-iron gate and ushered me through rooms filled with exquisite late-eighteenth-century pieces. Of course I had to compliment her on what I saw. That pleased her immensely, and instead of taking the elevator, we climbed the stairs in order that I might peek into even more rooms. By the time we reached the third-floor piazza we were fast friends. A glass of frothy pink punch made us even closer.

"So, you were invited to tea," she said. "I'm impressed."

"Yes. Mrs. Amelia Shadbark. *The* pillar of Charleston society."

"That, too, honey. What I mean is, Amelia didn't often entertain. Not since her husband passed away."

"Then I'm flattered."

"As well you should be." Evangeline downed half a glass of punch in a single gulp. Apparently now that she had a drinking partner, there was no longer any need to sip.

I smiled happily. The grand dame might be dead, and my presence in her house problematic, but at least one person had realized what a coup it was.

"To Amelia," I said, and raised my glass.

Evangeline drained her glass. "To hell with Amelia."

"I beg your pardon?"

"You heard me. The woman was a witch."

"Well, uh, I don't know what to say."

"No need to say anything, honey. But let me tell you, that woman was as mean as a snake. Somewhere there's a happy mongoose."

I took my first sip. A body my size can't handle much more than one drink, but I needed the fortification.

"I don't suppose you'd care to share more, dear."

Evangeline poured herself another glass and drained half of it before answering. "Sure, she came across as high society, and yes, her people settled Charleston when God was just a boy, but she had her share of problems, let me tell you."

I took another sip. "Tell away!"

8

Evangeline drained her second glass. That is to say, her second glass since I'd *arrived*.

"For one thing, her children hated her. Constance—the daughter—hasn't been by to see her mother in years. Of course the two of them haven't been on proper speaking terms every since Constance ran off to Chicago with a pencil eraser salesman."

"A what?"

"A pencil eraser salesman," she repeated irritably. "You have a hearing problem, honey?"

"No, ma'am. It's just that I never thought about that being a profession."

"Well, I suppose it is, because that's what he was. Anyway, the old bat nearly disinherited her."

"But she didn't?"

Evangeline shrugged and refilled her glass. When she was done, nothing but froth remained in the pitcher.

"I've heard it both ways," she finally said. "But what would you do if your daughter killed your husband?"

"I beg your pardon?"

She nodded. "Orman Shadbark died of a heart attack when Constance eloped. At least that's what Amelia claims."

I dug in my pocketbook for a pen and began taking notes on my cocktail napkin. Luckily, Evangeline La-Pointe was not adverse to using paper products.

"What do you mean by 'she claims'?"

"Well, he died of a heart attack—that's a fact. But I wouldn't blame it all on Constance. Lord only knows what grief the poor man was subjected to all along."

I would have loved to hear more details of Amelia Shadbark's shabby treatment of her husband, but that information was not going to be productive. Maybe some other time, and on a full stomach.

"You mentioned other children, dear. How do they fit in the picture?"

"There is just one other—a son. Orman Shadbark Jr."

"Did he get along with his mother?"

Evangeline took a swig of her concoction and then made a face. I didn't know at first how to interpret the grimace.

"Orman Jr. is a L-O-S-E-R."

"How so?"

Her face contorted again. This time a plethora of creases appeared seemingly out of nowhere, confirming my earlier suspicions that she was older than her surgeon would have you believe.

"The man's a drunk."

"You don't say."

She seemed oblivious to the irony. "He lives somewhere up in North Charleston. Or is it Hanahan? Anyway, he hasn't been able to keep a job for years. If it weren't for the handouts his mama gives him—or should I say gave?—he'd be living on the street. And that family thinks they're so all-fired special."

I took my second sip of punch. Some folks don't find courage until they hit the bottom of the bottle. I was fortunate enough to find it near the top of my glass.

"What did Amelia Shadbark do to you?" I asked.

Evangeline blinked. "I don't know what you mean."

I tried another tack. "We all have our dark sides. What was hers?"

She drained her glass for the third time. "She had this dog, you see. Some fancy breed—Irish wolfhound, I think it was. Tall, skinny thing. Anyway, you're supposed to keep your dog on a leash, clean up after it. That sort of thing. Well, Amelia's dog was too good for that. Came over every day and did its business. And guess who wouldn't come over and clean it up?"

"I'm sure that was aggravating," I said sympathetically. I'd had a similar thing happen to me, and I wanted to strangle the bitch. The neighbor, not her dog.

Evangeline eyed the froth in the pitcher. "Oh, that wasn't the half of it. I also had a dog back then. A little Pomeranian named Flossie. One day Flossie got out— just for a minute—and the wolfhound was over here like greased lightning."

I gasped. "Oh no. I hope it was quick and painless."

She glared at me. "It was neither. I couldn't separate them, try as I might. You wouldn't think such a thing would be possible, but it was. Anyway, the vet advised an abortion, but I wouldn't hear of it."

"You mean Flossie got *pregnant*?"

"Fortunately there was just one puppy, but she had to have a cesarean."

"Bless her heart."

"The puppy weighed almost a third as much as she did. We named him Huey. You know, after Baby Huey in the comic books."

I nodded. "So they both survived?"

"Yes, but Flossie was never the same after that."

I glanced around. There'd been no sign of a dog in that lovely house. Come to think of it, there'd been no dog at Amelia Shadbark's house either—at least not that I could see. Surely an Irish wolfhound would be hard to miss.

"Where are the dogs now?"

Evangeline turned the empty pitcher upside down over her glass, collected what few drops remained, and slugged them back. Then she set pitcher and glass down with a thud.

"Honey, Flossie's been dead for thirty-five years. Huey for twenty."

And I thought Mama could hold a grudge. Mention Cora Anne Sanders, and Mama will tell you that the former insulted her in front of the whole world, God included, by putting ketchup on Mama's casserole contribution to a church supper. That was back in 1976!

The only thing I remember that far back—that still got me worked up—was being stood up on a date by Blainey Edwards. If he had taken me to homecoming, as he promised, I never would have agreed to have my roommates fix me up with a blind date. That means I never would have met and married Buford Timberlake. Then again, we never would have produced two such lovely and loving children as Susan and Charlie.

I took my third sip. "I know it's none of my business, Evangeline, but—"

My hostess waved for me to be quiet. "Shhh! You hear that?"

"What?"

"That car."

"Which car?" We were in a city, for crying out loud, and it was evening rush hour.

"That car!" She pointed at a dark green Buick that seemed to have appeared out of nowhere and was turning into Amelia's driveway. "Well, well, well. I wonder what he's doing there now!"

"Who?"

"Her gardener."

The car pulled to the end of the short driveway, and sat idling for a few minutes before the engine killed. Finally, a tall dark man got out on the driver's side, glanced up at the deceased's house, and then disappeared behind some shrubs at the driveway's end.

"Surely he knows she's dead."

"Well—"

"I never trusted that man."

"Why, because he's African American?"

Her eyes flickered. "Don't be ridiculous. I'm not prejudiced against anyone. But for a gardener, that man spends an awful lot of time inside."

"Inside the house?"

"Oh, he goes around to the back, of course. So I've never seen him go in. But I know what's going on. He even brings her presents."

Since the man in question appeared to be in his late twenties, I wanted to shout, "You go, girl!" But, as C. J.'s granddaddy up in Shelby used to say, you don't spank a cow that's giving you milk. That expression finally made sense—well, sort of.

"Presents? You don't say!" I pretended to be shocked.

She nodded vigorously. "Sometimes as often as once a week."

"What does he bring?"

"I can't tell. They're always in a box."

"Are they wrapped?"

"Some are, some aren't. But always right out in broad daylight. It's like they didn't even care about the scandal."

"Is there a scandal?"

She shrugged.

"I mean," I said, "what do the neighbors have to say?"

"My neighbors don't have a whole lot to say, I'm afraid."

"Oh?"

"Well, the McFarlands"—she gestured with her chin to indicate the house on our left—"are getting up in years, and I almost never see them out. And the Graysons"—she jerked to the right—"are from off."

"I beg your pardon?"

"From off. You know, from off someplace else."

"But they live here now," I said incredulously.

"Honey, they've lived here only fifteen years. Why, they've hardly had time to unpack."

"I'm from off," I informed her, as if she hadn't figured that out.

"Yes, but they're from someplace up North originally. We just don't chat that much."

"I see." I stood. "It's been wonderful getting to know you, Evangeline."

She eyed the remains of my drink expectantly. "You

come back anytime, Abby. We'll have ourselves another little tea party."

I promised to return.

"Hello," I called. "Hello!"

The gardener appeared suddenly between two
camellia bushes, nearly giving me a heart attack. I
steadied myself against his car while catching my
breath.

"Sorry, ma'am. I didn't mean to scare you."

"That's okay."

I will confess right now to staring at him. He was the
most beautiful man I'd ever seen. Using Greg's height as
a comparison, I judged him to be about six feet tall. His
skin was smooth, the color of a good chocolate milk-
shake, his hair arranged in neat braids that fell below his
shoulders in back. But what made this man so gorgeous
was the symmetry of his features. It was as if a template
for his face had been cut from a single piece of folded
paper. I wanted to reach up and touch him; to trace the
outline of his eyes, nose, and mouth. The only other
time I've ever felt that impulse was on a trip to Florence,
Italy. There it was the statue of David I wanted to caress
(had I been able to reach it), and not some Italian man—
well, there were a few of those, too. But I digress.

"Can I help you, ma'am?"

I shook myself out of my reverie. "I was having tea
with a neighbor across the street," I said. If Evangeline
could call it "tea," then so could I. "I wondered if you'd
heard the news about Mrs. Shadbark."

The young man cocked his head and gave me an ap-
praising look. "Actually, I have. In fact, I was just
about to ask you the same thing."

"*Me?*"

"I thought maybe you wanted to sell her something." He was holding an oil lamp box, which he set carefully on the front passenger seat as he spoke.

"To the contrary! I, uh, I—"

"My name is Percival Franklin," he said and held out his hand. The ease with which he did, coupled with his youth, disarmed me.

"Abigail Timberwash," I said. "I mean, Timberlake. Or Washburn—that's my married name."

"Are you a friend of the family?" His tone was skeptical.

"Well—I knew her."

"Then you know she was one terrific lady. I can't believe she's dead."

"It's certainly a shock. Are you a friend of the family as well?"

He grinned. "Why are you playing games with me, Mrs. Timberwash?"

"That's Timberlake! And whatever do you mean?"

He pointed to Evangeline's house, which at that point was directly behind me. "I saw you sitting up there with that snoopy woman."

"You did?"

"That's all she does, you know. Just sits there and watches this house to see who comes and goes. She seems to find me particularly interesting. You don't suppose it's because of my color, do you?" He laughed. "Or haven't you noticed?"

My face burned. "You're making fun of me, aren't you?"

"Mrs. Timberlake, you're not from around here—"

"How do you know I'm not?"

"You have a different accent."

"It's pure Carolina," I wailed.

"It isn't Charleston. Mrs. Timber*lake*, are you with the police?"

One of the lessons I've learned surprisingly late in life is that virtually everything comes with a spin. The news, history, even the Bible, they all have somebody's viewpoint attached to them. There is no source of information that we mortals process that doesn't come with a bias. The question is, how much, and whose?

I could easily, and truthfully, have told the young man that I was indeed connected with the police. I am, in fact, married to a retired detective. Never mind that he works as a shrimper now. Granted, this might be a bit more spin than was prudent, but since truth operates along a continuum, what did it matter?

However, Percival Franklin seemed to be far more astute than I was at his age. I had nothing to gain by b.s.'ing him further, and possibly something significant to lose.

"No, I'm not with the police. In fact, the police questioned me this morning because I was one of the last people to see Mrs. Shadbark alive. Needless to say, this has made me a bit uncomfortable, so I decided to do a little investigating of my own. As for that snoop across the street, she said you were Mrs. Shadbark's gardener. Is that true?"

He didn't even blink. "Very good, Mrs. Timberlake. Not everyone can turn on a dime like that."

"It helps to be small."

We both laughed.

"You still haven't answered my question," I said. "Are you the gardener?"

"Ah, that! You mean 'just' the gardener, don't you?"

"Well—I—you're not so bad yourself, Mr. Franklin. You certainly cut to the chase."

"Saves time."

"I should imagine that a young man like you has plenty of time."

"I work three jobs, Mrs. Timberlake—well, I did, until this morning. I work the graveyard shift at a factory, I do the gardening here—when it needs it—and then I have my *real* job."

"Which is?"

He opened the car door and carefully removed the box. "Have a peek."

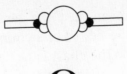

9

"That's beautiful! Where did you get it?"

"I made it." There was no attempt to disguise the pride in Percival Franklin's voice.

"Get out of town!"

"Excuse me?"

"I mean, this is incredible. Can you take it out of the box?"

The young man extracted the sculpture from its box with the delicacy of a surgeon. *It* was a sprig of camellia leaves, and a single blossom, carved from a dark wood, possibly cherry. The leaves gleamed like real camellia leaves after a rain, and on one of the flower's petals a drop glistened and appeared to shimmer.

"Wow!" I reached to touch one of the leaves, but he pulled the sculpture away.

"I had it hidden in the toolshed. I was going to give it to her today. It needed to dry a little bit more."

"The varnish?"

"Shellac. It was still tacky when I brought it." He tipped the box. "See?" He rubbed an area of the base with a long finger. "And here, where the cardboard stuck."

"You sell these?"

He nodded.

"Where? I mean, do you have a shop?"

"I have a stall at The Market."

He meant *The* Market, which runs the length of Market Street, between Concord and Meeting. It was built in 1788 and is at times referred to as the Slave Market, although slaves were never sold there. House slaves were, however, sent to shop for produce and dry goods at the many stalls on the lower level. Today many of the shoppers are tourists in search of a good deal on souvenirs.

"Are they all flowers?"

"I do dolphins," he said. "And seagulls. They're the easiest. They're also cheaper, so they sell better."

"If you don't mind my asking, how much does something like this go for?"

He shrugged. "Like I said, I do dolphins and seagulls. This is my first attempt at a flower."

I fished in my purse for one of my business cards. I have a little metal case for them, but it always manages to come open. I'm more likely than not to come up with a lipstick or comb. This time I found a card on my first dip.

"I own an antique store on King Street. The Den of Antiquity. I'm afraid I sell strictly antiques, and I haven't owned the shop very long. But when I get to know my customer base better—you know, their tastes—I'd love to recommend your work. Well— pieces like this flower. I don't know about the dolphins and gulls."

He took the card almost shyly. "I was thinking about two hundred and fifty. You think that's too much?"

"I think that's a steal!"

"Really?"

I longed to finger his flower. "It's museum quality."

His eyes shone. "I don't just carve wood—"

A gray Mercedes-Benz was trying to park along the curb. The driver was obviously inexperienced, or else very drunk. She made three attempts at parallel parking, then finally settled for the front left tire resting half on the curb.

"Well, gotta go," Percival Franklin said. He seemed tense, poised for flight.

"But you were about to tell me—"

He slipped the carving back into its box. As he did so, my business card fluttered to the ground. While I was stooping to pick it up, he thrust the box at me. It grazed the corner of my eye.

"Sorry," he said, "but you take this. It's yours."

Before I could react at all, much less thank him, he was backing his dark green Buick out of Mrs. Amelia Shadbark's driveway. I stared after him in disbelief. Then I stared into the box.

"I'll take that for you," a high-pitched voice chirped.

It was the driver, a pale woman in a cream linen suit, with matching heels and bag, and a broad-brimmed straw hat only a shade darker. She seemed perfectly steady in her four-inch spikes, as she clicked up the drive at an astonishing speed.

"That's all right," I said. "It's not a bit heavy."

She waved an armful of chunky jewelry at me and trilled like a canary. "Of course it isn't. But I'll take it just the same."

"I think not."

She clicked to a stop. "I beg your pardon?"

"What's in this box belongs to me," I said calmly.

She cocked her head, the brim of her hat resting on one shoulder, and studied me with eyes that were frank and unafraid. Her face was familiar, but I didn't know where, or how, I might have met her. It was like listening to one of those harmonies from the late sixties that was clearly not the Beatles, yet you couldn't place it.

"You got that box from *him*, didn't you?" she asked.

"Quite frankly, dear, it's none of your business."

Her head snapped to its normal position. "It is, if what's in there belonged to Mrs. Amelia Shadbark."

"Well, it didn't."

She clicked forward two steps and held out her hands. The chunky jewelry clanked obscenely as it settled into place.

"Let me be the judge of that."

I stood my ground. "I don't think so."

Physically I'm about as threatening as a stuffed kitten, but the Linen Lady seemed to be having second thoughts. She inched backward, until she'd relinquished the ground gained in her last advance.

"Who are you?" she demanded in a schoolgirl voice.

I've never actually played football, but I've been forced to watch enough on TV to pick up a few good moves. I considered feinting to the left, and then, since I could undoubtedly turn faster than she could, making a break for it to the right. The only problem was I didn't want to risk dropping the exquisite carving Percival Franklin had made. And then there was also the very small matter of my pride.

"I was here first," I said. "How about you identify yourself."

The linen crowd are practiced in giving cold looks, not glares, but the inept driver was able to give me a doozy. At least she was good at something. The climate on that Charleston driveway suddenly felt like a cold winter day up in Charlotte.

"My name is Mindy Sparrow, and I'm a friend of the family. Now, who are you?"

"My name is Abigail Timberlake, and I was a business associate of the deceased."

"Amelia didn't own a business."

"Maybe so, but that's how we met."

"Just what kind of business?"

"None of yours."

I spoke softly, and my tone was nothing if not polite. Nonetheless, Ms. Sparrow reeled in apparent shock. Had her spike heels been any higher, she would have been at risk for breaking a limb.

"Why, I never!"

"That's hard to believe, ma'am. You seem pretty good at being rude."

"Then I shall call the police."

"Please do. I'd like to level harassment charges."

That comment generated both teetering and twittering. "Why, I never," she said again. "This is just preposterous."

"I quite agree. This is the first time I've had a complete stranger demand that I give her a gift—one just given to me by a friend."

She emitted a series of strange sounds. The best way I can describe it is that it reminded me of a flock of birds settling in to roost for the night. I waited patiently until she was able to form words.

"That man is your *friend*?"

"A very dear friend. One for whom I wouldn't hesitate to lay down my life."

"But he's the gardener!"

I glanced around. "And a very good one too. You should see the backyard."

"I've seen it many times." She eyed the package. "Don't the police usually seal a house under these circumstances?"

"I suppose they do. Well, if you'll excuse me, I better be going." I nimbly sidestepped her. "I'll tell Constance and Orman that you called," I said over my shoulder.

"Just a minute!"

I turned, having gotten the desired effect. "Yes?"

"So you really know the family?"

"Do you?"

"Constance Shadbark is my best friend," she said. "We grew up together—in fact, I can't remember a time when I didn't know Constance. Funny though, but I can't remember her ever mentioning you, Ms. Timberquake."

"That's Timber*lake*. And I may as well come clean now—I never met your friend Constance."

"But you said—"

"Ms. Canary—"

"That's Sparrow! *Mrs.* Sparrow."

"Mrs. Sparrow, then. My intimating that I knew

Constance and Orman was just my way of finding out if you really knew them yourself. For all I know, you could have been just another nosy neighbor."

She smiled for the first time. "I see you've met Evangeline LaPointe."

"She was very chatty."

"I bet she was."

"No doubt she told you horror stories about Mrs. Shadbark. Did she mention the dog incident?"

"In detail."

"You believed her?"

"I took it with a grain of salt."

"Ms. Timberlake, who are you really, and what are doing here?"

There wasn't a trace of animosity in her voice, so the tide appeared to have turned in my favor. I decided to trot out the truth. Sometimes this strategy actually works.

"I'm an antique dealer. Mrs. Shadbark invited me to tea yesterday. She asked me to broker her Lalique collection."

Mindy Sparrow raised an eyebrow—well, what would have been an eyebrow, had it not been for some overzealous plucking.

"She contacted *me*," I hastened to explain. "I really am a legitimate antique dealer. My shop is the Den of Antiquity. It's on King Street." I fumbled for another one of my business cards, but fished out a dilapidated card for Manly Moe's Massage and Tattoo Parlor on the Isle of Palms. I have no idea how that got in my purse.

"That's all right, Ms. Timberlake. I believe you. It's

just that I haven't a clue as to what collection you're talking about."

"René Lalique."

"Really? I'm afraid I don't know her clothes. Are they available at Talbot's?"

Anyone who caries a crumpled card from Moe's Massage and Tattoo Parlor has no business snickering. I tried my darnedest not to.

"It's a glass collection."

"Like goblets and such?"

"There are a few of those, yes. But her collection contains mostly vases and perfume bottles. Although she does have a couple of nice hood ornaments. Lalique made those too."

Mindy Sparrow's nose wrinkled as badly as her skirt. I would have thought that all Linen Ladies loved Lalique, but apparently not this one.

"Oh, *that* collection. Well, from what I understand, Ms. Timberlake, whoever, uh, killed Mrs. Shadbark destroyed that. All those knickknacks broken to bits."

"They weren't knickknacks!" Perhaps I'd been a little too vehement. "They were highly collectible and quite valuable."

Her nose became as smooth as glass. "How valuable?"

"Well, that's hard to say—I just got an overall peek. The first thing I was supposed to do, you see, is appraise them."

"But off the top of your head. How much would they bring at auction?"

I shrugged. "Somewhere between a hundred thousand dollars and half a million. I know that's a broad figure, but it all depends on how limited the edition of each piece, and how well publicized the auction is. I was thinking Sotheby's, which should bring top dollar."

"I see. And do the police know this?"

"I tried to tell them."

She glanced at her car. She seemed suddenly anxious to leave.

"Are you in the book?"

"Not yet, but directory assistance will have the number." I assumed she meant the telephone book, and not the social registry. Unless I was cryogenically frozen and then thawed three centuries from now, I stood no chance of ever being listed in the latter.

"I may give you a call," she said. Without further ado she turned and clicked away. She seemed to have totally forgotten the box I clutched to my chest.

I watched her go. When her car was safely out of sight, I intended to do a little reconnoitering of the grounds. Since I didn't plan to enter the house—unless I "accidentally" found the back door unlocked—I had no expectations as to what I might find. But after all, isn't that the point of reconnaissance? Who knows, Mrs. Shadbark's killer might have left a trail of Lalique shards across the grass that the police—

My reverie was interrupted by a crash on the third story piazza across the street. I looked up just in time to see Evangeline LaPointe duck out sight. Unless my tired eyes were deceiving me, she had a pair of binoculars hanging from her neck.

It was time to cut my losses and get out of there.

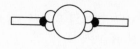

10

I was late getting back to work. Homer Johnson, bless his heart, remained at the shop until I returned. Although it was only ten minutes past my regular closing time, it had been an inexcusable and irresponsible thing for me to do.

"I'm really sorry," I said the second I found him.

He was dusting a carved mahogany bureau. *Dusting*.

"Think nothing of it, ma'am. But I used your phone again to call my wife. I hope you don't mind."

"Mind? You could have called the one who lives in Alaska, and I wouldn't have cared."

"Ma'am?"

"That was a joke, Homer." I looked around. Something was amiss; the shop looked much emptier than I remembered. Perhaps clean furniture took up less space.

Homer was astute, as well as tidy. "I sold the Renaissance Revival parlor suite, ma'am. And that Art Deco sideboard." He pronounced the word "deek-o."

"Get out of town! I've been trying to get rid of that parlor suite since I set up shop. Came with an estate I bought that couldn't be split."

"Did that big dresser with the chipped veneer come with that estate as well?"

83

I glanced over to where I'd last set eyes on that ugly piece. "You sold that, too!"

"Yes, ma'am. I told them it would be lonely without that parlor suite."

Had I been a good foot taller, I would have grabbed Homer Johnson by the jowls and planted a big wet smooch atop his shiny pate. Instead, I grabbed his hand and pumped it vigorously.

"I can't tell you how glad I am to have you working for me. In fact, I've just decided that instead of a straight salary, I'm going to put you on commission. How does ten percent sound? I'll even make it retroactive."

Homer smiled happily. "That sounds wonderful, ma'am."

"Great."

"Ma'am?"

"Yes, Homer?"

"I don't mean this to sound bad, or anything, but— uh—uh—"

"You want me to tell my mother to leave you alone?"

His chrome dome lit up like Rudolph's nose. "It's just that I'm a married man, and my wife's kind of a jealous woman. If she comes by the shop—"

"That's all right. No need to say more. I'll tell Mama to heel."

Homer made me promise not to be too hard on Mama. He also volunteered to open the shop for me in the morning; an offer I eagerly accepted. Thanks to an extra pair of pudgy hands, I was going to have time on my own to do the thing I do best.

*　*　*

I trudged through the front door of my new home wanting nothing more out of life than a nice long soak in the tub, and maybe a little food. Instead, I got Mama.

"Abby, you're late."

"Why, is Greg home already?"

"No. He called from Mount Pleasant. He said to tell you he had a good haul—whatever that means—and he'll be home as soon as he gets it unloaded and weighed."

"That's great, Mama!"

"If you say so, dear." She eyed the box Percival Franklin had given me. "What's that?"

"Nothing much. Where's C. J.?"

"In the kitchen making supper."

"What?" I set the box and my purse on the hall console. "Mama, C. J. can't cook. Besides, you told me you were making shepherd's pie."

"I changed my mind, dear. And C. J.'s not actually making supper, she's just helping Bob."

"What's *he* doing here?"

"Some sort of trouble with Rob, but he won't give me any details." She gave me an accusing look. "Things just seem to fall apart when I'm gone."

I kicked off my sandals. "What's that supposed to mean?"

"You know, dear."

"Know what?"

Mama patted her pearls. "Abby, don't make me say it."

I climbed wearily into the lap of my favorite William and Mary. It was no bathtub, but I knew from a lifetime of experience that Mama was going to have her say. My choice was to hear her out in the tub, in my birthday suit, or in the living room, while I was fully clothed. Since bubbles don't last forever, but Mama's lectures do, I chose the chair.

The second I was seated Dmitri appeared from nowhere and joined me. He immediately began kneading my thighs with his front paws. This cat has an unerring ability to tell when I'm agitated, no matter how calm my voice.

"Say it, Mama."

"All right, dear, if you insist." Mama sat in the chair opposite me. "It's just that—well, like I said before, Mrs. Shadbark was our perfect entrée into Charleston society. Why, a pretty woman like you, with a handsome husband like Greg—not to mention a mother like me—you would have climbed straight to the top."

Dmitri had stopped kneading and was lashing my face with his tail. I spit out a mouthful of hair.

"Mama, it wouldn't have happened that way."

"Sure, it may have taken a couple of weeks—a month or two at the most."

"Mama, this isn't Rock Hill. Or Charlotte, even. It's a whole different world down here. Charleston has secret societies—clubs, I guess you'd call them—that most folks don't know exist. I remember reading somewhere that even folks from the oldest and best families are on lists waiting to get in. Face it, Mama, we were deluding ourselves."

Mama shook her head vigorously. "You're forgetting, dear, that I belong to both the DAR and the Daughters of the Confederacy."

I pushed Dmitri gently off my lap. "Give it up, Mama. It wouldn't have happened."

"Well, if I had been there—" Mama's hand left her pearls and flew to her mouth.

"Oh, I get it! You think if you'd gone with me to the tea, that somehow Mrs. Shadbark would still be alive."

"You said it, dear, not me."

"What would you have done differently, Mama? Invited yourself to stay overnight?"

Mama shrugged. She looked on the verge of tears.

"Is it so awful to want to belong?"

"No, Mama. But we don't have to belong to every group. You have your friends from church, and there are plenty of people like us who have moved here from other places."

"A lot of them are Yankees," Mama said, her voice barely a whisper.

In fact, I wasn't sure at first that I heard right. "What did you say, Mama?"

"You heard me, dear."

"For shame, Mama. One of your granddaddies was a Yankee."

"He was from Maryland, dear. That's a border state."

"But he fought for the Union."

Mama dropped the subject, but it was not a satisfying victory for me. Clearly she missed her friends back in Rock Hill. That may have been a very small pond, a puddle even, but Mama had been a big fish—maybe not a grass carp, but at least a large-mouthed bass. In Charleston we were destined to be minnows.

Greg arrived in ebullient spirits; it had been his largest shrimp catch yet. He claimed he'd heard the critters calling to him from the bottom of the ocean. All he had to do was chug over to where they were and let down his nets. The crustaceans literally crawled into them. After he kissed me, he kissed Mama, and then C.J. He would have kissed Bob, except that the latter was too busy putting the final touches on dinner to be bothered by such nonsense.

I told Greg about hiring Homer Johnson, but I saw no need to put a damper on his spirits by telling him about the rest of my day. Instead, I coaxed him into the shower (whether I joined him is really not your business). Then I fixed him a scotch and soda, and we all, except for Bob, sat around in the living room and listened to Greg recount the events in *his* day.

Although we listened with varying degrees of enthusiasm, C.J. seemed particularly enthralled. At one point, when Greg was describing dumping the catch on the culling table, my young friend got so excited she fell off her chair.

Greg leaped to give her a hand. "C.J., are you all right?"

C.J. stood on her own power. "I'm fine. Ooh, Greg, would you take me with you tomorrow? Please? Pretty please?"

Greg looked at me. "You better ask the boss."

C.J. literally threw herself at my feet, barely missing the edge of the coffee table. "Please, Abby? With sugar on top?"

I sighed. It's not that I didn't trust the two of them together. Plus which, Greg's cousins would be there. It was just that Calamity Jane didn't come by her name in a vacuum.

"You have to promise to do what you're told," I said sternly.

C. J. threw her arms around my legs and gave them a tight squeeze. "Ooh Abby," this is going to bring back so many memories."

"I didn't know you'd been shrimping before."

"I haven't. But Granddaddy Ledbetter took me batting once when I was a little girl. I'm sure there are many similarities."

"I don't see what hitting a baseball has to do with shrimp, dear."

C. J. laughed. "Not that kind of bat, silly. The kind that hang upside down in caves. You see there's this cave near Shelby—"

"Let me guess," Greg said. "Your Granny made bat stew."

The big gal made a disgusted face. "That would be yucky, wouldn't it? No, Granny used to cut them into bite-size bits, dip them in a special bat batter, and deep fry them until they were nice and crunchy."

"Bat batter?" Mama asked. She was always looking for new recipes to submit to church cookbooks.

C. J. nodded. "I could give you the recipe if you want."

"Maybe later, dear," I said.

Bob was motioning us all to sit down. His pride in his gourmet meals is exceeded only by the control he exerts over those who partake of his efforts. Allow one of his soufflés to fall, and he'll pout for weeks.

Knowing him as we all do, we took our seats. Greg sat at the head of the table, yours truly at the foot—or, if you like, the other way around. Mama and C. J. sat on one side, Bob on the other. After Mama said her short Episcopal grace, we all dug in.

Some of us stopped digging almost immediately. "This is very interesting," Greg said diplomatically. "What did you call it?"

"It's grouper. I wrapped it in pancetta—which is sort of an Italian bacon—then broiled it."

"What's that stuff under it?" C. J. asked, as if she didn't know. After all, she'd been in the kitchen helping him.

Mama gave her the evil eye. We both knew we'd have been a lot better off with shepherd's pie. Possibly even with battered bat bits.

"That stuff," Bob said archly, "is pureed potato infused with goat cheese."

Greg turned as green as the Atlantic where it hugs the coast. Unless something happened to distract him, he was going to blow like a norther.

Mama, bless her heart, decided to take the initiative. "Abby, dear," she said almost cheerfully, "how is the murder investigation going?"

Greg went from green to white in a nanosecond. "What murder investigation?"

I gave Mama *two* evil eyes.

Mama has never been one to take hints. "Mrs. Shadbark, the woman Abby had tea with yesterday, was poisoned. Our Abby may have been the last person to see her alive."

"Except for our C. J.!" I wailed.

Greg's eyes, normally the color of fine sapphires, had turned a dark gray. "Abby, you're not involving yourself in this, are you?"

"*They* involved me!"

"Who is they?"

"Sergeant Scrubb and—who's the other one, C. J?"

"Bright," she purred. "He's dreamy."

Greg frowned. "What did the officers want?"

I swallowed hard. The pureed potatoes with goat cheese had formed a lump in my throat the size of Texas.

"They just asked some questions—like what was it we had to eat, who poured the tea, that kind of thing."

"They asked me questions about glass," Bob said.

All eyes turned to the cook.

"Glass?" Greg asked.

Bob nodded. "That Bright fellow had a box of shards. Said Abby told him they might be valuable."

"Not the shards," I hissed. "The original pieces. They were Lalique."

He shrugged. "They may have been at one time. It was impossible to tell."

"Lalique has a very distinctive look, Bob," I said, measuring my words like drops of cod liver oil.

"That's true, Abby, but none of the pieces I saw were signed."

"Well, they were." I jumped up from the table without excusing myself—thereby proving I didn't belong in Charleston society—and retrieved the peacock's head perfume bottle that had been sitting on my bedroom dresser. "Take a look at that," I said and thrust it under Bob's patrician nose.

He blinked. "Uh—"

"Look," I said. "It's right there. See for yourself."

"Abby," Greg said disapprovingly.

"That's okay," Bob boomed. He took the bottle, and

despite the fact that he was wearing glasses, held it inches from his nose.

"Well?" I demanded.

Bob handed the piece back. "Sorry, Abby, but it's not his."

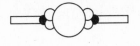

11

"What do you mean?" I try not to be shrill. The fact that a lonely seagull responded just outside the dining room window was sheer coincidence.

"Abby, how many L's are there in Lalique?"

"Two, of course."

"That has three. Forgers misspell all the time. Sometimes it's carelessness, some think it protects them legally. Of course they're wrong."

I stared at the base of the bottle until I was in danger of needing glasses myself. There *were* three L's. How could I have missed that? How could C.J. with her twenty-something eyes have missed it as well? Sure, she's an egg short of an omelet, but when it comes to this business she's absolutely brilliant.

You see what you want to believe, my daddy used to say. I can only hope he didn't see the seagull that dive-bombed him. Perhaps the one outside my window now was an omen.

"I can't believe this," I said. "How could I have made such a stupid mistake?"

Bob, whose generosity exceeds even his talent as a

cook, cleared his throat softly. "We've all been there, Abby."

"But I—I feel like such a fool."

C. J., who was sitting on my right, leaned over and patted my shoulder. Her hands are as big as oven mitts, and as heavy as oven doors. I had to struggle not to land facedown in the goat-flavored spuds.

"Don't worry Abby, I'm sure you'll straighten this all out. You always do."

"Shhh."

I'd said it quietly, but any man who can hear shrimp calling from the bottom of the ocean can hear his shushing wife the length of a dinner table. His eyes, still strangely gray, locked on mine.

"What did you say, dear?"

I smiled. "I merely said 'shhh.' C. J. needs to eat before her food gets cold. In fact, we all do. Bon appetit, everyone!" I speared a forkful of pancetta-wrapped grouper.

"Not so fast, Abby. You're skulking around like an amateur detective again, aren't you?"

I patted my cheek to indicate that it would be rude of me to answer with my mouth full.

Greg shifted his gaze. "C. J.? What do you know about this?"

I tried kicking her under the table, but my leg was too short. It wasn't too short, however, to connect with the table's leg. Sheer willpower kept me from howling, a fact for which my tablemates should have been grateful.

"Abby hasn't said anything about investigating this murder," C. J. said guilelessly.

"And I saw her in the shop today," Bob offered.

Mama touched the corners of her mouth with her

napkin. "But she did leave the store early. Over an hour, wasn't it dear? That nice Mr. Johnson had to cover for you on his very first day."

If looks could kill, I'd be an orphan now. "Mama," I growled.

Alas, the woman is not easily stifled. "I'm not saying I blame Abby for wanting to clear her name of suspicion. After all, Mrs. Amelia Shadbark was the pinnacle of Charleston society. And as long as there's any doubt at all, our pedigree will not be accepted in the right circles—although I still don't understand why the DAR isn't good enough."

Greg stabbed his grouper, and then let the fork sink to the plate, where it connected with a clank. "So *that's* why you suddenly decided to hire an assistant"

I smiled meekly. It is usually my best defense. Unfortunately, it's getting harder and harder to manipulate my dear husband.

"I'm going to have to put my foot down this time," he said, and actually stamped the floor. "This amateur sleuthing has got to stop. God knows it's dangerous enough for us professionals. I'll be damned if I'm going to let my wife get involved."

That was going too far. "Are you forbidding me?"

Greg stared silently. His eyes were blue again—an icy blue.

"Well, *are* you?"

"Don't make me say it, Abby."

"Ooh!" It was an involuntary response from C.J., and she was immediately mortified.

I smiled at her. "Not to worry, dear, the dinner theater is over." I turned my forced smile on Bob. "You simply must give me this recipe."

"Sure, Abby. As soon as I get home—"

"Now."

He did so in nauseating detail.

To his credit, Greg ate every last bite of his supper. In fact, we all cleaned our plates. C.J. was so nervous she even had seconds.

After coffee, I shooed Bob home at the earliest opportunity. Greg and C.J. went to bed early and at the same time—separate rooms, of course—which left just Mama to contend with. I'll confess to wishing that she'd be struck with a sudden case of acute laryngitis. Had I been something besides a lapsed Episcopalian, I might even have prayed for it.

"Well, I declare," Mama said, as she supervised me loading the dishwasher. "I never would have dared talking like that to your father."

I tried to remember that far back. I had a vague recollection of sporadic tension at the dinner table, but never any raised voices. And Daddy certainly never stamped his feet. Mama, either, for that matter. Although—and I don't mean to cast aspersions on the woman from whose womb I issued—it is harder to stamp pumps than wing tips.

"With all due respect, Mama, I refuse to discuss this."

"But Abby, I'm your mother. You're supposed to be able to discuss anything with me."

"Anything?"

"Anything but sex."

"I'm a mother, too, Mama. My rule handbook says to stay out of a grown child's business. Especially if she's married."

"Why, I never!"

"Then please don't start now."

"Thirty-four hours of labor, and this is the thanks I get?"

"It was six."

"What?"

"It was thirty-six hours of labor, not thirty-four."

"Are you sure?"

"You've only said it a million times."

"Well, nevertheless, the point I was hoping to make is that I think you should stand by your guns."

"What?"

"Don't let your husband tell you what to do. In the end, you'll only resent him for it."

I leaned against the upper rack of the dishwasher, and it slid away from me. Fortunately my reflexes are still pretty good. A year or two down the line and I might have ended up in the dishwasher altogether.

"I can't believe you're saying this, Mama."

She stared down at her pink-and-white-gingham apron with the eyelet ruffle. "I wanted to work when your daddy and I were first married, but he forbade it. It put a huge strain on our marriage."

"But you did work, Mama. You were a secretary—"

"That was a job, dear. I wanted to work at my vocation."

"Vocation?"

"Abby, sometimes I think you just repeat everything I say."

"Sorry, Mama. What was your vocation?"

When she looked up from her apron she was blushing. "I was going to be a lounge singer, dear. I sang—"

"Lounge singer?"

"There you go again!"

I clamped my hands over my mouth to show her I meant business.

She sighed. "Okay, but don't interrupt again." She sighed again for good measure. "I sang torch songs. I was good, too, if I have to say so myself. Some people even called me the next Patsy Cline."

I tried to imagine Mama singing in a smoky bar attached to some Holiday Inn, but I couldn't. At least not without imagining an empty bar, the bartender with *his* hands over his ears. You see, back in Rock Hill my mite of a mother sang in the church choir. She was what the choir director fondly called an "m and m" member. That's because everyone said "mercy me" anytime she opened her mouth. Once, in an act of misguided kindness, the director gave her a solo. At the conclusion of the service the ushers found a pack of dogs on the front steps. One of them was dead from a brain aneurysm.

"Well, Abby, aren't you going to say anything?"

"So, you wish you'd stood up to Daddy, huh?"

Mama stroked her pearls. "He was a dear, sweet man, and may he rest in peace. But just think where I might be today."

I gave Mama a big hug and sent her off to bed. Alone at last, I got out the Greater Charleston white pages and looked up the name Shadbark. There was just one.

"Hello, Constance," I said to myself with a smile. "I'll be seeing you tomorrow."

I slept fitfully and was wide awake when Greg left to

go shrimping with C.J. How could I not have been? The love of my life clomped about the bedroom like a pirate with two peg legs. He slammed dresser drawers, closet doors, and even the toilet seat. Poor Dmitri, unaccustomed to the din, wiggled his way under the covers and took refuge between my feet. It was a wonder Mama didn't come flying out of her room to mediate.

You can bet that I feigned sleep. Silence—and this is a lesson I've learned from all the men in my family—is far more effective than a raised voice. At any rate, after the bedroom door slammed for the last time, I tried hard to go back to sleep. I counted sheep, llamas, and chickens, but to no avail.

Finally I got up, took a long hot shower, and fixed myself a bowl of Raisin Bran—the kind with two scoops—and a cup of green tea. After eating, I remained in the kitchen nursing the brew, and brooding, until I heard Mama moving about in her room. Then I lit out of there like a coon dog with its tail on fire.

When I arrived at the shop, five minutes before opening time, Homer Johnson was waiting outside the door. With him were two anxious shoppers he'd snagged and already sold on the idea of redecorating their respective houses, using nothing but antiques. One of the two, a man with a Seeing Eye dog, had even agreed to buy a pair of Austrian lamps I'd been trying to unload for weeks.

I wisely let Homer do his thing, but when there was a lull in the lucrative activity, I pulled him aside. He came with me reluctantly. The mild-mannered man I'd hired the day before had metamorphosed into a merchandising monster.

"Homer, darling," I said, pouring on the sugar, "I know this is only your second day here, but you seem to be doing exceptionally well. Would you mind terribly if I took the day off?"

He blinked behind the square wire frames.

"Only for today," I promised. "Tomorrow you can have the day off."

He blinked again. "It ain't that, ma'am. It's just that—well, I'm surprised you trust me, what with me being new at this and all."

I laughed. "Homer, dear, you could sell the Grace Memorial Bridge."

He smiled happily at the compliment. The bridge of which I spoke was the terror of all who passed from Mount Pleasant into Charleston. It was nosebleed high and barely wider than a skateboard. Burly men have been known to wet themselves on the way over.

"Thanks, ma'am. I enjoy selling, that's all."

"Well, you certainly have the knack."

"There ain't nothing to it, really. All you gotta do is tell the truth. Like, take that corner china cabinet over there. See how it gets its shape, almost like a heart if you were to look at it from on top? You don't see that very often. And look at the wood—oak it is, but hand-rubbed with oil so shiny and smooth that every grain shows. Heck, you could put the crown jewels in that china cabinet they wouldn't look outta place. You know what I think?"

"What?" I was staring at the cabinet with a new appreciation.

"I think that there cabinet belonged to one of them *old* Charleston families. During the war—and I mean the War Between the States—the womenfolk stuffed their skirts and petticoats in there to keep it from breaking from all them vibrations when the Yankees were shelling the Battery."

"You don't say!"

"Yes, ma'am, I do. I think this here piece meant something mighty special to one of them blue bloods. Then after the war, what with the carpetbaggers and all, things got real tight and the lady of the house had to sell it. You can bet she carried on something awful, but it had to be done. Thing is, only one who could afford it then was one of them Yankees."

"What a shame!"

"Yes, ma'am, it sure is. So then this Yankee family has it for three generations. They put their laundry soap and what not in it, 'cause they don't know its true value. Then when the last one dies, some distant cousins up in someplace like Minnesota, inherit it. Of course they can't be bothered to haul it all the way up there, so they sell it at an auction." He walked over and began to stroke the polished wood. "No, ma'am, this here ain't just a work of art, it's a piece of history. This is Charleston."

"I want to buy it!" I clamped a petite paw over my pathetic maw. "I mean, don't sell it, Homer. I want to take it home with me."

He nodded. "There's a right nice little dressing table over yonder that the lady of the house sat at, combing her hair, while she worked up the courage to part with this cabinet—"

"Say no more! I'll take it as well!"

"Yes, ma'am. I'll put it aside. Will you be wanting the bench, too?"

I fled the shop while I still had inventory left to sell.

One thing for sure, with a man like Homer at the helm, I was certainly free to do a little poking around for clues to Mrs. Shadbark's killer.

I hummed with satisfaction as I drove over to Mount Pleasant to interview Constance. I'd show Greg, and while I was at it, I'd clear my name of any doubt, *and* establish a reputation as a woman to be reckoned with. Maybe even one worthy of inclusion in Charleston's coveted secret societies—as an honorary member, of course! Just as long as I didn't poke the wrong person, or at least poke too hard, there was no harm to be done. No harm at all.

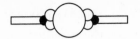

12

There are currently two bridges that span the Cooper River to connect Mount Pleasant with the Charleston Peninsula; the aforementioned Grace Memorial, which is one-way into Charleston, and the newer Silas N. Pearlman, which is two-way—*most* of the time. Although the latter is equally high, to allow for the passage of ships, the lanes are wider, permitting drivers to relax enough to enjoy the spectacular views.

With any luck one might pass directly over massive freighters from China or Malaysia, or spot dolphins feeding in the aquamarine waters of Charleston Harbor. On any given day one can gaze down on Shutes Folly Island with its intriguing Castle Pinckney, or wonder at the size of the *U.S.S. Yorktown,* a retired aircraft carrier that served both in World War II and in Vietnam, and which is now a museum in its berth at Patriots Point.

I have been to Mount Pleasant many times, beginning with when I was just a little girl. In those days it was a charming, if somewhat sleepy town, shaded by spreading live oaks festooned with Spanish moss. There never was a mountain—the highest point barely reaching twenty feet—and water has always been the defining feature, from the shrimp boats of Shem Creek, to the tidal marshes and the harbor itself.

Today this once bucolic village is one of South Carolina's fastest-growing cities. Beginning in the 1980s wealthy retirees from up North discovered the area's charm, as well as the fact that it is only half as far as Florida, making trips back to see families all that more feasible. Ironically, the very things that brought this influx of new residents—the romantic scenery, the slower pace of life—are being replaced by upscale housing developments and traffic bad enough to make a New Yorker blanch.

The Gullah people, descendants of black slaves who have retained many African customs and created a Creole language all their own, have lived in the area as long as any Europeans. Today, however, the young people find themselves rapidly being priced out of the housing market by wealthy newcomers. There are still enclaves of Gullah living along the upper reaches of Rifle Range Road, but gated communities continue to sprout up like mushrooms after a summer rain.

I fully expected Constance Shadbark to live in one of these new moneyed neighborhoods—perhaps Park West, or the Estates section of Charleston National— but much to my surprise, she lived in Fig Tree Apartments, a lower-income housing project just off Highway 17. The apartments had been in the news just a week ago, when a badly decomposed body had been found in an upstairs unit. Police suspected foul play. If I remembered correctly from all the TV coverage,

Constance lived just a few doors down from the scene of the crime.

Her apartment was on the ground floor, and as it lacked a working bell, I rapped on the peeling green door. When no one answered after several seconds, I rapped again.

"I'll just be a minute," a woman called. "I need to grab my purse."

After enough time had elapsed to cook up a mess of collard greens, the door opened. Clearly I had the wrong apartment, the wrong address altogether. This woman, with her stringy shoulder-length hair, dressed in a faded floral T-shirt from Kmart, and stretch pants that bulged obscenely in places skirts were meant to cover, could not be Amelia Shadbark's daughter.

"Uh, I think I've made a mistake."

The woman, who was leaning heavily on a cane, looked at me through eyes that were mere slits. "You're the one they sent to pick me up, right?"

"I beg your pardon?"

"You're from social services, right? You're here to give me a ride to the doctor."

"No, ma'am. I'm looking for a Constance Shadbark."

She pushed a greasy wisp away from her eyes with her free hand, the better to see me. "What do you want with Constance?"

"It's about her mother."

Her eyes appeared closed. "I'm Constance Shadbark Rodriguez. Prefer to use my maiden name. Who are you?"

"My name is Abigail Timberlake. I had tea with your mother the day before yesterday—the day before she, uh, passed on"

She nodded. "So you're the one."

"It wasn't my fault!" I wailed.

"Are you sure? Because I'd have to congratulate you if you did, and I'm not in a congratulatory mood."

I started. "What did you say?"

"You heard me." She began to back into the apartment, as deliberating as a semi-truck easing into the delivery bay of a supermarket.

"You're glad your mama's dead?"

"Glad isn't the word, Ms. Timberlake. I'm thrilled."

The door would have closed, but for the tip of the woman's cane. I planted one of my size fours beside the wooden staff.

"Look, I may not be from social services, but I can give you a ride just the same. To the doctor, to the grocery store—wherever you want to go. Just name it."

She paused. Her breath came in loud gusts through the narrow space created by my foot.

"Please," I begged. "I'm a very good driver."

"Let's make it IHOP then."

"Not the doctor?"

"You want your chance to grill me, right?"

I didn't argue again.

Constance informed me that she didn't like to talk on an empty stomach, so I drove as fast as I could without risking a ticket. This involved a lot of vehicular bobbing and weaving, around tourists who appeared pleasantly lost, or retirees whose massive cars were no more peppy than they. If it had been Mama with me, I would have had to put up with a lot of senseless gasping, possibly even a few screams. Constance remained placid, although she did grunt when I screeched to a stop at the red light where Mathis Ferry road joins the highway.

But we made it to the restaurant safely, and I was relieved to find a parking place. You see, the International House of Pancakes on Route 17 North is one of this burgeoning town's few spots where one can grab a bite of breakfast. As such, it is invariably crowded. Midmorning, however, seemed to be a fairly good time. Although there were several empty booths available in nonsmoking, Constance Rodriguez insisted on sitting in the land of hazy addiction. What made her choice really interesting is the fact that she didn't smoke. Or at least she claimed not to.

"I'm tired of all this political correctness," she grunted, and then proceeded to order the Farmer's Breakfast with extra sides of hash browns and bacon. I opted for just coffee.

True to her word, Constance didn't say a word—except for placing her order—until after she was through eating. That is, through eating her *first* breakfast. After ordering a second breakfast, this time the Rooty-Tooty-Fruity, hold the Fruity, she inclined her head in my direction.

"You may ask your questions now," she said imperiously.

I swallowed a mouthful of tepid coffee and took a deep breath. "Well, uh, okay. Did I understand you correctly before? I mean, are you actually thrilled that your mama is dead?"

She ran a pinky up the side of the boysenberry syrup bottle, and then licked it. The pinky, not the bottle. Although I wouldn't have been surprised to see her lick that too.

"I'm overjoyed," she said, her tone utterly flat. "The woman was insufferable."

I found myself wishing IHOP served something stronger than coffee. "Do you mind elaborating?" I asked.

"Where should I begin?" She dabbed a puddle of syrup on the table next to the bottle. "How about the day I was born? Mama thought she'd done her duty. Thought she'd produced a proper heir. A boy. She was so out of it—so hopped up on painkillers—she misunderstood the doctor and nurses. When she came to her senses and saw me, she literally turned away. Figuratively, too. Do you know, she never once changed my diapers?"

"You're joking!"

"I don't joke, Ms. Timberlake. She hired a nursemaid. A black woman named Betty. Until I was ten, Betty was more of a mama to me, than Amelia." She paused to clean the sides of the maple syrup bottle.

"What happened when you were ten?"

"Betty died," she said, in the same flat tones. "She was run over by a drunk while crossing King Street on New Year's Eve. New Year's Day actually. Mama wouldn't let her live at the house. Made Betty stay late that night to take care of me while she and Daddy partied."

I warmed my coffee from the thermos on the table and stirred in two miniature tubs of half-and-half, and a package of Equal. "Did your daddy treat you the way your mama did?"

For the first time her eyes were wide enough for me to see their color. They were palmetto-frond green.

"I didn't agree to talk about Daddy."

I nodded. "But what about your brother—Orman Jr., isn't it? I mean, how did your mama treat him?"

"Ha! Well, Mama hung the moon on him, of course. Guess who got to take care of the little monster when Betty died?"

I smiled. "I have a younger brother. His name is Toy, believe it or not. In my mama's eyes he can do no wrong."

I knew she was studying my face, but the fact I could no longer see her eyes again was disconcerting. It was like having a face-to-face conversation with a person wearing very dark, or reflective, sunglasses.

"So Toy really pisses you off," she said finally.

"Well, he's studying to be an Episcopal priest—hey, that's not fair. We're here to talk about your mother, Mrs. Amelia Shadbark."

"Right." The apricot syrup bottle was clean, so Constance was forced to dribble some directly on her finger. "But you brought up the subject of your brother, Ms. Timberlake."

"Well, let's get back to yours. Does he live in the area?"

She shrugged. "Last I heard he had an apartment in North Charleston. Off Rivers Avenue, I think. Close to Trident Technical College."

That didn't sound like a likely address for a Shadbark. But neither did the Fig Tree Apartments, even if they were located in prestigious Mount Pleasant.

"When's the last time you saw him?" I asked.

She screwed up her face to help her think. "Five years?"

It sounded more like a question than an answer, but I wasn't surprised. I'd have to stop and think if anyone asked me when I last saw Toy. It's not my fault he moved to California, and refuses to come East even for a short visit. If I had as much time on my hands as Mama does, it might be a different story. I'm not adverse to visiting La-La Land, mind you. I just can't take that much vacation.

"Mrs. Rodriguez," I said—she'd not yet invited me to call her Constance—"can you think of any reason someone would want to kill your mother?"

"Myself excluded?"

"Come on, surely you don't mean that!"

She laughed for the first time. It was surprisingly high and girlish, and reminded me of Mindy Sparrow.

"Do I look like the type who could kill—physically, I mean?"

"Your mother was poisoned," I said, perhaps a bit too sharply.

"Well, it wasn't me. I haven't seen her in years. I would have had to mail her the poison. But to answer your question, you might want to check out her heirs."

She pronounced it "hairs." I was on the verge of telling her that was the job of a real detective—one with a lab at his or her disposal—when I figured it out. But Constance might have inadvertently made a point.

A human hair will record toxins that have been ingested during its growing cycle, although it is unlikely Amelia Shadbark's hair grew very much after she was poisoned.

"Aren't you one of her heirs?" I asked.

"Ha! Now that's a good one. Mama wrote me out of her will the day I married Lorenzo."

"The pencil eraser salesman?"

It is possible to glare through slits. The blue-green eyes shone like twin laser lights.

"There is nothing disgraceful about selling pencil erasers. Somebody has to do it. But oh no, Mama wanted me to marry a doctor, or a clergyman. Even a lawyer, she said, was better than a salesman."

"Been there, done that—married the lawyer, I mean. It was a disaster. Now I'm married to an ex-cop shrimp fisherman."

"Really?" Her demeanor was suddenly much warmer. Now we were sisters; in status, if nothing else.

"Really. He operates out of Shem Creek, here in Mount Pleasant. He comes home every night smelling like the beach at low tide."

She smiled. "Lorenzo used to smell like rubber."

"What happened to him?" It was a reasonable question, given that she referred to him only in the past tense.

Constance gave the Very Berry jar a thorough cleaning before answering. "He died—it will be ten years next Friday. His sample van collided with a lumber truck."

"I'm so sorry."

She laughed, but that high girlish voice couldn't

transcend the bitterness. "Thanks, but it was kind of ironic, wasn't it?"

"How so?"

"Those logs were headed for a pencil factory. My Lorenzo was pummeled to death by potential pencils."

"So then you came back to the Charleston area." I didn't know what else to say.

"Yes, that's what brought me back. I got a job when I first returned—as a bookkeeper for a bakery up in North Charleston. I didn't count on being crippled by arthritis." She extended a clutch of sticky fingers. "See? I can't even close this hand properly. But it's even worse in my knees. And since I can't drive any-more, I have to rely on the mercy of strangers."

I grimaced sympathetically. I also felt guilty as all get out. Thanks to me, the woman was packing more weight on those knees, instead of keeping her appoint-ment with the doctor.

"I trust Mrs. Sparrow has been a big help."

She centered the slits on my face. "What the hell does that mean?"

"Well, it's just—I mean, she is your best friend and all. It must be a comfort to have a friend as close as a sister nearby."

"Mrs. Sparrow," she hissed, "is not my best friend. In fact, she isn't any kind of a friend."

"But she said—"

"Mrs. Sparrow is a bitch."

You can bet I would have gotten to the bottom of that, had it not been for the arrival of the Rooty-Tooty-Fruity, sans fruit. After that, my little interrogation was over. Although Constance allowed me to drive her to the doctor—where we had to wait for a cancellation—

and to the grocery store, she refused to say another word about herself, her mother, or her brother.

It wasn't a total loss, however, because while still in her syrup-licking stage, she'd given me a little something to go on.

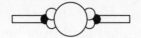

13

Orman Shadbark Jr. might well prove to be a big something to go on, if only I could find him. From Mount Pleasant I took the Mark Clark Expressway, crossing first over the Wando River, then Daniel Island, and finally over the Cooper River, which, despite the fact that it was low tide, was doing a remarkable job of forming its share of the Atlantic Ocean. I exited the expressway on Rivers Avenue, headed north, and as I approached Trident Technical College I kept a sharp lookout for apartments, but to no avail. Eventually I was forced to expand my search for an apartment building to both sides of Rivers Avenue, which is four lanes wide, and in the process gave my guardian angels, and myself, a good cardiovascular workout.

Common sense ultimately prevailed, and I suspended my sleuthing in favor of a hearty lunch at Binh Minh, a Vietnamese restaurant adjacent to a defunct miniature golf course. I'd eaten there before on several occasions, and knew their salty lemongrass chicken was to die for, whereas the traffic on Rivers Avenue was not.

I had no sooner turned off my engine when I noticed, tucked behind the little golf course, a red-brick, single-story building that looked too long and narrow to be a conventional house. It wasn't worth the effort of fighting traffic, not to mention losing my parking space, to drive over to the strange building, so I hoofed it instead.

It was worth every drop of dew (Southern women don't perspire) when I not only confirmed that the odd structure was indeed an apartment building—although only four units long—but that the tenant farthest from Rivers Avenue was listed on the mailbox as Orman. There couldn't be that many Ormans in the country. It had to be Constance's brother.

The bell was taped over, so I rapped with my knuckles. They may be tiny, but so are BBs. Both are hard, however, and can pack quite a wallop—not that I intended to hit anyone, mind you.

At any rate, the door opened presently, and when it did, it was all I could do to remain standing. The wave of alcohol fumes was that strong.

"Yes?" The man reeking of spirits was of medium height, perhaps in his late forties or early fifties, and was wearing the Charleston summer uniform of the upper class. That is to say, his suit was made of blue-and-white-striped cotton seersucker, and he sported a matching blue bow tie. White buckskin shoes completed the look.

"Mr. Shadbark?" I asked.

He peered over my head with eyes so red they added a patriotic touch to his ensemble. "Who wants to know?"

I proffered a petite paw. "My name is Abigail Timberlake." There was no point in confusing him with the Wiggins part. "I'm a friend of your sister."

"Sister?" He swayed like one of the harbor cranes in hurricane force winds. "Don't have a sister."

"Constance Rodriguez, sir. Isn't she your sister?"

The bloodshot eyes closed while he considered the possibility. When they finally opened, the red had turned to pink.

"Tell her I don't have any money," he said. "Not till the end of the month."

I turned my face long enough to fill my lungs with parking lot air. "Sir," I said while exhaling, "I don't think Constance wants your money."

"What does she want, then?"

It was time to 'fess up. While telling the occasional lie might be fun, it's also a whole lot of work.

"Constance doesn't want anything, Mr. Shadbark," I said, carefully omitting the D. "*I* do. I want to talk about your mother."

"Are you from the paper?"

"I beg your pardon?"

"The *Post and Courier*. There was a young lady here yesterday—"

"No, sir, I am not a reporter. I'm an antique dealer. I had tea with your mother the day she died."

He gave me the once-over, which took all of three seconds. "Come in."

"Well, uh—"

He snorted. Had someone lit a match just then, we would have both gone up in flames.

"Look," he said, "I can't afford to air-condition all of North Charleston."

He had a point. I had no business knocking on a strange man's door if I wasn't prepared to accept his hospitality.

"Just for a minute," I said. "My husband's waiting for me in the car."

"I'm not going to bite you, Mrs. Timbersnake." He laughed. "Given your name, that would be your job, wouldn't it?"

"It's Timber*lake*," I said through gritted teeth. "Actually, it isn't even that—never mind. Inside will be fine."

A Southern gentleman by birth, Orman Shadbark Jr., my impromptu host, stood gallantly aside while I entered. He even bowed slightly, if unsteadily, from the waist.

"Please," he said, "sit wherever you can find a spot."

That was easier said than done. The small room contained a sofa, two armchairs, and a coffee table, but they were all covered with empty bottles, dirty clothes, dirty dishes, and personal items I choose not to identify. I suppose the floor was an option, if I didn't mind sitting on a mat of food crumbs. I could only conclude that Orman had been lying in, or on, his bed, fully dressed in the seersucker suit.

"I don't mind standing," I said.

"Suit yourself." He looked longingly at an armchair, which, even if he cleared it, etiquette would prevent him from occupying. "Would you care for a drink?"

"No, thanks."

He frowned, causing the bow tie to bobble. "I hope you don't mind if I have one. It's this heat."

"By all means."

The apartment was frigid, however. No doubt he needed the alcohol in his veins to keep them from freezing. Pure alcohol doesn't freeze, you know—at least not at conventionally achieved temperatures. I had a roommate in college who proved that. We had a miniature fridge in our dorm room. I kept butter pecan ice cream in my half of the freezing compartment, Mary Beth gin in hers, away from the prying eyes of our dorm mother, who presumably had never been a college student herself.

At any rate, Orman disappeared into what I assumed was his bedroom, and returned just as quick with a glass half filled with a red liquid. I tried not to stare. At least he wasn't drinking booze straight out of the bottle.

"It's got tomato juice in it," he said, reading my mind. "That's good for your health, isn't it? Lots of vitamins."

I shrugged and smiled. "Mr. Shadbark, I'm really sorry about your mother's passing. I hope you don't think I had anything to do with it."

"Did you?" The bloodshot eyes regarded me calmly over the Bloody Mary.

"Of course not!"

"Then I don't blame you. Constance now—wait, didn't you just say you were her friend?"

"I fibbed. I just met her today."

"Oh, well, in that case"—he took a sip—"the woman is a bitch."

"I beg your pardon?"

"It was bad enough she broke Mama's heart like that, running off with a pencil sharpener salesman, but—"

"Erasers."

"What?"

"Her husband sold pencil erasers."

"It doesn't matter what he sold," he said, his voice as

cold as Mary Beth's gin. "The point is, it broke Mama's heart." He paused for a vitamin fix. "When I think of all the pain Constance caused, and her not even being Mama's daughter—"

"What?"

Orman smirked over the rim of his glass. "Oh, you didn't know that little detail, did you?"

I wanted to wipe that look off his face with his bow tie—*after* I throttled him with it. "Suppose you tell me about it," I managed to say calmly.

He took a swig of vitamins. "Daddy committed an indiscretion shortly after he and Mama were married."

"You mean he had an affair?"

"I suppose you could call it that, but it was only with the maid. Anyway, the girl didn't have any family— which wouldn't have been such a big deal, I suppose, except that she went and died on him." He laughed. "Well, not on him, exactly—not literally, but during childbirth. You know what I mean."

I got the picture all right. The Shadbarks didn't consider sleeping with the servants a sin, or even just plain unethical. It could, apparently, create inconvenient consequences.

"Let me guess," I said. It was a good thing the Orman's carpet was already ruined, because the sarcasm dripping from my voice would have done the job. "Your parents did the honorable thing and took the baby in, and that baby just happened to be Constance."

Orman chugged the rest of his health drink. "Well, it wasn't that simple, of course. They had to go through certain legal formalities. In fact, it could have been really tough, if Daddy hadn't known the right people. And I must say, it was really generous of Mama to go along with it all. I know it couldn't have been easy for her, having Constance always there as a reminder."

"Did no one in your parents' social milieu find it strange that they adopted the maid's baby?"

"If they did, they kept it to themselves. I'm sure you'll find Charleston a very civilized place, Ms. Timberlake."

I already did. Believe me, I didn't, for a minute, think the majority of the inhabitants, even the blue-blooded elite, were necessarily anything like the Shadbarks. Or their nosy neighbor, Evangeline LaPointe, for that matter. I'm old enough to know that no one group of people has the market cornered on vice, or virtue, for that matter.

"You know," I said, finding it hard to believe myself, "that Constance doesn't even know the circumstances of her birth. She thinks your mother turned away from her because she was a girl, and not the male heir your father desired."

The sneer was becoming a familiar landmark on Orman's pickled face. "Of course Constance knows."

"But she said—"

"Constance lied to you. She hated the fact her biological mother was the maid. She took those feelings out on Mama. Me, too. She used to pinch me when no one was looking. Until I got big enough to fight back, I looked like a purple-and-white checkerboard."

This new version of the Shadbark family's dysfunction sounded plausible, but that didn't mean I believed it. Constance had come across just as sincere. One thing both stories had in common, though, was that there had been animosity between mother and daughter.

"I'm sure the police have informed you, sir, that your mother was poisoned."

He waved the empty glass, sending dregs of tomato juice into the air. "A horrible way to die."

"Do you think your sister is capable of such a thing?"

"Constance?"

"Do you have another?" I asked with remarkable patience.

"Of course not." The red eyes turned into glowing slits, affirming for me that Constance and Orman shared at least some genetic material. "I hate to say this," he continued, "but the answer is yes. You see, I don't think the woman has a conscience."

"That's a pretty strong statement."

He licked a pinky and dabbed at the lapel of the seersucker suit, where a speck of tomato had landed. "But it's true. Did you ever watch the *Addams Family* on TV?"

"That doesn't mean I don't have a conscience," I said quickly.

He actually smiled. "But then you're familiar with the character Wednesday, the one who cut the heads off her dolls."

"Constance did that?"

"She cut heads off my G.I. Joe action figures, too."

I shuddered. *If* what he said was true, Constance had been one troubled little girl. Still, it was a long way from decapitating Barbie to poisoning one's mother. Well, at least for most folks.

"Mr. Shadbark, you mentioned something before about telling Constance she had to wait for her money until the end of the month. What was that about?"

He looked longingly at the empty glass. "Ah, that. You see, my daddy left us each a small trust fund, something to see us through hard times, should they ever come. He didn't want us sponging off of Mama. Anyway, Constance turned hers all over to that con man with the pencil sharpeners. Even though the two of us have never gotten along—well, I can't let her starve now, can I? She's still my sister."

I didn't know what to think. It couldn't have been very much of a trust fund. Even if he did give some of his money to Constance—I glanced around me again. Buford and I lived almost that well right out of college. (However, when Buford started law school, we gave up our cute ground-floor apartment and rented a third-floor walkup, where we shared a bathroom with a one-legged man who peed in the sink.)

"Are you retired, Mr. Shadbark?" It was meant to be a loaded question.

He recoiled. "I have a nervous condition, if you must know."

"What was your profession?"

"I am—well, I was—a gentleman of means. I guess you could say I was a philanthropist."

"I see. Well, I was inside your mother's house only once, but I daresay she appeared to have a lot of extra room. And seeing as how she was up in her years—"

He didn't touch me, but he used his breath to chase me to the door. "I wouldn't dream of sponging off my mama, Ms. Timberlake."

I felt behind me for the knob. "Well, it's been a pleasure talking to you, Mr. Shadbark. You've been very helpful."

"What the hell is that supposed to mean?"

"Nothing." My fingers found the knob. Seconds later my lungs were blessed with fresh air.

Orman followed me out to the concrete slab that served as a porch. "I didn't kill Mama, if that's what you think!"

I turned heel and scurried to the safety of my car.

C.J. was pacing back and forth across my driveway when I returned home. When she saw me approaching she waved her gangly arms in an exaggerated motion, as if to divert a herd of bulls. Since one of her dreams is to run in front of belligerent bovines in Pamplona, I thought for a second she might be practicing some sort of emergency procedure. When I stopped in the street to watch, however, she waved even harder. I stared dumbfounded as she ran right up to my driver's side window.

"Go, Abby, go!" she shouted.

I lowered the glass. "C.J., what on earth is going on?"

C.J. stuck her horse-size head in the car. I would have given her a sugar lump if one had been handy.

"Just go, Abby!" she practically shouted in my ear. "I'll meet you at Waterfront Park in twenty minutes with everything you need."

"What?"

"You know, things like food, water, and your jammies. Although, personally, Abby, I don't wear pajamas. Granny Ledbetter says it's healthier to sleep in the clothes we were born in, which, of course, is nothing, unless you're Cousin Alvin. You see, his mama had this bad habit of sucking on blankets, sort of like Siamese cats sometimes do. Anyway, she must have swallowed a lot of lint, because Cousin Alvin was born wearing a little pink onesie. Of course it didn't have any snaps, because Auntie Agnes hadn't bothered to swallow any of those."

I groaned. "What I meant, C.J., is why am I in such a hurry to get to Waterfront Park? What's happening there?"

"Hopefully nothing, Abby. That's why it will be a good place for us to rendezvous. Ooh, I just remembered, do you have a passport? If you don't, you can borrow mine, but you'll have to explain to customs officials that the picture was taken when you were having a good hair day."

"C. J.!" I screamed loud enough to scare a bull away, "what are we rendezvousing for? And why on earth do I need a passport?"

She backed from the car, looking as baffled as the bull would have been had I asked it the same question. "Abby, you mean you don't know?"

"Know what?"

"Abby, you're wanted for murder!"

14

"Don't be ridiculous, C.J.! Sergeant Scrubb knows I didn't kill Amelia Shadbark."

The big gal nodded vigorously. "That may be so, Abby, but what about Miss Point?"

"Miss who?"

"Point. I think that's what he said. Anyway, her first name is the same as the title of that Longfellow poem."

"Evangeline?"

"Yeah, that's the one. I had to memorize that in the sixth grade—"

"Get in!" I ordered.

C.J. clambered around to the passenger side, while I fumbled with the power door lock. I'm not saying I was nervous, but I gave all four windows a good work-out before I found the right switch.

The second she was belted—I always insist on that—I tore out of there like a greyhound from a cat show. When I got to the next block I made a hard right turn and then slowed down to conversational speed.

"Evangeline LaPointe is dead?"

"Ooh, Abby, you really *didn't* know?"

"Of course not!" I pulled over and parked in the

scant shade of a towering palmetto. "When did this happen? Where?"

"Sometime last night. The cleaning girl found her dead this morning. Ooh, Abby, I was so afraid for you."

I had no trouble composing a stern face. "Shame on you, C. J.! To think I would actually kill someone."

"But if you had, Abby, I was prepared to help you get away. You're my best friend, you know."

I was touched. "That's very loyal, dear, but helping a murder suspect escape is not only against the law, it's immoral."

"Maybe you had your reasons."

"C. J., you're a good friend, I appreciate that. But I'm disappointed that you think I'm capable of murder."

She hung her massive head. "Sorry Abby. I keep forgetting that you're not a Ledbetter."

"Y'all do a peck of murdering?" I asked in my best Shelby accent.

She seemed genuinely surprised at the question, which was meant entirely in jest, by the way. "Abby, don't tell me you've never heard of the Ledbetters and the McCoys!"

"That's the Hatfields and the McCoys, dear. And that was up in Kentucky and West Virginia."

"Oh no, Abby, that was in Shelby—"

I gave her a meaningful look, one I'd used many times on my own two kids when they were teenagers. C. J. was not my child, of course, and she was a grown woman, but she got the point.

"Still," she said, "I want you to know I would have visited you in prison."

"I suppose you would have baked me a cake with a file in it."

"Don't be silly, Abby, I've learned my lesson. I baked one of those for Cousin Alvin, and it only got him into a whole lot more trouble."

"Let me guess. The guards found the file when they put the cake through the metal detector."

Her head sunk until her chin was resting against her chest. "Naw, it wasn't that kind of file, Abby. It wasn't metal."

"Then what kind was it?"

"It was his IRS file. They audited him the next year, and he didn't have a thing to show them."

I sighed. I'd wasted far too much time humoring my friend.

"C. J., let's get back to Evangeline LaPointe. How did you hear she was murdered?"

"Sergeant Clean. He's here right now—I mean at your house. Didn't you see his car?"

"*Who's* at my house?"

"You know, the same detective that was there yesterday with Sergeant Bright. Sergeant Bright, by the way, is the cute one. Sergeant Clean looks like Matt Damon."

"You must mean Sergeant Scrubb! And it's Ben Affleck he resembles."

"I don't think so, Abby. Cousin Alvin looks like—"

I waved a hand impatiently. "He's there *now*?"

She nodded miserably. "Ooh, Abby, I think he's waiting to arrest you."

I made a U-turn, nearly clipping the palmetto trunk. It was time to face the music.

* * *

"There she is!" Mama sang out when I walked through my front door. "My firstborn, the boon of my old age. My Abby has never done anything but bring joy to those around her. Why, when she was only four years old she donated her entire allowance—all fifty cents—to the Salvation Army pot outside Woolworth's. When she was seven—"

"Mozella," Greg said gently, "she's not on trial here."

I stared at the tableau in front of me. Mama was seated in one of the yellow and blue William and Mary wing armchairs, Greg was standing in front of the other, and the good-looking Sergeant Scrubb was standing by a silk-covered settee that is said to have pampered the bottom of none other than Jefferson Davis, president of the Confederate States of America.

It was the sight of Greg that unnerved me the most. If he'd been summoned back to port on his shrimp trawler, then I was indeed in serious trouble. For a split second I regretted not having fled with C. J. One is forever hearing of innocent people ending up behind bars. This is a tragic thing to happen to anyone, but would be even worse for me than for most folks, because a woman my height simply does not look good in horizontal stripes.

"I'm innocent," I wailed.

Greg left his station, strode to me, and clutched me to his chest—actually, it was his stomach; yet another disadvantage of being four feet, nine inches. Since he smelled only a wee bit fishy, I concluded he hadn't had a chance to haul his nets in even once.

"He hasn't charged you with anything, hon." He kissed the top of my hard little head. "He only wants to ask you a few questions."

I pushed out of his arms so I could see his eyes. While not exactly sparkling, they were pretty much their normal sapphire-blue.

"You don't sound angry, dear."

That brought on a few twinkles. "I'm not always a grouch, Abby."

"But I didn't listen to you. I was off meddling again this morning when they called you in from the boat. I think I may be getting somewhere though because—"

Greg finished my sentence with a kiss. He has incredibly full lips for a man his age, and I adore kissing him. It's possible that on this occasion I was so relieved to discover he wasn't angry that I got a little carried away.

"Please," Mama begged, "can we stop with the CPAs?"

I stopped. "That's PDA. It stands for public display of affection. A CPA is someone you hire to do your taxes."

Mama scowled. "I know of which I speak, Abby. Ever since your daddy died I've been taking my taxes to Stanley Mucklehouse, that CPA over on Cherry Road. And every year, when we're done going over the forms, and I'm saying good-bye, he grabs me and kisses me."

"He *what*?"

"You heard me, Abby. Last year he even tried to French kiss me."

"Mama!" I shrieked and slapped my hands over my

ears. They stayed on a full two seconds. "Why do you keep going back?"

Mama patted her pearls. "I'm a widow woman, Abby, why else do you think? Each year I tell myself, this might be the last time I'm ever going to be kissed like that by a man. Of course I hate myself afterward, but then the following year when Stanley tries his moves—well, I find that I can't resist. Who knows when I'm going to get another chance."

"But he only kisses you, right?" My head was bobbing up and down with the rapidity of a jackhammer. I was willing her to agree with me.

Mama looked genuinely shocked. Her hands hovered above the pearls in mid-pat.

"Why, Abigail Louise Wiggins Timberlake Washburn! Shame on you! Don't you listen to a word I say? I said Stanley *tried* to put his tongue in my mouth. Of course I didn't let him. That would have been going too far. That would have been dishonoring your daddy's memory."

"How did you stop him?"

Mama smiled. "Let's just say Stanley Mucklehouse speaks with a lisp now."

"Oh, Mama," I moaned. And to think I tried to discourage her that time she ran off to Dayton, Ohio, to become a nun. Thank heavens they caught her wearing curlers under her wimple and singing on the stairs.

Inspector Scrubb coughed, presumably to get our attention.

"Abby," Greg said, "Sergeant Scrubb would like to speak with you alone." Greg nodded at Mama and C.J., indicating that it was time for them all to leave.

It was a wasted gesture. Mama had suddenly found her pearls even more fascinating than ever, and C.J. had picked up Dmitri and was nuzzling him, and cooing as if my ten-pound feline was a human baby.

"Let's go," Greg said with surprising authority. He headed to the door and held it open.

The two recalcitrant women inched from the room. C.J. cast me a pitying look, but Mama mostly looked miffed. Frankly, I was glad to see them go.

Sergeant Scrubb seemed relieved as well. He loosened his tie and accepted the glass of sweet tea I offered him—although it was clear from the collections of plates and glasses in the kitchen that Mama had already done her social thing.

The investigator sat when I did. "Well then," he said brightly, "shall we get down to business?"

"Grill away!" I cried.

He laughed. "Abby, we've been through this before. I'm not interested in grilling you. I just want to ask a few questions."

"Then let me say flat-out that I'm sorry. What I did wasn't right and I apologize."

"Apologize?"

"For giving you the wrong phone number."

"You did?"

I hung my head in shame. "The number I gave you for my shop is incorrect."

He shrugged. "It's really not such a big deal, Abby. People often forget their phone numbers. It's not like you call your shop a lot, is it?"

"No, of course not." I could feel the color saturate

my face. What a certifiable fool I'd been to think that the cute sergeant had the hots for me. Oh well, at least I hadn't shared that fantasy with anyone.

"So, Abby, you mind if I get to my question now?"

"Ask away," I said as I jumped blithely to yet another conclusion. "But I'm telling you now, the answer is no."

He took a sip of tea. "Well, then that's a shame."

"Excuse me?"

"I was hoping you'd say yes. That would make my job a whole lot easier."

"And I want the merchandise in my shop to sell itself." Actually, with Homer Johnson on board, my wish had pretty much come true.

Sergeant Scrubb grinned. It was definitely Ben Affleck he resembled, C. J. be hanged.

"I'm afraid you misunderstand me, Abby."

"Oh, I understand you quite well. But just for the record, I did *not* kill Evangeline LaPointe. What would have been my motive? Except possibly to cover my tracks. *If* Ms. LaPointe had witnessed me killing Mrs. Shadbark—which I assure you didn't happen, since I didn't kill the woman. What would have been my motive in that case? I have money—maybe not as much as she had, but enough to buy me anything I really want. And even if I was as poor as my children will be when they first get out of college, how would murdering a wealthy widow solve that problem? It's not like I was in her will. No, I'm sorry to disappoint you, detective, but you're barking up the wrong tree here."

He was grinning again. "Somehow I don't think so. Abby, you're just who I want to be my eyes and ears in this case."

Fortunately I was sitting on my center of gravity. Otherwise I would have fallen out of my chair, and quite possibly induced a concussion from hitting my forehead against the Italian marble coffee table.

"Would you mind repeating that?"

"Permit me to expound, instead. Abby, it is clear to me that you are a woman who found herself in the wrong place at the wrong time—or even the right place at the wrong time. It doesn't matter, so take your pick.

"The bottom line is, like it or not, you found yourself involved in the details of Amelia Shadbark's demise. In order to prove your innocence, you involved yourself even further. Now, either we can have an adversarial relationship in which I grill you—as you so charmingly put it—or else we can work together. Sort of a partnership, if you will."

I gasped. "You want to hire me on the force?"

Sergeant Scrubb laughed. "I wish I could, but you'd have to go through the academy first. No, I was hoping you'd function in an unofficial capacity. And sorry, but without compensation, I'm afraid."

"I see. You want me to be an unpaid informant. A stoolie."

"Well that's one way to put it, I guess."

"Don't worry, I accept."

"You *do*?"

"I don't suppose there's a chance I get to pack a pistol?"

"No, ma'am."

"I'm kidding, of course. It's just that I saw *Annie Get Your Gun* when I was in high school. I wouldn't really want to shoot anybody. Buford—that's my ex— and I went target practicing once. I couldn't even bring myself to aim at the cardboard cutouts. But listening and looking—well, I can do those in my sleep."

Ben—I mean, Sergeant Scrubb—smiled warmly. "Good. Now here's what I would like you to do."

A taller woman would have scooted her chair—even if it was a William and Mary—forward a bit, just to indicate she was giving the matter her full attention. I, on the other hand, had to content myself with leaning forward on my aforementioned center of gravity, and then cocking my head like the old RCA Victrola dog.

"Yes?" I asked raptly.

"I'd like you to fill me on who you've talked to so far, and what, if any, conclusions you've drawn."

"No problemo."

I filled him in on the cocktail I'd shared with the newly departed Ms. LaPointe; my encounter with Percival Franklin, the artistic gardener; the words I'd exchanged with the epitome of Linen Ladyship herself, Mindy Sparrow; the breakfast I'd bought for the considerable Constance; and the surprising circumstances in which I'd found Orman Shadbark Jr. And it goes without saying that I reminded him of my earlier run-in with Brunhilde Salazar, the cantankerous housekeeper, who, in my humble opinion, was still the most likely of the bunch to kill Amelia Shadbark.

Sergeant Scrubb was a good listener, and this time when he took notes, he asked me to stop so he wouldn't miss anything. He was still using the pencil stub from the day before—either that or he had a collection of the miniature markers. Perhaps he bowled regularly, or played Put-Put golf.

"So, that's about it," I finally said. "Oh, except that it just occurred to me that since Brunhilde Salazar is a housekeeper, she's also the most likely to have poisoned poor Ms. LaPointe. The two women must have known each other—at least they were aware of the other's existence. It would have been a simple thing for Brunhilde to stop by with a lethal cake or something and—"

"Abby," Sergeant Scrubb said, waving his notepad to get my attention, "Evangeline LaPointe was not poisoned."

"She wasn't? Then how did she die?"

"She was suffocated."

15

I shuddered. "How?"

"With her bedroom pillow most probably. There were lipstick marks on the case, and minute pieces of lint on her tongue."

I shuddered again. Collaborating with the police, at least in this situation, was not a task for those with weak stomachs.

"Abby, are you okay?"

"I'm peachy. I was thinking—I mean, a woman could have smothered her just as well as a man, right?"

He nodded. "Your account of how much she'd been drinking jibes with our lab reports. She might have already been passed out."

"What time did it happen?"

"Between three and four A.M. That's as close as we can get it at this point. But whoever did it picked a good time to commit a crime. Almost no one is on the streets at that hour—not in Ms. LaPointe's neighborhood, at any rate. And if you drive a decent car, and obey the speed limit, the police aren't going to bother you. They'll just assume you're a doctor who's been called to see a patient at MUSC."

"So there were no witnesses—no Evangeline La-

Pointes, so to speak." I chastised myself silently for having spoken ill of the dead. According to Mama, just thinking such a thing put my own demise imminently near.

"Well, you're right on that score. Most people are asleep by that time. And anyway, suffocation is generally a fairly silent means of killing someone. Especially since the subject was too drunk to put up much of a fight."

In an effort to appear sophisticated in the ways of crime detecting, I pretended to ponder a moment. When I was ready to pontificate, I crossed my legs, folded my hands, and cleared my throat. A brilliant deduction deserves a good *intro*duction, does it not?

"We can assume then—since we have two means of dispatching our victims—that we have two killers on our hands, possibly even two very different motives for murder."

Much to my astonishment, Sergeant Scrubb shook his head. "We can't assume that at all. The means in the second case may have been totally unplanned."

"Oh."

"For instance, the person who poisoned Mrs. Shadbark could well have intended to poison Ms. La-Pointe—perhaps inserting a lethal substance into her breakfast marmalade. Or, more likely, in this case, her beverage of choice. At any rate, it may have been that when he or she found the intended victim in a stupor, he or she decided to capitalize on the opportunity. Smothering her there on the spot avoided a lot of potential complications."

"I see." This time I did. If the killer had, for instance, intended to crank up the toxicity of Evangeline's hooch a notch, a third party—such as myself—might have taken a sip or two and lived to call the paramedics. How handy to be able to just smother her into eternal oblivion.

"Abby," Sergeant Scrubb said, "I hope you're getting the picture, that the mind of a successful criminal is nothing if not adaptable. And every criminal not yet caught is successful. I'm sure you've heard a lot about M.O.—modus operandi—and while there is truth to that, the really dangerous minds are unpredictable."

"I've got the picture."

"Good. Now a few ground rules. First, at no point are you to try and apprehend a suspect. Is that rule understood?"

"Of course. That would be plain silly of me." I laughed pleasantly, and for just the right amount of time. "Do I look like a linebacker?"

"Your size has nothing to do with it. I'm telling you not to break the law."

"But what about a citizen's arrest. That's legal, isn't it?"

"Please, Mrs. Washburn, you're to take no action of any kind."

"But—"

"Rule number two, you may not mention to anyone—particularly anyone you suspect of either murder—that you suspect them. And under no circumstances are you to mention that you have any connection to the police."

"So then what is there left for me to do?" I wailed.

"Like we discussed before, just keep your eyes and ears open, and report to me."

"But that's just what I was doing before—except for the reporting to you bit."

"Exactly. Oh, and Abby, this conversation never happened."

"Well, maybe not officially, but unofficially it did."

He stood. "I was never even here," he said softly.

I hopped to my feet. "Oh, but you were. I have witnesses. Besides, you probably left some of your DNA right there on that sweet tea glass. I could clone you as proof."

Sergeant Scrubb gave me a courtly, if somewhat surly bow and strode to the door.

I can't claim that the much loved threesome was waiting at the front door, with glasses of their own pressed to their ears, but they trooped back inside within a matter of seconds.

"Ooh, Abby," C. J. cooed, "did he make you a detective?"

"Not hardly, dear."

"He couldn't have made her a real detective," Mama said knowingly, "but he could have deputized her."

"Actually, he couldn't," Greg said, "not unless it was an absolute emergency, and the circumstances were extraordinary. And that's only if he were the county sheriff. A homicide detective doesn't have that power."

C. J. shook her big shaggy head. "Back home in Shelby—"

"He didn't do anything," I said, heading her off at the pass, "except to tell me to keep my ears and eyes open."

"Which you were already doing," Mama said. "So,

what did he really want?" She was not only twirling her pearls, but her eyes were attempting to drill into the side of Greg's handsome head.

I didn't fall off the turnip truck. I knew Mama like only a daughter could. What she was really saying was *Look out, Greg. That cute Sergeant Scrubb has designs on your wife.* In fact, I was so sure of it that I decided to put myself to the test.

"Mama," I said, "he isn't the slightest bit interested in me."

"Of course he is dear, didn't you see how he—" Mama turned the color of cranberry relish. "For shame, Abby, playing a trick on your dear old mother that way."

Greg turned and laughed. "Reading your mother's mind again, hon?"

"Yes, but it's getting harder. She's so transparent I can see right through her to C. J."

"Very funny, dear." A blindfolded bat could have read Mama's mind just then. She wanted to ground me to my room, with no TV for a week.

"Ooh, Abby, read my mind!" C. J. was jumping up and down like a six-year-old on Christmas morning.

I turned to the big gal, put my fingertips to temples, and pretended to concentrate. "Hmm. I see a woman in Shelby, North Carolina, and her initials are G. L. She was the best mind-reader who ever lived."

"Abby, that's right!" It's a good thing I don't live in an apartment with neighbors downstairs, or they might have called the police.

"That's cheating," Mama said. "Everyone who knows C. J. knows all about her Granny Ledbetter."

"Ooh, but it wasn't Granny Ledbetter, Abby was

talking about. She meant Gizella Ledbetter, Cousin Alvin's first wife. Isn't that right, Abby?"

I took the shameful route and lied. "Absolutely. That Gizella was really something else."

C. J. nodded vigorously. "She reads minds even better than Granny. In fact, Hollywood used her as an adviser on the set of a movie that just came out. It's called *What Men Want*—you know, where this woman gets to hear what men are thinking."

"You mean the silent movie everyone's talking about?"

"That's the one."

Greg grinned. "Ladies," he said good-naturedly, "how about we all go to lunch? I hear Poogan's Porch is having rollback prices to the 1970s this week."

That got everyone's attention. Poogan's Porch makes the best biscuits in the world—even better than Mama's. All their food, which is Lowcountry in character, is quite yummy. A price rollback at this eatery is like getting an invitation to buy a Mercedes at Escort prices.

Then there is the ambiance of the place. Poogan's Porch, at 72 Queen Street, was built as a spacious home in 1888, surrounded by a lovely garden and enclosed by a wrought-iron fence. In 1976 the owners sold their home and moved away, leaving behind their faithful dog, Poogan. The charming Victorian structure was subsequently turned into a restaurant, but Poogan remained, claiming a perch on the front porch, from which he greeted customers. The heartbreaking story alone makes this establishment worthy of a visit.

"Count me in!" C. J. and Mama shouted at the same time.

"Sounds great to me," I said agreeably, although now that everything was hunky-dory between me and my hunk, I would just as soon dine a duo.

"Then," Greg said, his grin broadening, "we can drive over to the Palmetto Grande—you know, the theater with the stadium seating—over in Mount Pleasant and take in a matinee. We can see the flick C.J. was talking about."

"I'll even pay for the movie," C.J. said.

It was a done deal.

I begged everyone's indulgence and while they headed for Poogan's Porch, I made a slight detour. The Den of Antiquity is less than a three-minute walk from the restaurant, and I really felt an obligation to check in on Homer. Mama wanted to come with me, until I reminded her, in front of the others, that my new employee was married.

Of course I'd been foolish to worry. Homer was busy helping a Linen Lady load a set of medical textbooks into her car. The massive tomes had come as part and parcel of an estate sale, and even though they were well over one hundred years old, it was a very common edition, and the books were of surprisingly little value. I hadn't had the heart to dispose of them, and had been considering dropping them off at the library on the theory that those folks had more experience in such matters, and were therefore perhaps a bit more dispassionate. Meanwhile, the volumes, which were lined up atop an armoire, collected dust.

How Homer had managed to unload—well, load,

when you come to think of it—this set of books was beyond me. The man was truly gifted. So gifted, in fact, that walking into my shop took my breath away.

"Homer," I called when he came back inside, "can I see you for a minute?" There were three other customers lined up at the register waiting to pay for purchases, but I took precedence. The customer may be always right, but the owner is always first—at least in a good employee's mind.

He trotted over, the dome of his head glistening with sweat. "Yes, ma'am?"

"Homer, you're going to have to slow done a bit."

"I'm fine, ma'am, really. I'll catch my breath here in a minute."

"No, Homer, what I mean is, if you don't stop selling things so fast, I'm going to run out of merchandise."

"Ma'am?"

"You see, Homer, I go to auctions and estate sales no more than once a week. Sometimes, if business is slow, I go only once a month." I gestured at the space around me. "I had more furniture than this when I first got married."

He chewed on that for a minute. "Ma'am, maybe I could go to these sales for you."

I didn't need to chew on that, however. Homer was a natural-born salesman, that much was clear, but that didn't mean he had the ability to buy. That takes an eye that is years in developing.

"Maybe someday, Homer. But for now, tone down the sales pitch a notch. Just until I get a chance to replenish stock. If folks see an empty store, they may not bother to come back."

He yawned, neglecting to cover his mouth. Since yawns are even more contagious than summer colds, I yawned as well.

"Excuse me, ma'am," he said.

"Certainly, dear. I didn't sleep so well last night myself."

"Ma'am, I was reading in that little trade paper you have on your desk that there's going to be an auction tonight over on James Island."

"Yes, the Delrumple estate. It's supposed to contain a number of eighteenth-century English pieces. I'd been planning to go until—well, it doesn't matter, I don't have time. Anyway, the preview was last night."

"Yes, ma'am, but I was at the preview and—"

"But it's a dealers-only auction. That's why it's at night. How did you get in?"

"I showed them one of your cards, ma'am. The ones you keep in that little plastic box up by the cash register. I told them I was your new assistant."

I shook my head in amazement. "Won't wonders ever cease?"

"Ma'am, I was wondering . . . would you trust me to buy for you tonight?"

Apparently wonders never cease. I'd only just hired the man. What did I know about him—except that he was capable of selling appetite suppressants on a cruise ship?

"Well, I—I mean—you see, Homer—"

"Ma'am, what if you give me a budget—which I'll stick to, of course—and what if I sign a paper, or something, that says if what I buy doesn't sell in a certain amount of time—you name it—I promise to buy it myself, at retail prices. Or you can garnish my wages. Whichever you prefer."

"You sound so confident!"

"Yes, ma'am, I am."

So this is what came of offering the man a ten percent commission. Even though I have a state-of the-art register that's virtually as silent as a dead snake, I could hear it "ka-ching" as my coffers filled. Here was a foolproof method of making a profit, the alternative of which was to watch my stock dwindle, and in the process scare off some potential repeat customers. I didn't have to ponder that one very long.

"You've got yourself a deal, Homer. And even though it's none of my business, I've got to ask you, what's Mrs. Johnson think about you being gone so much?"

Some bald men, bless their hearts, blush first across the pate. Homer is one of these.

"She's glad to have me out of the house, to tell the truth, ma'am. The retirement thing was not quite what either of us expected."

I nodded. I know a number of women who pray for sunny days so that their husbands will get out and play golf, fish—anything, just as long as they are out from underfoot. This is particularly common among the couples I know who have relocated. It seems that, in general, women are quicker at establishing new social ties. Besides, as the old adage goes, women's work is never done. How many retired men can you name who clean bathrooms and do laundry on a regular basis?

Homer walked back with me to the front of the shop, despite the looks from the women waiting—some of them not so patiently—for his services. "You won't re-gret this, ma'am."

"I'm sure I won't."

We said our good-byes and I stepped out into the heat and humidity that a summer's day on King Street has to offer. I took two more steps and plowed right into a peck of trouble.

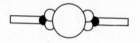

16

I gasped. "Excuse me!"

One of the drawbacks of being diminutive is that folks don't always see you coming until the last second. This can be problematic when you don't bother to look at all.

"Unnh!" The tall, dark woman with whom I'd connected did a little hopping dance until she caught her balance.

I gasped again. "Ms. Salazar! I'm so sorry. I didn't realize you were there."

Brunhilde looked remarkably placid for a woman whose solar plexus bore the imprint of my cranium. Given her personality, she looked downright comatose.

"Eeth okay. I vas coming to zee youth anyvay."

"Youth? How nice, do you have a grandchild who lives nearby?" Brunhilde didn't look old enough to be a grandmother, but then again, neither do I. I'm *not* a grandmother, by the way, but I am old enough. At any rate, grandparents of any age are easily distracted when their descendants are mentioned.

"I haff no enkelkinder."

"I beg your pardon?"

"Zee grunchildren. I vas newer married."

147

"But the youth—ah," I said as it dawned on me. "You're looking for the College of Charleston. Just go right back up King Street and hang a left on George. Now if you want the frat houses turn left on Wentworth—"

"I don' vant zee cullege. I vant to shpeek wiz youth." She extended a long tanned arm and prodded me on the chest with a finger the size of bratwurst, only a good deal firmer.

"Oh! Vell—I mean, well—would you like to step into the shop? It's a good deal cooler in there, I assure you."

"Zee polyeshter," she muttered. "Eeth hot."

"This isn't polyester," I wailed, tugging at my dress, which was nonetheless sticking to me. "It's one hundred percent cotton!"

Brunhilde rolled her eyes. "Vee talk here, yah? Een shop eez too many pepples."

"Have it your way. What's on your mind?"

The truth is I was delighted to see the Amazonian—or Rio de Janeiroan, or whoever she was. She was the next person on my list to pay a little visit to. I was thinking that after the movie I'd cut out from the group and do my civic duty.

"Youth haff been talking to zee poleeth, yah?"

That took me aback. How did she know? Surely Sergeants Scrubb and Bright wouldn't have mentioned my observer status. Perhaps the woman with the hybrid and somewhat variable accent had been staking out my house.

"Why do you say that, dear?"

"Eeth yooth a gueth, but a goot vahn, yah?"

"It's preposterous," I said.

"Vaht eeth zeeth perpotherouth?"

I couldn't have gotten any more wet had I stood in the sun all day. "It means ridiculous."

"Zo, youth don' talk to zee poleeth?"

"Well, of course I talked to them." Thank heavens I'm an Episcopalian, and not a Mennonite like my buddy Magdalena Yoder up in Pennsylvania. Lying, for me, is only a minor sin. "But we never talked about you. What would be the point in that?"

"I shtink maybe you shtink I haff zumshting to do weeth Meeshus Shadbark's dess."

"Absolutely not! But if we continue to stand here in the broiling sun, we'll both shtink for sure. Why don't you join me for lunch? I'm meeting my family at Poogan's Porch."

She cocked her head, her mane casting a much welcome, albeit temporary, shadow on me. "Voo veel pay for zeeth loonch?"

"Why, I will of course." I hadn't intended to, but what the heck? When Buford dumped me in favor of the second Mrs. Timberlake—the one with silicon ta-tas—I was so poor I found myself checking the coin returns on vending machines and public telephones. I've come a long way since then financially, but sometimes I forget to be generous.

"Goot. I veel koom zen."

Greg had secured us a table for four in the front dining room, but as our party had yet to receive their entrées (believe me, they'd already placed their orders), it was really no trouble for them to move to the more accommodating back room. That I had a guest with me did a lot to ameliorate their annoyance at the small fact that I was late.

After proper introductions had been made, and we had settled in at our new table—I squeezed between Greg and C. J., across from Mama and my guest—I began the difficult task of extracting from Brunhilde the information I wanted to know, without making her feel like she was at an inquisition. The task was made more difficult by Mama.

"It's pity," she said, while we waited for our entrées to arrive, "that a beautiful woman like you isn't married."

"You're not married, either, Mama," I snapped. "Neither is C. J."

"It's not for want of trying, dear," Mama said, with a flip of pearls, "but a woman my age has no real need for a husband. And C. J. is too young to even think about the subject." She turned to Brunhilde with a smile. "Now, a beautiful woman like you, Ms. Salazar, I would have thought you'd be spoken for."

"Yeth?" Mama had said the B word twice, and Brunhilde was positively beaming.

"Oh yes. But a woman your age—uh, whatever that is . . ." Mama let the sentence dangle because she was counting on the unemployed housekeeper to answer it for her. It was clear to me now what the wee Wiggins woman was after; she was trying to conduct her own investigation. One that had nothing to do with Amelia's death, but everything to do with personal statistics and just plain nosiness.

Too well brought up to ask personal questions directly, my mini-madre was an expert at beating around the bush. This may be a Southern trait in general, but Mama excels at it. Strangers who don't want their bushes beat around shouldn't even be in the same room with her. Friends who are tired of having their bushes beat around know to guard them with both hands.

I turned to Greg for help, but he was engrossed in studying the flatware pattern. Whereas Brunhilde had heard the B word, Greg's ears had picked up the M word and automatically shut down. He is happily married now, I assure you, but years of confirmed bachelorhood have conditioned him like Pavlov's dogs.

My only recourse was C. J. Yes, the big gal is a Moon Pie or two short of a party, but she's got an otherwise brilliant, if somewhat oversize, head on her broad shoulders. I knew for a fact that she speaks seventeen languages.

"Help me," I begged.

"Sure thing, Abby." She turned to Brunhilde Salazar, who no doubt was about to share with Mama, along with her age, her green card number, height, weight, and even her bra size. "*Desculpe-me por interromper. O senhora fala ingles?*"

"*Sim!*"

"What are they saying?" Mama wailed.

"They're speaking Portuguese—I think. You are speaking Portuguese, aren't you, C. J?"

"Yes. Only now, of course, I'm speaking English. No offense, Abby, but you really should learn more languages."

"I intend to, dear. In fact, Portuguese is next on my list. German comes right after that." I put my mouth to

C. J.'s ear. "Please ask her—in anything but English—
how she heard about Ms. Evangeline LaPointe's death
last night."

My young friend did as she was bid. Brunhilde answered in a torrent of mellifluous if somewhat sibilant
syllables, which C. J. then whispered in my ear.

"No fair!" Mama cried.

"This is business, Mama."

"But Abby, it's rude to speak in a foreign language
in front of others, especially when there is no need."

"Sorry, Mama."

"Greg, do something!"

Greg looked up from his fascinating flatware, but I
slipped my right hand under the table and placed it
lightly on his muscular thigh. My darling and ofttimes
loquacious husband, who would normally walk bare-
foot on hot coals for his mother-in-law, was suddenly
struck dumb.

Of course I'd already eaten at the Vietnamese restaurant, but before my family's lunch (or dinner, as it is
properly called in the South) arrived, I learned the following. Brunhilde Manheim Salazar had, in fact, been
married, and was now a widow. How her husband died,
however, was unclear. C. J.'s Portuguese was quite
flawless, I'm sure, but even after she switched to German, and then briefly to English, I was expected to believe that Joao Salazar was the victim of spontaneous
combustion.

"That's a bit hard to believe," I said. "That sounds
like something you read in the *National Intruder*."

"Ooh, Abby, it happens more often than you think."

Alas, my gal pal had forgotten to whisper, and

Mama was not in the least bit distracted by her forks. "What happens more often than you think?"

"Nothing, Mama."

My petite progenitress patted her pearls petulantly. "I may as well just be at home, for all attention I'm being paid."

I sighed. "Ms. Salazar claims her husband spontaneously combusted."

Greg glanced up from his cutlery, but said nothing.

In her past lives—all nine of them—Mama had been a cat. That's the only way I can explain her incessant curiosity.

"What does that mean?" she asked.

"It's a bit gruesome, Mama, especially for dinner table talk."

"I gave birth to two babies," Mama reminded me, as if I could ever forget.

"Well, supposedly there have been cases where people spontaneously catch on fire—although investigations tend to show that they were already dead, and that it was their clothing that ignited first. Anyway, if they're not discovered, they sometimes burn for hours—like giant human candles. You see, the human body has a lot of fat, and apparently the clothing acts like a wick."

Mama wrinkled her nose. It was more an act of dismissal than disgust.

"I told you it was a little farfetched."

C. J. shook her massive head vigorously. "My Great-Uncle Cyril Ledbetter spontaneously combusted, and he was stark naked." It may have been the N word, but all eyes turned to look at her. "He was at a church picnic and they were skinny-dipping, you see. He had gotten out of the pond and had dried off, but hadn't had time to put his clothes back on. Anyway, suddenly he went poof—just like that he burst into flames. There was nothing anyone could do to help them. Later on some of the teenagers wanted to roast marshmallows over him, but the pastor said it wouldn't be right."

"Why didn't they just throw him back in the pond?" I asked. "You know, to put out the flames?"

"Because Uncle Cyril couldn't swim."

"Which denomination is it," Mama wanted to know, "that allows its members to swim in the nude? It's not the Methodists, is it?"

"Noots," Brunhilde declared in English. "Zeeth voman eez noots."

Mama looked stricken. "Me?"

"Hur!" Brunhilde stood and pointed the bratwurst finger at C. J. "Youth ur all noots."

"Why I never!" Mama twirled her pearls.

Brunhilde pushed her chair back and turned to me. "I don know vhat I vas shtinking, cooming to loonch weeth youth."

"But I'm not finished with the interview," I cried.

"Vell, I am. Eef eeth shuspects youth vant, den I sugget zat youth shpeek weeth Meeshus Shparrow."

"Who?"

"I think he's a violinist with the New York Philharmonic," Mama said. "I saw him on TV the other night."

Brunhilde's wild orbs burned into mine. "Meeshus Meendee Shparrow. She vas shuppposedly a friend of Mrs. Shadbark. But I don shtink zo, yah?"

The former housekeeper than turned and strode

away, nearly colliding with the waitress who was loaded down with a tray bearing our meals.

"So what do you think?" I asked Greg. I'd just polished off a biscuit and was eyeing another. Yes, I have a small stomach, but the biscuits at Poogan's Porch have to be tasted to be believed.

Greg groaned. By mutual agreement we'd tabled any discussion of Brunhilde Salazar until after the meal was over. Actually, only the three of them had agreed to that. I was all for talking with food in our mouths, but was overruled. Now, however, it was time to pay the petite piper.

"I think there's something rotten in Sweden," C. J. said.

I gave her a disapproving look. "I was speaking to Greg, dear. And anyway, the correct expression is Denmark."

"Not if you're living in Denmark, Abby. My cousin Lars Ledbetterson in Copenhagen—"

"C. J.!" I said, perhaps a bit too sharply.

It was Greg's turn to quiet me with a gentle hand on the thigh. His hand, my thigh.

"Let her speak, Abby. She may be on to something."

C. J. tossed her mane triumphantly. It was all I could do to refrain from tossing the second biscuit at her.

"She's not from Brazil," C. J. said with annoying confidence.

"How do know?"

"Because of her accent."

"I know she has a strange accent but—"

"Her Portuguese accent, silly. She's definitely not a

native speaker. Besides, she knows only a few words. The rest of the time we talked in Spanish—and frankly, Abby, even that wasn't very good."

"German, then?"

"Nah, she barely knew that at all."

"So it's possible you were wrong about the spontaneous combustion then?"

C. J. shrugged.

"Why did you reference Sweden?" Greg asked. It seemed like an obvious question to me, but sometimes he actually picks up on things. Perhaps it's his training as a real investigator.

"Because she's Swedish," C. J. said with another toss of her head.

"She didn't look Swedish to me," Mama said.

"Not all Swedes are blond with blue eyes, Mozella. Cousin Lars Ledbetter—"

"Was Danish," I said, my patience wearing as thin as Calista Flockhart at a weight loss spa.

"Her fingers, Abby. Didn't you notice her fingers?"

"Of course I did. They looked like bratwurst."

"They were the fingers of a masseuse."

"Not all Swedes are masseuses, either," I reminded her.

"Ooh silly, I know that. But Brunhilde is. Only her name isn't Brunhilde, but Ingebord."

"Are you pretending to be psychic again, C. J.?"

Once on a trip to Savannah, a voodoo priestess had labeled my young friend a psychic, claiming that C. J. had something called the second sense. The idea of possessing special qualities had really captured the girl's imagination, making her practically unbearable. It wasn't until well after the priestess confessed to being a phony that C.J. backed off her claim that she could read minds.

"I *know*, Abby," C.J. said indignantly, "because Ingebord once gave me a massage."

17

"When did that woman give you a massage?"

"That time we were in Savannah."

The mention of that beautiful Georgia city made the hair on my arms stand on end. Fortunately Greg was looking at C. J., and not my limbs.

"Why didn't you tell us earlier?" I demanded.

"Because I just now made the connection."

"But you're sure? That she's Swedish, I mean?"

C. J. rolled her eyes. "Abby, I know Swedish when I speak it. That's what we talked in, of course. Ingebord is from Jukkasjarvi, up above the Arctic Circle."

"That sounds weirdly familiar," I said. I wasn't being sarcastic.

"Maybe that's because you read about the ice hotel." C. J. took a deep breath, always a dangerous sign. "It's built out of just ice, you know. Walls, ceilings floors, everything. There's even an ice chapel. It sleeps a hundred guests—not in the chapel, of course, but in the rooms. And do you know what, Abby? The temperature in that hotel is always below freezing. Between minus four and minus nine centigrade, as a matter of fact. Ooh, and the really neat thing is that they tear down the entire hotel every spring and build a new one the next year."

Mama rolled her pearls instead of her eyes. "Are you sure this ice hotel is in Sweden and not Shelby?"

"No, Mama, this for real," I said. Then, realizing how disrespectful that might have sounded to C.J., slapped my mouth gently. "I've read about the ice hotel in travel magazines. I think it's an interesting idea, but I couldn't stand to be that cold."

Greg gave my thigh a slow squeeze under the table-cloth. "There are ways to stay warm," he murmured.

I couldn't believe how amorous a single day off was making my hubby. I had half a mind to sneak over to the shrimp boat docks in Mount Pleasant some night and cut an irreparable hole in his net.

"Why, sugar bear—"

"Ooh, Abby, you're not going to get all yucky on us, are you?"

My sugar bear blushed. "Ladies, excuse me a minute," he said, and got up.

I watched him walk in the direction of the men's room. "C.J. how could you?"

"How could I what, Abby."

"Embarrass him like that!"

"She's right," Mama said, much to my surprise. "Abby and Greg haven't you-know-what for ages. You should have let them be."

"Mama!"

"Well, it's true, dear."

"Even if it was, how would you know?"

"I don't hear the bedsprings," Mama said. "Lord knows, when you get to be my age, sleep doesn't al-ways come easy. Some nights I lie awake until three in the morning."

I must have been the color of port wine. "Maybe we keep the springs oiled."

"I don't hear the headboard either. Why, your Daddy and I—"

"Stop it!" I had both hands clamped as tight as I could over my ears. The part of me that believes my mother is still a virgin wanted to keep it that way.

I hummed softly to myself, and C. J. and Mama continued to discourse—I could see their lips flapping—until Greg returned. They so distracted me, it took me a minute to realize Greg was talking as well.

My ears rang when I finally released them. "Say that again, please, dear."

Greg laughed and nuzzled the closest ear. "I said, your mama must be talking about sex again."

"You got that right," I growled.

Greg laughed again. "Hey, I was just on the phone to Sergeant Scrubb, and C. J. was absolutely right."

"She *was*? I mean, about what?"

"Brunhilde Salazar is an alias for Ingebord Simonson. She is indeed Swedish and from that little town with the ice hotel—and don't think for a minute I'm going to try and pronounce it."

"You see?" C. J. cried.

"But why the ruse then?" I asked. "Is she in the country illegally?"

He shook his head. "No, it's apparently because she has a horrific employment record."

I was all ears, even if they weren't quite up to par. "Details, dear."

"Well"—Greg glanced at the other two women— "maybe it's best if I wait until, uh—"

"Until we vamoose?" Mama said. She answered her question by standing, which meant that Greg stood, too. "Come on, dear," Mama said to C.J. "Let's you and I do some shopping. "I hear that the vintage clothing store on King Street—Granny's Goodies, I think it's called—sometimes has crinolines for sale. Do you know how hard it is to buy knee-length crinolines these days?"

"But we're supposed to all go to the movies in Mount Pleasant," C.J. whined.

"You can still go," I said. "Just let me have a few minutes alone with Greg."

"You said *you*. Abby, does that mean you're planning not to come?"

"I'll certainly try."

"She'll be there," Mama said. "Greg, you make her come."

"I can't make Abby do anything she doesn't already want to do," Greg said.

Despite a little residual ringing in my right ear, I could hear the pride in my husband's voice.

It was decided that Greg and I would meet Mama and C.J. in front of the Palmetto Grande at four o'-clock. We would take pot luck with the movies. Whichever one began closest to our arrival would be the one we watched. All three of us women were pulling for the silent movie about men; Greg, on the other hand, yearned for spilled guts and a few broken bones.

Mama and C.J. elected not to eat dessert in favor of popcorn and candy later at the show. Mama, I knew, continuously watches her weight in order to look good in cinch-waisted fifties-style dresses, but C.J., I am convinced, had finally figured out that by skipping out now, she could get out of paying for lunch. No doubt she regretted having already offered to spring for the movie. (Please don't get me wrong; the girl is as generous as a busload of nuns when it comes to her time, but when it comes to her pocketbook, C.J. can be as tight as last year's blue jeans.)

At any rate, since Greg couldn't decide between the pecan pie and the bread pudding, he ordered both. I ordered just coffee, but reserved the right to sample each dessert an unlimited number of times. If I recall correctly, that privilege was stated in our wedding vows.

"So tell me everything," I said, as soon as the coast was clear. By that, I mean more than just the absence of C.J. and Mama, but the diminished likelihood that either of them would return. Just to expedite their second departure, I'd checked under the table and on the chairs to make sure neither had left any props behind—purses, glasses, and such.

Greg had reseated himself across the table from me so that we could talk face to face. Squeezing my thigh was going to be a bit more of a challenge for him, but playing footsie was definitely less awkward.

"Abby, you're not going to believe the kind of luck that Swedish housekeeper has had."

"Try me." Chances are she'd never been rendered unconscious and stuffed in a suit of seventeenth-century Italian armor like I once was.

"Well, she was right when she said her husband combusted—only it wasn't so spontaneous. He fell asleep smoking. He was dead drunk at the time." He held up a hand, knowing, perhaps from experience, that I might interrupt. "That was her first husband. And that was in Sweden. Her second husband was an American, a tourist in fact, who had come to see the ice hotel. He brought her to the States to live, but then, just a couple of months later, he fell off the roof while cleaning out gutters. Broke his damn neck. Husband number three, also an American, got the radio-in-the-lap-while-you're-bathing treatment."

"Electrocuted?"

"Yeah. What a way to go, hunh?"

"Was it her fault? And that fall from the roof?"

"No evidence, Abby. In none of those three cases. But it gets even better."

"No, wait, let me guess. Husband number four got his tie caught in the garbage disposal and by the time she could get there and turn it off, he was mincemeat."

Greg smiled. "You're getting the picture. Only this time it wasn't a husband, but a client. Like C. J. said, Ingebord trained as a masseuse. She was giving a massage in Savannah when the table collapsed."

"That killed him?"

"The man had a history of heart problems. Slamming into the floor like that sent him into cardiac arrest."

The desserts arrived. We held off conversing until the waitress left, and it was then I discovered she'd put the bread pudding in front of me. Not wanting to hurt her feelings—in case she turned around—I took a bite. It was warm and covered with a gooey sauce that made my teeth invite calories. Gladly, in fact.

"Anything else?" I asked when the bowl was half empty.

Greg was grinning like a cat at a mice convention. "Isn't that enough?"

"So, no more victims, eh?"

"I mean," he said, "haven't you had enough of my dessert?"

I pushed the dish across the table. "What about my question? Were there any more victims?"

"No, that appears to be it."

I have an agile tongue and was able to lick that part of my face adjacent to, but outside, my lips. I was even able to manage a quick lick to the tip of my nose. Don't ask me how breading pudding got all the way up there.

"So, how does a woman with that kind of history secure employment with one of the finest families in Charleston?"

"Because none of the deaths could be linked to her."

"Even the collapsing massage table?"

"Manufacturer's defect."

"If she's so innocent, then why the alias?"

"Good question, and Scrubb is working on that. The suspect—"

"Aha! So she is a suspect!"

"Unofficially, yes. He did question her, of course, and she said it was to escape the bad publicity associated with the table incident. That, given Savannah's proximity to Charleston, it might have made it in the *Post and Courier.*"

"Did it?"

"One small paragraph. No picture. Nothing except the name to link her. She said she was desperate for a job, and didn't want to go back to Sweden. Too cold and too many taxes."

"Still," I said skeptically, "Amelia Shadbark, scion of Charleston society, didn't bother to check the woman's references?"

"She asked for them, of course, but only gave them a glance. That's all most folks do, in fact. We all like to think we're pretty good judges of character. Face it, Abby, in the normal course of events, a housekeeper does not have to do brain surgery."

"True, but the Brunhilde Salazar persona is every bit as abrasive as industrial grade sandpaper."

"Which, apparently, is exactly what the grande dame needed at that point in her life. What better way to keep malingerers from pestering you?"

I retrieved the now-empty bread pudding dish and gave it a good wipe down with my index finger. I know, that was the height of bad manners, but as long as I was never going to be fully accepted into Charleston society, what did it *really* matter? It's not like I was being unkind.

"Would two of these malingerers"—I smacked my lips—"just happen to be her children, Constance and Orman?"

"I didn't hear the whole case, Abby; I talked to Scrubb for only a few minutes. But speaking of a few minutes, we—we don't have to be at the theater for another hour and a half." He waggled his eyebrows playfully.

"But on a full stomach?"

"I'm game if you are."

"You're on."

What goes on behind my closed doors is not anyone else's business. I will say, however, that it was of such high caliber that Greg didn't seem to mind in the least giving my regrets to Mama and C. J. at the movie theater. Perhaps he even assumed that would be the case from the get-go, because he merely warned me to watch my back before departing to meet the ladies.

I left the house a few minutes after my beloved did, fully outfitted for the job at hand. I was wearing a fresh dress—and yes, it was linen—and carried with me a large designer tote bag; large enough to contain a bottle of Evian, a small pair of binoculars, my cell phone, and a Three Musketeers candy bar. The last item had been plucked from the freezer, sealed in a small sandwich bag, and now nestled in a large freezer bag with numerous ice cubes.

There was, of course, a method to my madness. The water was to guard against thirst generated by the hot Charleston sun, the binoculars were for spying, the cell phone in case I got into trouble, and the chocolate because even a well-fed girl can never have too much of a good thing. Besides, when the ice cubes melted I could pour the runoff on my toasted tootsies. I was, after all, wearing open-toed sandals. I just didn't expect to jump out of those sandals before I'd even reached my front gate. "Jeepers-creeper!" I cried, dropping the tote so I could clamp both hands over my pounding heart in order to keep it in my chest.

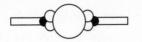

18

"Sorry, Abby. I didn't mean to scare you."

Bob Steuben had apparently been standing right next to the wrought-iron stair railing. Maybe it's because he's so thin, but I didn't see him until he reached out and touched me.

I plopped my behind on the nearest step until I could catch my breath. Unfortunately, that step was hot enough to fry not only an egg on, but a rasher of bacon as well. I picked my bacon up in a hurry.

"Bob, what *is* it?" At least with me, pain and annoyance tend to go hand and hand.

"He's gone!"

"Who's gone?"

"Rob, of course."

I grabbed one of Bob's manicured hands and pulled him up the steps and into the house. Then, before I did anything else, I stashed the Three Musketeers back in the freezer.

"Now then," I said, taking a much more comfortable seat, "where has Rob gone?"

"That's just it, I don't know. We always spell each other for lunch. Usually we take turns on who goes first—depending on who's hungriest, or has a doctor's

appointment, that kind of thing. Rob asked for an early
lunch today so he could get his oil changed and tires
rotated before the lunch crowd arrived. Anyway, he left
just after eleven and hasn't come back."

I already knew that the Rob-Bobs do not brown bag
it in the back of their shop like so many other dealers
do. Heavens, that was far too déclassé for the gour-
mand Bob. As for Rob, he'd rather eat my cooking than
have to suffer through two of Bob's meals in one day.
Emu salad sandwiches and yak butter tea do not float
his culinary boat.

"Did you call the car dealer?"

"Yes, and he wasn't there."

"Jiffy Lube?"

"Not there, either, Abby. I called every establishment in the Charleston phone book that was likely to
provide those services. Nada."

I thought of suggesting he call the Medical University of South Carolina—our nearest hospital—and in-
quire about accident victims, but the idea of a car
wreck had to originate in Bob's own highly suggestive
mind. There was obviously no need to suggest Rob
might be having an affair.

"How can I help you, Bob?"

"Well, uh, I don't know." Bob buried his face in his
large bony hands. For the first time I noticed he had the
hairiest knuckles I'd ever seen.

"Would you like me to come over to the Finer
Things and hang out with you until he gets back?" I
asked. "We could confront him together when he
does."

He looked up. "No!" he said with surprising vehe-
mence. "I'm not a baby."

"Needing a friend doesn't make you a baby. I'd be happy to do it."

Sometimes, and I'm sure my friend Magdalena Yoder would agree, being a friend requires one to fudge a little on the truth. And the truth in this case is that I wanted nothing more than for Bob to solve his own problem, and leave me to solve mine. Bob, who is frankly a bit on the homely side, has always been jealous of Rob's friends and acquaintances. Rob Goldburg is, after all, a very handsome man. I think he looks like James Brolin back in his *Marcus Welby* days.

"No, Abby, I don't need you to baby-sit me. But please tell me how you managed to get through it when Buford cheated on you?"

I suppose there are those who would say there is no equating a twenty-year heterosexual marriage that produced two children to a six-year-long gay relationship that doesn't even include a pet. I say they're wrong. Love is love, and pain is pain.

"It hurt like hell when I found out Buford had been cheating on me," I said. "But I found out because he told me—when he announced one night, just after we'd made love, that he wanted a divorce."

"Ouch."

"You're telling me. He pretty much said that he was trading me in for a younger model because she had a firmer body—silicon though it was. Anyway, my point is, I had proof my husband was cheating on me. It came from the ass's—I mean, horse's—mouth himself. There was no speculation involved."

"Abby, you really had no clue that Buford was seeing Tweetie?"

"None. Of course the kids were both in high school, so there was already a lot of drama to keep me distracted—but Buford was sneaky. He got away with it because he's smart. And Rob's smart as well. Too smart, in fact, to make up alibis that he knows can be easily checked out—unless what he's up to is a surprise. I mean a good surprise. Even smart men can screw up big time when it comes to planning surprises. I think it's because they're so often clueless themselves when we plan for them. Men! Go figure!"

"Nu, so what am I? Chopped liver? Thanks a lot, Abby!"

I smiled. Bob is a WASP from Toledo, Rob a Jewish man from Charlotte. Bob will most likely never acquire a Southern accent, but he has managed to pick up the odd Yiddish phrase.

"Sorry, dear. I guess I forgot you were, uh—"

"A man?"

My feet may be only size four, but they're still a mouthful. "Don't put words in my mouth!" I cried. "There's no room! What I'm trying to say is, you and I are buddies. By not lumping you with other men, I was paying you a compliment."

He grinned. "I'll settle for that. So, Abby, what is your advice for me? Just go back and reopen the shop? Carry on like it's business as usual? But when Rob returns—if he does—then what?"

"He *will*. Trust me on that."

"But do I confront him? What do I say?"

"That's a hard one. If you can stand it, wait a couple of days. But only if you can manage to not act all weird about it. If you can't—well, at least try to listen to what he has to say."

"I'll wait."

He gave me a look that said it would be my fault if, indeed, Rob proved to be unfaithful. So be it. I'd raised two teenagers; I was used to being blamed for everything. Besides, what did one man's erroneous opinion really matter, when Charleston's aristocracy thought me capable of murder?

Bob's visit not only left me in a crunch for time, it left me distracted. I drove to Mindy Sparrow's house on Tradd Street, even though it is just two blocks from where I live. I'd looked her up in the Charleston white pages, you see, and there had been just one Sparrow listed south of Broad. There were a couple of Hawks, and a Starling, but just the one Sparrow—Beauregard. That had to be Mindy's husband, I reasoned. At any rate, that short drive made my linen dress look like a piece of origami that had been balled up and discarded. Even chain-smoking California sun worshippers seldom get that wrinkled.

I was tugging on my dress when Mindy answered the door. She didn't seem at all surprised to see me.

"Love your dress," she chirped.

For a second I thought she was making fun of me. Then it dawned on me that she was being as sincere as a preacher on Judgment Day.

I waved my wrist. "And I'm wearing chunky jewelry too."

"Beautiful!"

"And designer shoes." Actually, I'd bought the sandals at Payless for $12.99, but they looked like I'd paid at least twice that for them.

"Interesting. Ms. Timberfake—"

"That's Timber*lake*."

"Yes, of course. Would you like to come in?"

I could hardly believe my good fortune. "I'd love to."

She stepped aside to usher me into one of the most tastefully appointed salons I'd ever seen. The key, as often is the case, was understatement.

With the exception of a late-eighteenth-century Chinese rug, which served as the room's focal point, the furnishings were English. The rug, however, was outstanding. Its center field bore the representations of nine mythical lion-dogs. The colors employed were a rich deep blue, tan, ivory, and persimmon. There was a good deal of wear—Charlestonians use their antiques—but still, I would estimate that at a properly advertised auction, the rug would easily fetch fifty thousand dollars.

The English pieces were also notable. They were all eighteenth century as well, and of the finest workmanship. I wouldn't be surprised to learn that they were all signed. There weren't many pieces; just a settee, two chairs, and an inlaid satinwood game table, but that's what gave the room its exceptional beauty.

"How lovely!" I gushed.

Mindy permitted her aristocratic mouth to form a smile. "They were all brought over from England by my husband's great-great-great-granddaddy, Phineas Sparrow, in 1798."

A less arrogant woman would simply have said "thank you." There was no need to trot out the generations of Charleston forbears. Well, two could play that game as good as one.

I shook my head in mock sympathy. "Post–Revolutionary War immigration. You must be so embarrassed."

Beady bird eyes bored into mine. "Just when did your ancestors come over?"

"About a century before that."

"But not to Charleston!"

"Not right away."

"But they did move to Charleston?"

The truth is, my family first settled in North Carolina, and North Carolinians are, incidentally, modest folk. They consider their fair state to be a valley of humility between two mountains of conceit. Although my family eventually spread to the Upstate region of South Carolina and parts of Georgia, no one, to my knowledge—until I came along—ever dared call Charleston home. I couldn't exactly tell Mindy the truth, now could I?

"Well, they landed in Virginia," I said, trying to keep a straight face, "and built a home in Richmond. They gave that a try for a couple of years, and then decided to move on down to Charleston. As you can imagine, they'd heard so many nice things about this place and were anxious to compare the two cities."

"And?" She was waiting with bated breath.

"They were bitterly disappointed. They found Charleston to be unworthy of their affections, so they moved to the Upstate."

Perhaps I'd gone too far. Mindy teetered on her four-inch spikes. If she fell, I'd have to catch her, and I was sorely out of practice.

"I'm just kidding!" I cried.

She stopped swaying. "Which part were you joking about?"

"That they'd found Charleston to be unworthy of their affections. To the contrary, it was they who were unworthy."

She seemed only minimally relieved. "But has your family really been in this country that long?"

"I'm afraid so. Great-Great-Great-Great-Great-Great-Great Granddaddy Cornelio Wiggins landed in Philadelphia in 1690."

"Ah, so they were Yankees."

"For about a year. He waited there until my great-great-great-great-great-great-granny could join him. Then they headed South."

"Phineas Sparrow was the youngest son of a duke, and my great-great-great-granddaddy on my mama's side, Baron Munchausen by Proxy, was the second son of an earl." At least that's what it sounded like.

"Is that so?" She had yet to ask me what I was doing there, much less offer me a place to sit.

"Oh yes, and my husband's branch of the Sparrow family is related to three American presidents, but the Proxys can claim four."

If you can't beat them, then adore them. "I certainly admire your bloodlines, dear. Good breeding may not be everything, but it's almost everything, and you, my dear, look very well bred."

"Thank you—I think."

"Tell me, is it true that old-time Charlestonians, like you, are not allowed to receive transfusions from those of us who hail from off? You know, on the grounds that it might dilute the blue in your blood, possibly even turning it an unsightly shade of fuchsia?"

"Ms. Timberbake," she trilled, teetering dangerously once more, "did you come here just to poke fun at everything I hold dear?"

"That's Timber*lake*," I said, "and it's about time you asked the nature of my visit. As it happens, I came to ask you a few questions of my own. Questions that have to do with Amelia Shadbark."

Mindy Sparrow appeared to be not the least bit surprised. She gestured at a Chippendale chair.

"Please, have a seat. Would you care for something cold to drink? Some sweet tea maybe?"

"That would be lovely. In the meantime, do you mind if I use the powder room?"

She smiled wanly. "It's the second door on the right."

For your information, I didn't have to use the facilities. But as long as Mindy was going to be in the kitchen pouring my tea, I might as well be doing something interesting. And, I don't mind telling you, my curiosity was rewarded.

The Sparrows had solid gold bathroom fixtures. Although I have enough money of my own to live comfortably, it occurred to me that an unscrupulous version of myself could walk around with faux gold faucets in her purse, ask to use the bathrooms of the super rich, and then make a switch. One might not get away with it, but at least the bailiff would twist his tongue when he read the charges.

I tried unscrewing the sink spigot—just to test my idea—but these hands, which can barely crack open a boiled peanut, were useless in that regard. I flushed the toilet to give my visit credence, mussed up the guest towel, and returned to the salon.

Mindy appeared seconds later bearing a sterling tray with two tall glasses of tea.

"Do you like benne cookies?" she asked. She was referring to the sesame wafers so popular in Charleston. The cookies, like Gullah, have their origin in West Africa, where sesame seeds are believed to bring good luck.

"I love them," I said without hesitation.

My answer seemed to disappoint her. No doubt she hoped I'd never heard of this Charleston treat, thereby reaffirming my status as a stranger.

Since there was no coffee table, she handed me my drink and let me select a few wafers, before she whisked the tray back to the kitchen. By the gleaming looks of that silver platter, there was a maid standing by with a polishing cloth at the ready.

"Now then," she said when she'd returned and taken a seat, "perhaps we can start over."

I'm all for peace. "Absolutely," I said.

"So, Ms. Timbershake, ask me your questions about Amelia. I want, just as badly as you do, to have her killer found."

I decided, in the interest of expediency, to let her mispronunciation of my professional name pass. Therefore, I swallowed my irritation along with the remains of my wafer.

"I understand you were a close friend of the family."

She smiled. "Very close. Like I told you when I first met you the other evening, Constance Shadbark was my best friend growing up."

"Are you still close?"

"Yes, of course."

"That's very interesting, you see, because just this morning Constance said the opposite."

She blinked. "Surely you misunderstood."

"I don't think so. In fact, Constance rather vehemently denied any sort of friendship between the two of you."

"Are you sure you have the right Constance?" Mrs. Sparrow's smile had tightened to such a point that it looked like her face might crack. If she ever tired of being a society dame, she'd have a nice future on a home shopping channel.

"I'm quite sure," I said. "I mean, how many Constance Rodriguez née Shadbarks could there be? Besides, she admitted to eloping with the pencil eraser salesman."

The smile slipped and was replaced by a smirk. "That's the one."

"So, like I said, she denies being friends with you. Why do you think that is?"

"Because she's jealous."

"And what is Constance jealous of?"

"The fact that I was Amelia Shadbark's daughter. Her biological daughter."

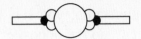

19

"I beg your pardon?"

"You heard me, Ms. Timberstake. Amelia Shadbark was my mother."

"But—but—that doesn't make any sense."

"Don't you think we looked alike?"

"Mrs. Shadbark had a lot of wrinkles," I said kindly, "and they weren't just on her clothes."

"Our bone structure," Mrs. Sparrow chirped. "And even the way we carried ourselves. Everybody could see it. Constance was no exception."

"Whoa! Do you mind starting at the beginning?"

Mindy Sparrow's smile was genuine now. "Where should I begin?"

"The beginning?"

My facetiousness was lost on her. "Oh, that would take all day. Let's just say that Amelia Shadbark experienced a mild period of teenage rebellion, and I was the result."

"Gracious me," I said, somewhat taken aback. "I suppose we can be glad it wasn't a serious teenage rebellion. How old was she?"

"Well, actually—strictly speaking, that is—she

wasn't a teenager. You see, Amelia had the unfortunate experience of being sent away to college. It was a private girls' college—which I won't name—but it was up *North*."

I shuddered in sympathy. "Go on."

"Well, she was twenty-one at the time, and a senior, when she met a boy from Boston. He was from one of the best families—a Brahman."

"Mrs. Sparrow, I'm a lapsed Episcopalian. I can assure you that his religion doesn't concern me."

"Boston Brahman are not a denomination," she twittered. "They're the cultural and intellectual elite. And for the most part, they are *old* money."

"But still Yankees," I mumbled.

The look she gave me was so cold it made her air-conditioner stop running. I swear it's true. I could hear the fan cease abruptly.

"Do you want to hear the rest, or not?"

"I do!" I pressed a petite palm over my mouth.

"In that case, I'll continue. Now, where was I?"

I mashed my errant lips into my face. I wasn't about to say a word.

"Oh, yes, shortly after she began to date this young man, Amelia found herself, uh, in the family way, as they used to say in those days. Unfortunately she was in a bit of a quandary because—"

"There was a chance the Brahman boy was not the father?"

"Don't be ridiculous! Of course he was the father. I'll have you know Amelia was not a slut."

"But you said she became pregnant *shortly* after she met him. One can infer—"

Another blast of arctic air made me mash my lips even flatter. I was going to need collagen injections just to speak again.

"Ms. Timbermake, I refuse to cooperate if you're going to continue to be so rude."

I unfurled my lips and gave them a good flap before speaking. "I'm sorry. I really am. I won't do it again, I promise."

Mindy cocked her head and regarded me with one icy orb. "You had better be, or this conversation is over." She paused an interminable length of time, presumably to see if I was going to interrupt. "Well, as I was *about* to say, Amelia was in a quandary because she knew her family would never approve of her marrying a Bostonian—even if he was a Brahman. Then, too, there was the small matter that his family looked down on Amelia because she was Southern. And, just in case you're wondering, abortions were very difficult to obtain, even had Amelia seen that as an option.

"At any rate, this wasn't the first time something like this had happened at the school, so the college was prepared. They found a home for Amelia's baby with a local couple. That sweet little baby the Hansons took in, of course, was me." She paused again, this time for dramatic affect. "Anyway, the Hansons were wonderful parents to me, even though they were—how shall I put this—blue collar.

"They saved their pennies, and when the time came for me to go to college, they didn't even object when I insisted on attending the College of Charleston. You see, I knew that my birth mother had been from Charleston, I even knew her name. Well, to make a long story short, I looked Amelia up and introduced myself." She waved her tapered fingers as if to shush me, although I hadn't uttered a peep. "I know, these blood reunions don't always go over big, but I was discreet. And, as it turned out, Amelia had just been going through a period of self-examination, so the timing was fortuitous."

I had just had to put my two cents' worth in. "It must not have been so discreet, if Constance found out."

Ms. Sparrow smiled smugly. "That was Amelia's doing. She was so proud of me, she let everyone and their gardener know who I was. So, of course, my new brother and sister were no exception. Constance is just three years younger than me, by the way. Orman Jr. four."

"But I don't get it. She was shamed into giving her baby away in the first place. What changed that?"

"The sixties. Oh, it still wasn't proper to have a child out of wedlock—and probably never will be. Not in Charleston. But certain things could be intimated, just never spoken directly. Still, folks knew the score. Although I don't think Amelia really cared at this point, because of what Orman Sr. was up to."

"Which was?"

"Another maid." She pointed one of the long manicured digits at me. "Ms. Timberrake, I'm only sharing this because Amelia's death concerns you. Otherwise—well, as I'm sure you've already noticed, we Charlestonians do not engage in gossip."

"I've certainly noticed something. But tell me, how did you manage to marry into society? I mean, given your rather unorthodox beginnings."

"Bloodlines," she hissed. "I have good bloodlines."

Having finished my tea and cookies, I stood. "Well, this has certainly been illuminating. But I am still confused about one thing; earlier when you trotted out your list of illustrious ancestors—the Munchausens, or whomever—were they Amelia's people, or the Hansons'?"

"Amelia's, of course!"

Mama worked hard to raise me as a Southern lady, and I try not to disappoint her. I extended a petite paw.

"Thank you. You've been very helpful, Mrs. Narrow."

"That's *Sparrow*."

"Whatever, dear."

I got out of there while I still had a few manners left.

I hate running into people. It can be so damn uncomfortable at times, especially if they have abs of steel.

"Excuse me," I said, using the last of my good manners.

"Oh no, ma'am, excuse me," said the tourist. The Bermuda shorts and camera told me he was a tourist, but his accent told me that the place he called home was no more than a full day's drive away.

I jockeyed to get around him, and as I did so I noticed he was holding a fistful of brochures. *Upsidedown.*

"Can I help you?" I asked.

"Beg pardon, ma'am?" He regarded me with clear gray eyes set in a deeply tanned face. I figured him to be in his late twenties.

"Which historic home are you looking for? Perhaps

I know where it is. The tiny little maps they supply on those brochures are all but worthless."

He flushed and righted the bunch. "Uh, well, the Heyward-Washington House looks kind of interesting."

"Oh, it was. Too bad they tore it down."

"Ma'am?"

"Oh yes, the city put up some first-class condominiums. I hear they're selling them for two million dollars each."

He frowned and smiled simultaneously. "Ma'am, I don't think that's the case."

"Oh?"

"I mean, uh, the brochure doesn't mention that at all."

"Those are old brochures, dear. These condos just went up in the last several months. You should see them, especially the penthouse. The view stretches from Folly Beach to the Isle of Palms. *That* one sells for three million dollars, and last I heard it's still available. You should really take a look—it won't cost you anything just to take a peek."

He was all smiles now. "Thanks, I might." He started to walk away.

"And they offer a huge discount to private investigators!" I called to his back.

He turned. "Ma'am?"

"PI's get a fifty percent discount."

His was a hearty, refreshing laugh. "So I'm busted, am I?"

"You betcha."

"What gave me away?"

"What didn't? Besides, I'm married to a former detective—wait just one cotton-picking minute! Greg hired you, didn't he?"

The gray eyes turned as somber as Charleston Harbor on a cloudy winter day. "If you'll excuse me, ma'am—"

"I'll do no such thing." This time I jockeyed to stay in front of him. "It makes perfect sense to me now. First he blows a gasket when I get involved in this case, then suddenly he's all peaches and cream. That's because he hired you to watch out for me, right?"

The hapless PI stared at me, at a loss for words.

"So, you're not so much a PI as you are a bodyguard. Am I right?"

"No comment, ma'am."

"Are you armed?"

He shifted from one sockless Nike to the other. "Ma'am, I'm not at liberty to say."

I shook my head. "Well, you've got your work cut out for you young man. I detest being followed, even if it is for my protection. Good luck keeping up with me."

"Please, ma'am, I'm only doing my job."

The poor guy was practically down on his bare knees begging. He had a point—although what did that really have to do with me? It was not my responsibility to see that he met the terms of his arrangement with Greg. If I chose to take my life into my own two tiny hands, that was my right. This is America, after all. Even in the Confederate States of America we had that right—well, those of us who were white and male.

"Okay," I said. "That's my car over there, as you well know. My plan is to drive up to Georgetown."

"Georgetown? But that's over an hour away."

That charming port city is indeed an hour and a half drive up coastal Highway 17. It's worth visiting if one is a tourist, by the way. Settled by rice planters in 1729, it is the third-oldest city in the state. There are many buildings of interest, including a rice museum, which once served as the old slave market.

"Yeah, I should really get a move on. I want to make sure I get back before dusk. All those deer along the highway make me nervous."

"What's in Georgetown?" I was surprised to hear him whine.

"You have your secrets, dear, I have mine."

"But your husband will be back from the movies by then—"

"Aha! So it *is* Greg you're working for!"

He couldn't have squirmed more had he been a worm presented with a fishhook. "But ma'am, the Braves are playing tonight, and I've already made plans to go over to a buddy's house to watch the game on his digital TV. The first pitch is at seven."

"Then I suggest we get cracking. Where's your car?"

"Around the corner, ma'am. That way." He pointed in the opposite direction.

"Well, I could offer you a ride, I suppose, but that would be taking hospitality a bit too far. What say we meet at the visitor center on Front Street in downtown Georgetown in exactly an hour and forty-five minutes—that should allow for traffic over the Silas N. Pealman Memorial Bridge. Anyway, I'll fill you in when we get there."

Without waiting for his reaction I walked calmly, if

a bit quickly, to my vehicle. My guess is that the tail Greg had hired to protect my tail hesitated a tad too long. When I glanced in my rearview mirror he was running in the direction of his car. Then I turned the corner. That was the last I saw of him.

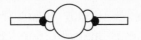

20

Yes, I should feel guilty for what I did, but a bodyguard who could be ditched that easily was not going to do me a whole lot of good. To the contrary, a really clever killer would spot my shadow, making everything I did just a waste of time. Still, it was sweet of Greg to want to protect me. I would remember to tell him that—if he didn't yell at me.

At any rate, I parked my car in the city garage off Concord Street, near the South Carolina State Port Authority. I wound my way up the ramp to the roof, on the theory that only a very determined PI would bother to search for me at such dizzying heights. Besides, the view from on top is invariably quite splendid. Today, despite the fact there was hardly a breath of wind, the harbor was dotted with sailboats. Further out, toward Fort Sumter, a lone figure was parasailing across the cloudless sky.

I paused to admire the scene, vowed to myself that I would someday be brave enough to go parasailing, and then scampered down the steps as fast as I could go. Although parking garage stairs give me the creeps, I find the elevators even worse. At least the odds of stairs malfunctioning are close to nil.

Due to the exceptional heat, there were fewer tourists about than usual, but I blended quickly into the stream of the sweaty if somewhat sparse crowd. Perhaps it is the charm and grace of the city, or perhaps it is simply the euphoria brought on by spending, but one almost never sees a cross face in downtown Charleston. A smile and a shopping bag are all one needs to become virtually invisible. Lacking the latter, I scurried toward The Market.

This historic shopping site was built on land deeded to the city in 1788 by Charles Cotesworth Pinckney, among others, on the stipulation that there would always remain a market. The main building, Market Hall, is a two-story Roman Doric structure designed by Joseph Hyde in 1840. The upper level, now under renovation, houses a Confederate museum. The arcade, at street level, stretches for several blocks toward the harbor, becoming progressively more simple in design.

I ducked into the harbor end of the arcade. At this point The Market consists of a single row of semi-open sheds that can be bitterly cold in the winter and sizzling hot in the summer. The vendors here rank among the hardiest souls on the planet. Any one of them could lead an expedition to the poles, or a jaunt, at sea level, along the equator. I can't visit this part of The Market without being propelled by guilt to purchase at least *something*.

The first among equals, and the hardiest of the lot, have got to be the Gullah women who sell their home-made sweetgrass baskets at the entrances to the sheds, where they endure the broiling summer sun, and cold damp winter winds. The baskets are veritable works of art, made in tradition of West African basketmakers, a tradition that, like benne cookies, was imported along with the slaves. One can also see the baskets for sale in Mount Pleasant, in little sheds along Highway 17. Sweetgrass baskets are highly collectible and have become popular with both tourists and long-term residents, and prices can reflect that.

I resisted the temptation to peruse the sweetgrass baskets at The Market in search of a bargain, and made my way as quickly as possible down the single aisle that runs the length of each shed. To either side were stalls that sold T-shirts, postcards, souvenirs, jewelry, handbags, binoculars, beach towels, videotapes, and a thousand other things that appealed for a split second, but for which I really had no need. There was no sign of Percival Franklin, or a stall displaying hand-carved dolphins and seagulls.

I hopped across the street and popped into the second shed. There was plenty of bric-a-brac on display, but nothing remotely resembling art, unless you count the velvet paintings of Jesus Christ, Elvis, Marilyn Monroe, the original Three Stooges, *and* galloping horses. One imaginative painting had the first three of these icons all in the same painting, seated astride galloping horses. The artist was, I am sure, not trying to be disrespectful, and had placed Jesus Christ on the lead horse. Marilyn Monroe brought up the rear.

"How much is it?" I asked, just out of curiosity.

The vendor, a squat woman with a semi-full contingent of teeth, grinned happily. "Four hundred and fifty dollars. Five fifty if you want to add the Stooges. We're all sold out of them at the moment, but I can get you one by tomorrow."

"Maybe just Curly."

She scowled. "Whoever heard of splitting up the Stooges? It's all three of them or nothing."

"In that case, nothing."

"Then like I said, four hundred and fifty. With the tax that comes out to—"

"No thanks."

"What?"

"Look, I'm a dealer myself—an antique dealer over on King Street. I was just asking out of curiosity. One never knows. My customers might ask where they can buy some beautiful contemporary artwork. I need to know whom to recommend."

She beamed and handed me a card. "Name's Connie Beth. I'm here every day. And on the days I can't make it, I send my husband, Elmer. He's the one that does the painting."

"Thanks, Connie Beth. Say, would you happen to know if there's a young man in one of these buildings who sells exquisitely beautiful woodcarvings?"

Connie Beth shook her head. "But there is a young fellow over in the next shed who sells these God-awful carvings. Birds, fish, that kind of thing. I told him if he'd take up carving important stuff—you know, like them praying hands—he could make all kinds of money."

Birds? Fish? Seagulls were birds. Dolphin weren't fish, although a lot of people assumed they were.

"Is he a very handsome African American? Maybe in his early twenties?"

She giggled. "Yeah, he is kind of cute, isn't he? Still,

it's what you got that sells, not how you look."

"Do your husband's paintings sell well?" I asked, struggling to keep a neutral tone to my voice.

Connie Beth nodded vigorously. "Like I said, we're all sold out of that one of Jesus, Elvis, Marilyn, and the Stooges. My Elmer can't paint them fast enough."

"Thank you, Connie Beth," I said. She had been very helpful.

I didn't mean to sneak up on Percival Franklin, but he was talking to a customer when I approached, and his back was turned. Even though I waited until the young man was through conducting business before I spoke, he jumped.

"Lord have mercy, Mrs. Timberlake! You scared the pis—tachios out of me."

"Nice recovery. Sorry about the scare. Sometimes I think I should wear a bell around my neck."

He laughed. "So, you still like the carving I gave you?"

"I love it! Unfortunately I didn't come here to talk to you about that."

"What do you want to talk about?"

There was something about the way he said it that made me blush. I could feel the crimson spread across my face.

"Oh, I'm a happily married woman, Mr. Franklin. Which is not to say I don't find you attractive—hey, did you know that woman who sells the velvet Jesus paintings has the hots for you?"

"She does?"

"Well, she said you were cute." Leave it to me to dig myself into a hole while standing on a concrete pad.

"Look, I came to see you about Evangeline LaPointe. She was murdered last night."

He stared at me. I wasn't sure he'd understood.

"Amelia Shadbark's nosy neighbor," I said. "The one who drank too much. She's dead."

His dark eyes flickered. "Not here."

"Not here, what?"

"We can't talk about this here." If I hadn't had the experience of raising a mumbling teenage son, I wouldn't have been able to understand a word Percival Franklin said.

"Then where?"

"Give me half an hour to close my stall. Then meet me at Waterfront Park—say in another fifteen minutes. You know where the Pineapple Fountain is?"

I nodded. This enormous, but spectacular, water feature lives up to its name. It's impossible to a miss a sixteen-foot granite fruit.

"I'll be there," I said, "with bells on."

"Just one will do the trick."

I laughed, but he'd already turned away to help a customer.

Instead of wandering back through the market I exited onto Market Street and headed straight for the park. Charleston has so many treasures, most of them of great historical interest, that it is easy for the casual visitor to miss some of the more recently created gems. Waterfront Park should be on everyone's list.

For one thing, it has what Charleston's Mayor Joseph P. Riley Jr. calls the "best gravel path in America." The mayor himself took an active part in selecting the stones, which hail from both Texas and South Carolina, and together form a surface that works well for both wheelchairs and high heels. It certainly felt good under my feet as I followed the walk that leads to the Pineapple Fountain.

I parked my keister on the nearest shady bench. For the first few minutes I kept a sharp lookout, in case I'd been followed. The park, however, was virtually deserted, and I soon found myself getting drowsy. I fought the feeling for a good five minutes and then—perhaps it was due to the soothing sound of splashing—succumbed to sleep.

"Mrs. Timberlake!"

I jumped, precipitating an uncomfortable reconnection of keister and bench. "What!"

Percival Franklin smiled. "Sorry, Mrs. Timberlake. It's just that I wouldn't do that if I were you."

"Oh Lordy, is it considered bad manners? I mean, was my mouth open?"

"No ma'am. I mean your purse. It's just sitting on the bench besides you. Someone could have walked away with it."

I grabbed my bag and held it to my still pounding chest. "Well, there was nobody around."

He gestured to the space where my pocketbook had been. "May I?"

"By all means. Sit. But you must call me Abigail."

"Call me Percival," he said, taking his seat. "The only people to call me Percy are dead." He meant it as a joke, I assure you.

One has to give us Southerners at least some credit. We've come a long way from my grade school days when not only was my school segregated, but the drinking fountains on the public playground were segregated as well. It would have been unthinkable back then for a white woman and a black man to share the same park bench. Today an interracial couple can stroll through Waterfront Park, pushing their mixed-race baby in a stroller, and no one will give them a second look—except possibly to smile at the baby.

Yes, I know, there are still a few cretins out there who are woefully behind the times. But there are enough reasonable, fair-minded folks—at least here in Charleston—that bigots are, by and large, afraid to give voice to their poison. I certainly didn't feel the least bit self-conscious about having Percival Franklin share my bench. Not on account of his race, at any rate. Now his looks—it is hard to sit that close to someone that good-looking, and not feel at least a trifle on edge.

"What's in that white bag?" I asked.

He glanced at the plastic sack between his feet. "I'll get to that in a minute. First tell me about Miss La-Pointe."

"There's not much to tell, except that she suffocated to death. Apparently someone smothered her."

Percival grimaced. "When?"

"Early this morning. Probably between three and four. That's all I know for sure—except for the fact that my dear sweet husband put a tail on me."

"Excuse me?"

"I was being dogged by a private investigator—a bodyguard, really. But then I ditched him."

The young man's head swiveled. "You must have done a good job, because there isn't a soul in sight. Not even a tourist."

"You don't see any tourists because there's nothing to buy here in the park. Only a mad dog or an Englishman—well, you get the picture. Anyway, Percival, I wanted to ask you a few questions if I might."

I couldn't see him tense, but I could feel the back support of the bench vibrate as his spine straightened. "I was in bed," he said flatly.

"Oh no, that's not what I meant! The questions are about Amelia Shadbark's children."

He looked at me through eyes still shining with suspicion. "I don't know them, Abby. I worked for Mrs. Shadbark three years, and I never saw the daughter—not to my knowledge. The son stopped by a couple of times, but we were never formally introduced. That didn't stop him from criticizing the way I clipped the hedges."

"How did you know he was the son, if you weren't introduced?"

"Brunhilde told me."

"Ah. Well, that brings me to my next question. What do you think of Ms. Salazar?"

"How do you mean? Are you wondering if I think she killed Mrs. Shadbark? Or Miss LaPointe?"

"That, too. I was going to have you start with your impressions in general—but please, plunge right in."

"Bruney is okay," he said, choosing his words deliberately. "Maybe we didn't see eye to eye when she first hired on, but I guess you can say we got to be friends."

"Bruney?"

"That's what I call her."

"Does she call you Percy?"

His glare, I'm sure, was all for show. "She can come across as mean, but she's really not. She doesn't have it in her to kill."

I looked him right in the eye. "Did you know she was really Swedish?" I asked.

He blinked. "Excuse me, Abby, but that's crazy."

"It's true. Brunhilde Salazar's real name is Ingebord Simonson."

Percival grinned. "Okay, so I'm busted. Yeah, I knew that."

"She told you?"

"Look, she isn't trying to get away with anything illegal. Bruney—and that's what I really call her—just needs a break. It's not her fault those husbands died. I would have married her myself—just to keep her in the country—except that I already have someone in my life."

"Oh." I didn't mean to sound disappointed. It just came out that way.

"And she's female, in case you're wandering."

"I wasn't." I swallowed enough irritation to give me a bellyache. "Okay, this leaves me with just one question; what do you know about Mrs. Mindy Sparrow?"

"The society lady who hates my guts?"

"That's the one. Although I think the word 'distrusts' is more accurate."

"Yeah, well, it's all the same to me."

"Yes, but what do you *know* about her?"

He shrugged. "Besides the fact that she's skinny, wears wrinkled clothes, and sounds like a, uh, like a sparrow?"

I smiled. "Besides that. For instance—and I know this is going to sound preposterous—do you think she could be Amelia Shadbark's daughter?"

"You've got to be kidding! Mrs. Shadbark was a tough old lady—kinda reminded me of my grandma in that way—but she was fair-minded. That society lady was always jumping to conclusions."

"Yes, but was there talk?"

"Among?"

"Well—you and Brunhilde, for instance."

"Abby, you're not getting it. Bruney and I liked the old lady. We had other things to talk about."

"Such as?"

He frowned. Clearly the young man did not understand that proper sleuthing required a goodly number of questions.

I moved on. "Did the police question you yet—I mean, in regard to Mrs. Shadbark's death."

"Yeah, they did their thing. Frankly, Abby, they didn't seem half as suspicious as you."

"I'm not suspicious of you!" I wailed. "I'm just trying to get the big picture. You've got to do that first, if you want to see the missing pieces."

"This Sherlock Holmes stuff is really important to you, isn't it?"

"It would be to you, too, if you were from off. Mrs. Shadbark was the first person south of Broad to invite me into her home. Then she dies. I don't think the police suspect me, either, but what do you think this does to my social standing?"

He chuckled and shook his head. "Man, I can't believe I'm hearing this. Social standing!"

"That's easy for you to say. You're not from off."

"From what?"

"From away, from someplace else. You mean you've never heard that expression?"

"Yeah, I suppose I have heard it, but it doesn't mean anything to me. In case you haven't noticed, Abby, I'm black. The society you're talking about doesn't care how long my people have been in Charleston. In that regard, I'll always be more off than you."

I pondered that for a moment. "But you have your own society, right? Your own pecking order."

"Yeah, I suppose we do. Not that I give a damn—excuse my language. I make friends with people I like, not based on where they're from, or who their ancestors were. This society stuff is just a bunch of bullshit. Again, excuse my language."

"You young people can afford to be cavalier," I said. But I knew he was right. There were hundreds, maybe thousands, of "offers" moving into Charleston County every year. I could start my own little society. Of course a lot of the newcomers were Yankees, with hurried ways and harsh accents—I slapped my cheek.

"What's the matter?" Percival asked. "Mosquitoes out already?"

"Something bit me, but I think I got it." There was no need to explain that the bug was called "envy."

"Hey," I said, forcing a brighter tone, "you ever going to show me what's in that bag?"

"This seems like as good a time as any." He handed me the bag carefully. "Go ahead. Take a peek."

21

"Oh my God! Where did you get this?"

"I made it."

"This isn't a joking matter. This belonged to Amelia, didn't it?"

"The hell it did." He stood angrily. "You think I stole it?"

"No! I didn't say that! But—but—it's Lalique. I mean—well, where did you get it?"

Percival snatched the bag from my hands. "I didn't steal it, that's for damn sure."

I stared up at him, and he stared back down at me. I knew he was lying, but what could I say? There had to be a reason he'd chosen to show me the piece, and alienating him was not going to get me the information I wanted.

"You ready to back off?" he finally asked.

"Yes." Perhaps I mumbled. Then again, the fountain had a loud splash.

"I asked you a question, Abby."

"I said yes!"

He remained standing, but took the piece of glass out of the bag and balanced it on the palm of his hand.

199

"You only saw it for a second, Abby. What made you think it was Lalique?"

The work in question featured a mermaid in opalescent and blue-stained glass. She was about six inches high, but in a crouching position. Her face was partially buried in a sweeping bunch of flowers.

"I've seen that motif," I said evenly. "It was one of his favorites. Besides, just looking at the quality of the glass, you can tell it's his."

Percival smiled slowly. "Do you think this piece is signed?"

"It should be. I know there are some exceptions, but—may I see?"

"Certainly." Percival tilted the statuette so I could see its base, but he didn't offer to let me hold it. I stood to get a better look.

"You didn't!" I cried. "How could you?"

"But that's my name."

"I know it's your name, damn it! How could you deface a piece of art?"

Percival's answer was to rear back and pitch the figurine, as if it were a baseball, right at the Pineapple Fountain. Then he took off running.

"You're crazy!" I screamed to his disappearing back.

The Pineapple Fountain has a twenty-foot diameter catchment basin and, mercifully, the mermaid landed in it. She made quite a splash in fact, only not quite as big as the one I made. The basin consists of a series of circular steps, and the statue came to rest in the deepest level, under the bulge of the monstrous fruit. I slipped while climbing down to retrieve it and, I'm ashamed to say, went totally under.

I came up sputtering and spitting—the city keeps its fountains clean, but not potable—and mad as a wet hatter. Perhaps I even swore a little bit before searching for the statuette. But find her I did, and to my great relief, she was still in one piece. I hugged her gratefully to my chest.

It was wonderfully cool there in the water, and since I was as soaked as I was ever going to get, I saw no reason to climb out right away. On many occasions I have seen children playing in the catchment basin of this and the park's other fountain, and no one seems to mind. So who was going to object if a very small adult sat quietly in the water on a scorcher of a summer day?

"Abby, is that you?"

I slid back under the water until just my head protruded. Although it was as slippery as a politician's tongue, I managed to hang on to the mermaid.

"Abby, that is you!" Rob Goldburg was standing not three feet away from the fountain's base. He had one long arm draped around the shoulders of a stunningly beautiful woman.

"No it's not." I took a deep breath and plunged beneath the surface. I'm quite good at holding my breath, you know. Buford, my ex-husband, and I courted at a water park up in Fort Mill, South Carolina. I couldn't swim very well at the time, but was too embarrassed to admit it. I let Buford take me out to the deep end of the pool on numerous occasions. Buford, who was so full of himself he should have been twins, didn't seem to notice that every now and then I'd sink below the surface. You can bet I learned to hold my breath quickly. In fact, I learned the lesson so well that I have—at times when I needed a change—contemplated moving to Japan and becoming a pearl diver.

But even a loggerhead turtle needs to come up for air sometime. When I came up, sputtering and spitting again, Rob and the beautiful stranger were still there.

"Having fun?" Rob asked.

I pushed streaming tresses out of my eyes with one hand, while grasping the Lalique with the other. It is hard to glare through chlorinated fountain water.

"I'm having a ball," I said. "You two want to join me?"

The handsome man laughed. "No thanks. These are eighty-dollar slacks."

"How about you?" I said to the woman. "Your slacks obviously cost a whole lot less."

"Abby!" Rob reprimanded me.

I stood. "Don't use that tone on me, Roberto. It's one thing to cheat on Bob, but to cheat on him with a woman! How could you?"

That sent Rob and his bimbo into paroxysms of laughter. They laughed so hard they staggered, and the bimbo came dangerously close to joining me in the drink after all.

"What is so damn funny," I demanded.

Rob clutched his well-toned chest. "Abby, do you think I'm straight all of a sudden?"

I shrugged. "A picture is worth a thousand words, isn't it?

"And that picture would be what? Me walking in a public park with my arm around a pretty lady?"

"There's more to it than that. How about all the sneaking around you've being doing? Don't think Bob hasn't noticed."

Rob flinched. "Bob said something?"

"Can you blame him? When I first learned that Buford had cheated on me with Tweetie, I talked to everyone with ears. Don't you remember? You ought to—you and Bob spent that whole first night holding my hands." I narrowed my eyes and looked at the bimbo. "The whole first night."

"But Abby—"

"Don't you 'but Abby' me!" I waded to the lip of the catchment. "The man is beside himself. He may be on the verge of a nervous breakdown."

"He's my brother!" the bimbo practically shouted.

It was my turn to yuk it up. "*Right*. Like I believe that. Rob only has one sister, and I've already met her. No offense, Rob, but your sister is nowhere near as pretty as this—this—"

"This is *Bob*'s sister, Abby."

"Say what?" I could feel the blood draining from my face. Or was that just more fountain water?

"My name is Wendy Steuben. I'm Bob Steuben's baby sister."

"Don't be ridiculous. Bob's sister won't even speak to him because he's gay."

Wendy smiled. "That was the case. I led a pretty sheltered life in Toledo, Abby—may I call you that?" She didn't wait for an answer. "I had a hard time accepting that my brother was gay. Whenever he tried to talk about it, I refused to listen. Then, a couple of months ago, Rob called. At first I didn't want to listen to Rob any more than Bob, but Rob put me in touch with a support group called PFLAG. They helped give me some perspective."

Rob nodded. "Wendy's still not okay with the idea of Bob and me as a couple, but she'd like to see him again. I flew her down here for a birthday surprise."

"It's your birthday?" I asked just to be polite. I couldn't see how someone so pretty could have a brother who looked like Bob. Not that Bob is ugly, mind you. Thanks to a great wig and a skillful makeup job, he made an uncanny Barbra Streisand at my Halloween party—albeit one with an enormous Adam's apple. But as himself, the man is agreeably homely.

"It's Bob's," she said. "Tomorrow."

"Tomorrow?"

Rob nodded again. "You got the invitation I sent, didn't you? It said 'regrets only.' "

"Yes, of course, but things sort of got in the way."

Rob frowned. "How can you forget a free dinner at Magnolias?"

He had a point. If the food in heaven isn't as good as the entrées chefs Barickman and Drake serve up, I'm sending it back. Every dish I've sampled is a party for the mouth, except for the Mocha Crème Brulee, which is a downright orgy.

"I think Bob's forgotten it's his birthday," I said. When one has a weak defense, it sometimes works to point out the guilt in others. "If he remembered, he would have guessed that your mysterious ways were somehow related."

Much to my relief, Rob agreed. "Bob's in denial. It's the big Four-O, you know. I remember when I turned forty I was so depressed I went bowling with my sister. We drank beer—straight from the bottles! Anyway, Abby, don't forget. It starts at six o'clock, and you want to be there for the big surprise." He gave Wendy's shoulder a squeeze.

"I wouldn't miss it for the world."

"Great. You don't think Greg, C. J., and your mother need reminding, do you?"

"I'm sure they don't." I smiled ruefully. "They haven't been as self-absorbed as I have."

"Abby was climbing the social ladder," Rob said, "when one of the rungs broke."

"It was the *top* rung," I hastened to explain. "And I didn't do it! I'm just trying to make sure no one accuses me of vandalism."

"Perhaps we've taken this ladder analogy far enough. Remind the others for me, if you will—" Rob had spotted the little mermaid cradled in my arms. "What's that?"

I held her out for him to take. "This, you'll have to agree, is vandalism. Just look what someone has done to this perfectly lovely Lalique."

Rob turned the piece over in hands worthy of a surgeon. He handed it back almost immediately.

"That isn't Lalique."

"Of course it is. It's just that it's been defaced by the forger's name."

"Look closer, Abby. Even without my reading glasses I can see that the name is not engraved in there. This signature—P. Franklin, whoever the hell he or she is—is part of the mold. Otherwise, it's a pretty good fake."

I reexamined the underside of the sculpture. It is amazing what one can miss while jumping to conclusions. Rob was absolutely right; Percival Franklin's signature was not inscribed.

"Why, slap me up the side of the head and call me whopper-jawed," I cried. "I can't believe I missed that."

Rob smiled. "Where did you say you got this?"

"I didn't say. But I got it from Amelia Shadbark's gardener."

"Her *gardener*?"

"He's an immensely talented young man. He has a stall in The Market—you may have seen it—where he sells wooden sculptures of local wildlife. Mostly porpoises and seagulls. They're really good, but not even in the same class as a carved camellia blossom he gave me yesterday. That one is museum quality."

"Ah, yes, I think Bob mentioned that. I tuned it out I guess." He gave Wendy a merry wink. "No offense, but he was whining a lot."

"No offense taken."

Rob tugged the statuette out of my grasp. "Like I said, it's a damn good fake. I would have been convinced of its authenticity, had it been signed by René himself. Or had I at least known its provenance. But this"—he rubbed a thumb over the telltale signature—"is incredible."

"If you think this is incredible, you should have seen Amelia Shadbark's collection. She had an entire room filled with this stuff."

Rob grabbed one of my arms with his free hand. "Wait a minute. Are you saying the grande dame had a collection of forgeries?"

I remembered my prized peacock perfume bottle,

which was indeed a forgery. "I didn't actually look at the signatures—I was there for tea. And anyway, I was supposed to come back to appraise them."

By that time the sun had dried everything but my sandals, and they were only the least bit damp. That's more than I can say for Rob and Wendy. The latter, not being a Southern woman, had not been informed that we females of the gentler latitudes never sweat; we merely dew. There wasn't enough dew in Dixie to account for her perspiration.

"Hey, how about we head for the shade," Rob said, "and continue the conversation there." Still gripping my wrist he steered me to the very bench that had been the scene of my little disagreement with Percival Franklin. The pretty girl from Toledo trotted amiably after us, dripping all the way.

"Now," Rob said, when we were all seated, although nicely spaced out so that we didn't touch in the heat, "do you think this gardener you mentioned really has the skill to do this?"

"The artistry, yes. But where would he learn glass-making skills?"

Rob fondled the statuette with admiration. "Maybe you should find out."

"Now *you* wait just one cotton-picking minute. You're not suggesting Percival had anything to do with Amelia Shadbark's death!"

He gave me a quizzical look. "Abby, I daresay you sound a little protective of this man."

I gasped. "He's young enough to be my son!"

"Hey, take it easy. It was just an innocent observation."

"Besides, he's a very bright young man. He wouldn't

sign his name on a piece of glass and then try and pass it off as a genuine Lalique."

"Unless," Wendy said, "he wanted to get caught. That happens sometimes. I read mystery novels, you see."

I resisted my temptation to glare at her. Charlestonians are known to be among the most courteous folks in the nation, and I would not be the one to sully our reputation. But mystery novels indeed! The girl had too much time on her hands if she could waste it reading fiction. I mean, what is the point, when it's all made up? Now, a good solid text on antique restoration—that was something worth reading.

Rob sensed my exasperation. "Well, Wendy and I really have to get going. She needs to get back to the hotel—she's staying at the Charleston Place, incidentally—and I better get back to the shop before Bob blows a gasket."

"I understand. I'll see you tomorrow evening."

"Ciao, Abby." Rob gave me a brotherly kiss on the cheek.

"Toodle-do," Wendy from Toledo said.

They left me sitting on a park bench that was warm enough to roast a brisket. I waited until they were out of sight before hauling my brisket off the bench and getting back down to work. I wasn't headed back to my shop, however, but to pay a second visit to the most likely suspect in Amelia Shadbark's untimely death.

22

The traffic to Mount Pleasant was light that time of the day and I enjoyed my ride over the Silas N. Pearlman Memorial Bridge. A Chinese container ship was approaching the span, and I waved. I know, it was a silly gesture. I'm sure the crew had better things to do—like avoid the pilings—than wave at a car passing overhead, but I wanted them to feel welcome. After all, if I was from off, they were from *way* off. Hopefully someone would get the impression that the natives were friendly.

Not a total fool, I reappeared on Constance Rodriguez's doorstep fully armed. I had a carrot cake from the Mount Pleasant Publix supermarket in one hand, and a cheddar loaf from the Atlanta Bread Company in the other. I rang the doorbell with my nose.

This time Constance took so long to answer the door that I was tempted to eat the gifts I'd brought to keep from starving to death. I could have kicked myself for not having brought something to drink.

"It's only you," Constance said when the door finally opened. "What do you want this time?"

"To give you these," I said, and held out the goodies.

She eyed the carrot cake. "Who told you that's my favorite?"

"No one, but Publix makes the best carrot cake in the world. I didn't think I could go wrong. See, it even has a carrot made out of icing on top."

"Ms. Timberlake, are you implying that we heavy people can be bought with food?"

"No ma'am. It's just that I know you don't get out much."

"Is that cheese bread fresh?"

"Atlanta Bread Company makes it fresh every day."

"You can come in," she growled, "but just for a minute."

I stepped gratefully into the air-conditioned apartment. It was furnished simply, in what can best be described as Early Goodwill decor. This is not a judgment call, mind you—we must all make do with what's available to us—but merely an observation. It was also my observation that Constance had recently had a guest. There were two plastic tumblers sitting on the fake cherry coffee table, and both were approximately half full of ice tea. Despite the cool air, the ice in the drinks was producing more sweat than Wendy Steuben.

"I hope I'm not interrupting anything," I said.

Constance caught me glancing at the tumblers. "Oh no. I get a little absentminded sometimes. I'd forgotten I'd already fixed myself a drink. Then, as long as I had two made, I decided I might as well drink them both." She paused, as if pondering the problems of the world. "Would you care for something to drink?" she finally asked.

Afraid that she might offer me one of the two teas, I

requested water. She was happy to oblige, but did I mind getting it for myself?

"And cut me a nice slice of that cake, while you're in the kitchen. Feel free to have one, as well. You'll find knives and forks in that drawer to the right of the sink, and there are some dessert plates in the left cabinet on the bottom shelf."

"What about the bread?"

"I'll be saving that for supper."

"No, I meant, where do you want me to put it?"

"Just leave it on the counter by the refrigerator. And speaking of which, pour me a little milk. It will go better with the cake. You'll find the glasses on the shelf above the dessert plates."

I did as I was bade, although I resolved not to do any laundry, if asked. Constance might not be happy to see me when I showed up at her door, but she had no compunctions against putting me right to work.

When I returned with her snack (I'd passed on the cake) she graciously allowed me to sit. I chose an armchair upholstered in faded purple-and-green-plaid polyester. Constance had already staked out a matching couch, and my only other option was a black painted kitchen chair that looked like its previous owner had thrown it into a wood-chipping machine, and then changed his mind.

"So," she said, and took her first bite. Before continuing she licked the icing off her lips. "To what do I owe the honor this time?"

I took a sip of water. "I went to see your brother, Mrs. Rodriguez. And then Mrs. Mindy Sparrow. They had some interesting things to say."

Constance jabbed a finger into her cake, and licked the icing off that, too. "I just bet they did. Bet they both badmouthed me to hell and back."

"I wouldn't say that—"

"You don't have to sugarcoat it for me, Ms. Timber-lake. Tell me exactly what they each said."

"Well, your brother had a very specific message. He said to tell you he wouldn't have any money until the end of the month."

"What the hell is that supposed to mean?" Actually, her language was a bit stronger than that, but I'm too much of a lady to repeat it word for word.

"I don't know what he meant."

"The hell you don't! He meant—as you damn well know—that he sends me a monthly check. Well, let me tell you something, little Miss Mess in Everybody's Business, he doesn't send me a dime. Once, just *once*, I borrowed two hundred dollars from him to get from Chicago back to here—by bus. I have long since paid that money back."

I said nothing, although I was tempted to tell her what Orman Jr. had said about her behavior being the cause of their father's death. The only reason I refrained was that I knew my motive was now wrong. I no longer wanted just to get information; I wanted to hurt her for calling me a name. The "little" part I was used to—but Miss Mess in Everybody's Business had really struck a nerve.

I'd served the piece of cake with the largest section of carrot-shaped icing on top. After waiting impatiently for a few seconds for me to respond, Constance swiped the decoration off in one piece and licked her finger. The cake itself disappeared in three bites. Then, for no reason that I could see, she licked the remaining fingers on that hand. Perhaps in a previous life she'd been a cat.

"So what did that lying Sparrow have to say?"

"Mrs. Rodriguez, she seems to be under the impression that Amelia was *her* mother."

"That lying piece of—"

"More cake?"

"Later. Tell me exactly what she said."

I told her. Constance listened with remarkable impassivity. I mean, one minute she was as fractious as a mule with a burr under its saddle, and the next, her features were as placid as a stone Buddha's.

I was beginning to think my cat diagnosis had been correct when she snapped out of her reverie. "It's all lies," she hissed. "The two of them are in cahoots. They want me committed." She wagged a moist finger. "No, I'll tell you what they *really* want—they want me to drop dead like Daddy did."

"Why would they want that?"

"So that they could inherit more money, of course!"

"But if Mrs. Sparrow isn't one of your mother's heirs, how does she stand to inherit?"

Constance snorted. "By marrying Orman Jr. Please, Mrs. Timberlake, this isn't rocket science."

I stood my ground. "It may not be rocket science, but its about as clear as a bowl of she-crab soup. Mrs. Sparrow is already married."

"That marriage is a sham. Mindy only married Beauregard Sparrow because she couldn't get my brother to commit. She was trying to make him jealous, but he was slow to react, and the plan backfired on her. But make no mistake, Mrs. Timberlake, Mindy and Orman Jr. have been lovers for years."

"Then why didn't she get divorced and marry him?"

"Because my brother is a loser. He's never been able to keep a job, and Mama and Daddy didn't believe in trust funds. We had to make it on our own. Mindy knew which side her bread was buttered on. Only now all that's changed—Orman Jr.'s side suddenly has more butter."

I tried to imagine the chic Mrs. Sparrow I knew cavorting with a broken-down drunk like Orman Shadbark Jr. Unless the latter stood to inherit a whole lot of money—more than a flock of Sparrows could supply—I just didn't see it.

"Forgive this indelicate question, Mrs. Rodriguez, but how large is your mother's estate?"

She regarded me through the slits that served as eyes. "Mama could buy and sell all of Charleston County."

"As rich as that? Well, Mrs. Sparrow would have me believe that you hated your mama."

"More lies! Take me to her, Mrs. Timberlake. Drive me over there right now, and I'll rip her lying tongue out."

"Okay by me. But I have to warn you, it's awfully hot out there."

I could tell Constance wasn't expecting to have her bluff called. She turned the color of a peeled rutabaga.

"Oh, then I shouldn't go out," she moaned. "Ever since the cradle, heat and I have been enemies."

"You sure you don't want to come? We can stop at Sticky Fingers restaurant on the way," I said, referring to a popular barbecue joint on Route 17. "Their Memphis dry ribs are to die for."

The woman seemed torn between following through on an empty threat or forgoing another meal at my expense. She gazed wistfully down at her hands.

"Youth eez mean!"

I nearly fell off the purple-and-green-plaid chair. I'd plumb forgotten about the two glasses of iced tea sitting on the coffee table when I came in.

"Brunhilde!" I exclaimed, as a hulking figure emerged from a back bedroom.

"Youth," cried the masseuse, shaking a sausagelike finger at me, "youth ur being oonfeer. Zeeth voman haff asrhritis. Eeth eez deefeecult fur her to valk."

"Drop the phony accent," I said calmly. "I know all about you, Brunhilde—I mean, Ingebord."

She stopped mid-stride. "Yah?"

"Yes. And I don't care that three of your husbands died under mysterious circumstances—wait, that didn't come out right! What I meant to say is, I don't hold that against you."

"You don't?" she said, with just the slightest trace of a lilt.

"These things happen," I said. Under my breath I may have mumbled something about her having Ledbetter blood. "I'm delighted to find you here. You're just the person I want to talk to."

Her normally dark and brooding face lit up like a jack-o'-lantern with two candles in it. "I am?"

"Absolutely. I don't suppose I could steal you away for a few minutes. Maybe we could take a walk."

"In this heat!" Constance struggled to rise from the couch.

"Don't worry," I said. "I'll take her someplace cool. Like maybe the mall."

"There is no covered mall in Mount Pleasant. You have to go all the way up to North Charleston."

"You're right. So, we'll make it a restaurant."

Constance had found her feet. "Then I'm coming too."

I didn't want to be rude, but having Constance along would defeat the whole purpose of my little excursion. I had to think fast.

"Make that the library. I have a trunk full of books that are overdue."

"But you live in Charleston, Mrs. Timberlake. You can't return Charleston books to our library."

"As it happens, they're Mount Pleasant books, ones my husband checked out to read on his shrimp boat. He berths it here, at Shem Creek."

Constance sank back down into the couch. "Then y'all can go on without me. Just don't believe everything you hear."

I had the impression that remark was directed at both Ingebord and me.

I grilled Ingebord over steaks at T-Bonz on Johnnie Dodds Boulevard. The early supper was her idea, by the way, not mine. She had two steak platters, and I had coffee. Clearing my name of any associated guilt in the death of Mrs. Amelia Shadbark was getting to be an expensive undertaking. Perhaps there was a way to write these expenditures off on my income taxes. If I got into trouble with the IRS—well, too bad the Bushes were now in the White House. Otherwise I could always donate an antique bed—maybe a nice

Queen Anne—to replace the worn out one in the Lincoln Bedroom.

I waited patiently until Ingebord had started in on her second steak before commencing the grilling. A full stomach is the best way to maintain peace, if you ask me.

"So tell me about the ice hotel in Sweden," I said pleasantly.

"It is cold."

"I imagine it is. Have you ever spent the night in it?" She looked up from her food. "I am an unlucky woman Mrs. Timberlake, but I am not a fool."

"I was just trying to make small talk," I cried.

Ingebord Simonson didn't suffer fools either. "The ice," she said emphatically, "what kind of foolish person is this that sleeps on ice?"

"An adventurer? Besides, the hotel supplies sleeping bags."

"It is crazy." She shoved a piece of meat the size of an impala into her mouth. "So what is it you really want to talk about, Mrs. Timberlake?"

"Everything—that is, in regard to Amelia Shadbark's death." I held up a hand to silence any protest. "But just so you know, I don't suspect you. And you, apparently, don't suspect Constance. Why is that?"

The bad news was that when Ingebord scowled she had only one eyebrow. The good news was that it was full enough that, with a little shaping, it would be rather attractive.

"Mrs. Timberlake, it is not that I do not suspect Mrs. Rodriguez, but where else am I to stay? The police tell me not to leave the area, and I cannot afford these Charleston hotels."

"Ah, so you were living in the Shadbark mansion, correct?"

She sighed. "There I have my own bathroom. A Jacuzzi even. And in the bedroom, a private telephone."

"You must have known Constance pretty well—I mean, to get her to take you in."

Ingebord shook her head vigorously. "I did not know her at all."

"You'd never even met her?"

"No, I had not met her. I was a servant, Mrs. Timberlake. I did not associate with the family or their guests."

"But you waited on them, right? I mean, you served my friend C. J. and me tea."

"Yah, this I do, but Mrs. Rodriguez, she does not even come for tea. Then, the day after her mama dies, she calls me at the motel I am staying in, and invites me to come stay in her apartment. I think at first maybe this is a joke, but she calls many times. Finally, I say yes. I told you before, Mrs. Timberlake, I am not stupid." She shuddered. "But we must share just one bathroom, yah?"

I took a sip of my coffee, which had gone tepid, but I didn't care. Ingebord Simonson was a lot more forthcoming than Brunhilde Salazar. I was finally getting somewhere.

"Tell me, dear," I said, "what's her game?"

23

Ingebord's English, while fluent, did not stretch to include all the nuances of the language. The eyebrows rose in questioning manner, pulling the scar on her left check into a taut thin line.

"Poker?"

"That's not the kind of game I mean. *Why* do you think she invited you to stay with her?"

A chunk of steak the size of an eland disappeared down her gullet. "Because she is lonely."

"That's it?"

"And she is kind. There is much hospitality in the American South."

"We do our best. But has Constance tried to influence you in any way?"

The scowl returned to Ingebord's swarthy forehead. "You think I can be—how do you say—bought?"

"Not at all. By the way, the desserts here are fabulous."

"Yah, I think maybe I will get one. Or two. It is hard to decide."

"Get them all. So, back to my question. While I know you can't be bought, is Constance trying to get you to see things her way?"

Ingebord looked up from the meat, like a lioness from her kill. "There is no need for her to do this, Mrs. Timberlake. I agree with what she thinks."

"Which is?"

"That it is the brother and Mrs. Sparrow who wanted my employer dead."

"You really think they're capable of murder?"

"Yah. Everyone is."

"Not me!" I honestly don't think I'm capable of murder. Killing, however, is another matter. If my children's lives were at stake, or Mama's, or Greg's, and maybe even C. J.'s—well, there's no telling the lengths I'd go to protect them.

Ingebord eyed the dessert menu. "Even you, Mrs. Timberlake."

My face burned. "And what about young Percival Franklin?"

She started, dropping the menu. "He is a good boy!"

"I figured you'd say that. From what I hear, you two got along famously."

"Yah, we got along okay. Mrs. Timberlake, there is no—how do you say—uh, motive?"

"Perhaps that's your word."

"Yah, it is. There is no motive for Percival to kill Mrs. Shadbark."

"There's no chance he managed to get himself written into her will?"

Ingebord stopped laughing when I snatched up the menu. "Mrs. Timberlake, Percival and I were servants. It is only in the movies that servants get written into the will."

Not only, I thought. "Percival is a very talented young man, dear. He's shown me some of his work."

She made no comment.

"He gave me a carved wooden flower," I said. "It was exquisite. He also gave me a glass mermaid."

Again no comment.

"Have you seen his work, Ingebord?"

She pursed her lips, as if just having tasted lemonade that was a tad too tart. "This style of art is not my cup of coffee," she muttered.

"I think you mean tea, dear. Anyway, did Percival give—or even sell—any pieces of art to Mrs. Shadbark?"

The eyebrows fused. "I did not concern myself with such matters, Mrs. Timberlake."

I sighed. For all the progress I was making, I would have been better off going to the movies with the gang. I could be snuggling up next to my honey pot, and if we'd let Mama pick the movie, I could be having a nice long nap.

"Do you at least know where Percival lives?"

It may have been my imagination, but I thought I saw her sallow color lighten a shade. She was now a pleasing pale yellow, not unlike my teeth.

"He lives in North Charleston, I think. Or maybe it is Hanahan. He is in the telephone book."

The woman was being as cagey as the Riverbanks Zoo up in Columbia. I held the menu as far away from her as I could.

"Can you at least tell me why you were so hostile to my friend C.J. and me, when we arrived for tea?"

"I was?"

"You practically bit our heads off. What was that all about?"

Ingebord shrugged. "Well, that seems like a long

time ago, yah? Maybe it was because there were others who tried to become friends with Mrs. Shadbark. It was obvious to me that they were after her money."

"You don't say! Like who?"

She lunged at the menu, and I didn't react fast enough. Ingebord flashed me a triumphant smile.

"Like Mrs. Sparrow."

"You seem to be fixated on that woman." I stood and fished a pair of twenties out of my pocketbook. "Hey, you don't mind paying, do you?"

"Are you leaving?"

"Yes. Duty awaits me at home." Not to mention three disgruntled loved ones, if you include my cat Dmitri. Fortunately, I'd left Greg with enough good-will to see him through a couple more hours—even if he discovered I'd ditched the bodyguard he'd hired.

"But how will I get home?" Ingebord whined. "How will I get back to Mrs. Rodriguez's apartment?"

I fumbled for another five. "You can either call a cab or I'll take you there now."

Ingebord had only to glance back at the menu to reach a decision. She grabbed the five. "This will pay for one dessert, yah? But what about the cab?"

I threw her a ten.

Mama threw herself at me the second I walked in my front door. "Oh, Abby, you're alive!"

"Of course I am, Mama. Why would you—" I gasped. "What happened here?"

Mama stepped back so I could view the scene of destruction. My parlor now looked like a teenager's room—one in which an atomic bomb had just been detonated.

"We've been burgled, Abby, that's what."

"Where are Greg and C. J.?"

"We're here, Abby." Greg strode quickly across the room from the hallway and threw his arms around me. C. J., who was trailing him, threw her gangly arms around the both of us. Not to be outdone, Mama wormed her way into the center of this human tripod. Thank heavens Dmitri was a cat and stayed appropriately aloof.

"I can't breathe!" I cried.

The group hug broke up. "Abby," Greg said, concern written all over his handsome face, "we didn't know what to think. You were supposed to be, uh—"

"Protected by the bodyguard you hired?"

"Damn it, Abby, you shouldn't have ditched him. He was only doing his job."

"And so was I. Only I can't do it with a shadow scaring off the folks I want to interview."

"Your job, Abby, is to sell antiques."

"And to be a good wife," Mama said, and then patted her pearls. June Cleaver's clone realized she'd gone too far.

I glared at her for good measure. "Well, y'all, here I am, and very much alive. Your worries were unfounded. Now this"—I waved at the devastation—"is another matter. Did anyone call the police?"

Greg appeared mildly miffed that I would even ask such a question. "Scrubb and Bright are on their way."

"But Abby," Mama said, her fingers still resting on her beads, "it's not as bad as you might be thinking. It's only this room that's been burgled."

"Mozella," my hubby said, "I don't think there's been a burglary. Nothing seems to be missing."

Mama's single strand of ancient pearls began a slow rotation around her neck. "Don't be silly, Greg. What do you call this?"

"Vandalism. That's what it looks like to me."

"But why would anyone want to vandalize our house?" Mama dropped the necklace as both hands cupped her cheeks. "It's because of something Abby did, isn't it?"

"*Me*? All I've done is to ask a couple of people a few questions."

If I hadn't seen C. J. put her fingers in her mouth, the ear-splitting whistle that followed would have propelled me right out of my sandals. Mama, who didn't see it coming, jumped so high that as she descended, her crinolines and full circle skirt filled with air and she floated gracefully back to the floor.

"Please people," C. J. begged, "I hate to see my family argue like this."

We stared at her.

"We weren't arguing," Mama said. "We were discussing."

"Nobody's in the least bent out of shape," Greg agreed.

C. J. could read my mind, as small as the print was. "Still, y'all are like family to me. You," she said to Mama, "are the mother I never had. And you, Greg, are the brother I never had. And you, Abby, are the daughter I'll probably never have."

"*Daughter?* I'm old enough to be your mother!"

The big gal shrugged. "Well, that's how I feel. So, are you three going to apologize to each other and promise to get along?"

Our stares turned to glares.

"Or not," C. J. said, with another shrug of her shoulders. "But can we all agree to count our blessings?"

Mama's pearls began another rotation. Fortunately for her, she has very small wattles, and the orbits are smooth and apparently painless.

"Which blessings would those be?" she asked.

"That nothing was stolen. Once back home in Shelby we were vandalized—"

"But something was stolen!" My shriek had Mama airborne again.

"What, hon?" Greg's sapphire eyes swept the room.

"That beautiful camellia carving I brought home yesterday. It was right here on the coffee table when I went out this morning."

Greg scooped up a couple of *Architectural Digests*, a wooden Balinese carving of a man sitting cross-legged, his arms folded, and a Rookwood Pottery vase. The items had been artfully arranged on the heavy marble table along with Percival Franklin's exquisite sculpture. The table had been overturned, and all my decorative items dumped on the floor, except for the wooden camellia blossom.

"Are you sure it was on the table, hon? I remember you showed it to me, but I don't remember you putting it on the table."

Of course I was sure. And even though he was a retired detective, it didn't surprise me that my helpful hubby hadn't noticed the rearranged objet d'art. After all, the day I came home from the beauty shop with an eighteen-inch weave attached to my short dark hair, it had taken Greg a full three hours to process the change. It was only when I dangled my new locks inches above his precious chili that they registered with him. I had the weave removed the next day.

"I'm sure, Greg," I said, drawing on my reserve pool of patience. "Mama—C. J.—y'all remember it being there, don't you?"

Mama nodded. "I thought it looked a little tacky there, next to those fancy magazines, but I wasn't going to say anything, dear."

"You just did, Mama."

C. J. must have thought another tiny tiff was in the offing. She jockeyed into position between me and my mini-madre.

"Ooh, Abby, I've been thinking. Maybe that camellia carving is still here in the house. Maybe it's just been hidden."

"And who would do that, dear? C. J., you didn't!"

The poor girl looked mortified. "Not me, Abby! I meant, hidden by the ghost."

"Ghost?"

"The one I've been telling you about. The one who jangles his keys in the hallway outside your guest room."

If exasperation was a virtue, I stood a good chance of being canonized after my death. "First of all, C. J., they don't like to be called ghosts anymore. The correct term is Apparition American. And in the second place, what would an Apparition American want with a carving of a flower?"

"Maybe the ghost—I mean, Apparition American— didn't have flowers at his funeral. And I know it's a male, Abby, I can just feel it. Anyway, maybe he was just trying to make things right."

Mama gasped, her pearls frozen in mid-stream. "Your daddy," she said to me. "I knew it!"

"What?"

"How can you forget, dear? There weren't any flowers at your daddy's funeral!"

I moved considerably closer to sainthood. "There weren't any flowers at Daddy's funeral, Mama, because it was his wish that the money be donated to York Place, the home for boys."

"Well, he could have changed his mind the day he died, and not gotten around to telling me. Besides, Sudie Mae up in Rock Hill had an Apparition American living in her house, and she—this one was a female—hid things all the time."

C.J.'s enormous head was bobbing up and down with all the vigor of the paint mixer at Home Depot. I knew from experience that the only way to get her to stop was to let her share the experience she wanted so desperately to relate.

"Spit it out, dear," I said.

"Well, Granny Ledbetter's house was haunted, you see. Things were disappearing all the time. Then they would reappear—just like that."

"How did you know it was an Apparition American who was responsible for this phenomenon?" Greg asked. My husband, bless his heart, tries to keep an open mind.

C.J. rolled her eyes at the question. "Because Granny's sister, Miss Mulva Jenkins, contacted the ghost—or whatever—during a séance. She—the ghost, not Granny or her sister—admitted she borrowed certain things. It was *her* house, after all. And she always put them back."

"Well—"

"Ooh, except for one thing, and that was Granny's teeth. They disappeared one night and we didn't find them for months. Then on National Clean Out Your Refrigerator Day, I found them in the very back of the freezing compartment. You won't believe this, you guys, but Granny's teeth were embedded in a frozen Snickers bar. Who knew Apparition Americans liked sweets?"

"Sounds more like your granny liked sweets," I growled. "Look, y'all, this conversation about Apparition Americans has been absolutely fascinating, but I can assure you that none of them were responsible for the missing sculpture."

"But how do you *know*, Abby?" C.J.'s chin jutted out so far, I could have balanced a broom on it, bristle end down.

"Because Apparition Americans aren't capable of killing anyone, are they?"

"Of course not, Abby. Don't be silly."

"There you have it, dear. Whoever took that flower is the same *person* who killed Mrs. Amelia Shadbark. And I just happen to know who it is."

24

"**W**ho?" My loved ones sounded like a Greek chorus. Even Dmitri got into the act by yowling

I suspected Mindy Sparrow. The woman had demanded I give the flower to her. She couldn't wait to get her well-bred hands on the entire estate. But I needed to talk to Percival again. Maybe he knew something about this Linen Lady that I didn't.

"Well, I can't prove it just yet, so I'm not sure I should tell—"

The doorbell rang and I skipped to get it.

"Deus ex machina," the Greek chorus cried. Dmitri, who doesn't speak Latin, merely meowed.

I ushered the sergeants in. They surveyed the mess, took notes, and asked a few questions. For a moment it looked like I was going to be able to hustle their bustles out of there before one of the gang told on me. I might as well have hoped that the Hope Diamond flew out of its display at the Smithsonian and landed in a locket around my neck.

"There's really no need to waste time asking any more questions," Mama said, patting her pearls. "Our Abby knows exactly who did it."

"I do not!"

"Ooh, Abby, but you do," C.J. said, nodding her huge head like a somnolent draft horse.

"They're making this up," I cried.

"Abby," Greg said, an uncharacteristic sharpness to his tone, "it's better if you come clean with the sergeants now."

Just when I thought I couldn't feel any more betrayed, Dmitri nipped my ankle and scampered from the room, his tail erect and bushy.

"Et tu, Brutus?" I wailed.

Detective Bright looked puzzled, but the Affleck look-alike treated me to a boyish grin. Since I no longer believed he was in the least bit attracted to me, I found it more annoying than charming.

"Well, Abby, it would appear that you're outnumbered."

"Maybe so, but might does not make right. I have a theory about who did this—I certainly don't have any proof. It would be wrong of me to point the finger now."

"But that finger," Mama said, "would be pointing at both the thief who stole the sculpture and Mrs. Amelia Shadbark's killer."

"Mama!"

Scrubb scribbled with his stub. "Is this true, Abby?"

"I plead the Fifth."

Sergeant Scrubb sighed heavily. Sergeant Bright was bright enough to feign interest in a post-Impressionist watercolor hanging askew on the wall.

"Abby," the unhappy detective said, "holding back information could be dangerous."

"True," I said, "but giving you the wrong information could be damning."

Sergeant Scrubb turned to Greg. "Can't you talk sense into her?"

The Greek chorus gasped.

"He's my husband, not my father," I said, drawing myself up to my full four feet nine.

"Her daddy couldn't talk sense into her, either," Mama said, and then, realizing the error of her ways, clapped a hand over her mouth. Had she been wearing gloves, I had no doubt she would have popped one in first for good measure.

Sergeant Scrubb spread his hands in a gesture of defeat. "In that case, it appears we've done all we can do here." He scribbled again on the miniature pad. "This is my personal cell phone number. Don't hesitate to use it."

The Greek chorus was relentless in their persecution of me. They claimed, repeatedly, that their blathering stemmed from their concern, but I didn't care. To put it bluntly, I was pissed off.

I went to bed right after supper—which I cooked, by the way—and I went to bed alone. I tried to get Dmitri to join me, but *he* was pissed at *me*, and all because at supper I'd made the mistake of mentioning my plan to take him to the vet the next day for his rabies shot. No doubt there are those who will scoff at the idea of a cat understanding English, but those folks have never met Dmitri. A house guest once referred to my ten-pound bundle of joy as "that four-footed fleabag." She made the mistake of saying this in Dmitri's presence, and that very same afternoon the "fleabag" in question made his daily deposit in one of her shoes.

At any rate, as I lay in bed waiting for Greg to join me, I heard the three humans talking, laughing, and generally carrying on, as if there was a party in progress. I'm sure Dmitri, who has a silent laugh, was out there yukking it up as well. In a futile effort to block out the sounds of revelry, I put my pillow over my head. It was still there the next morning when I awoke. Greg, however, had come to bed and gone.

I was surprised to see that it was already nine o'-clock. Thank heavens I'd hired Homer. Having an assistant was like owning a debit card. I couldn't imagine how I'd gotten along without one for so long.

C. J. was still asleep; I could tell that without even checking the guest room, thanks to her snores. And since the big galoot hadn't sought asylum in my room from the resident Apparition American, I assumed that Mama had taken mercy on the girl and spent the night in there as well. It wouldn't surprise me to learn that the two of them had stayed up until the wee hours bonding. If that was the case—well, bully for them. C. J., who had been abandoned as a baby on Granny Ledbetter's porch, could benefit from a little extra mothering, and Mama could always use another daughter. One who wasn't so pigheaded.

I showered and dressed, grabbed an untoasted Pop Tart, and headed straight for the Den of Antiquity. I couldn't wait to learn what treasures Homer had purchased for me from the Delrumple estate. Of course he wouldn't have had time to transport, much less display them—

"Homer!" I cried, startling a flock of Linen Ladies

who were gathered around him, as if he were their guru.

Seeing me, Homer sauntered—if the word may be applied to a man of his girth—my way, sporting a grin as wide as the Cooper River. "She's a beaut, isn't she?"

At first I thought he was referring to one of the Linen Ladies. Perhaps one of them was his wife—although I hadn't pegged Mrs. Homer Johnson as one of the wrinkled set. Then I saw the eighteenth-century breakfront bookcase, the true object of the bevy's admiration.

"Oh, Homer! It's just gorgeous. Did you get a good deal?"

He nodded, his trademark jowls obscuring his collar with each downward movement. "You bet I did. I spread me a little rumor."

"I beg your pardon?"

Homer's pate turned petunia pink. "I told a couple of the dealers that I thought this breakfront was a fake. This is a Massachusetts piece, you see, and the drawer bottoms are hand-hewn pine. So I told folks that pine wasn't used for drawer bottoms up there— and guess what? They believed me. They're nice folks, most of these dealers, but they're no *Antique Road Show* experts. No sir, not by a long shot. They can't afford to take big risks. All you got to do is plant a little seed of doubt in their brains and they're more than happy to set their sights on something else. Anyway, they all spent their budgets on other lots earlier in the auction, and when this came up—it was the second-to-last piece—they were plumb out of money. We—I mean you, Mrs. Timberlake—picked this baby up for a song."

"Well, I love that tune!" I cried. Then my conscience took over. "Was what you did legal?"

He shrugged and the jowls quivered. "Why not? I wasn't selling anything, just buying. And I was only making an observation that I may—or may not—have believed."

It certainly sounded like something one could get away with. Still, if I ran this scenario by the rector at Mama's church—well, I could imagine what he would say. There is legality, and then there is ethics. The two are not necessarily synonymous.

"Homer, I'd really rather you didn't pull this stunt again."

"Yes, ma'am." His color deepened. "You wouldn't be wanting me to try and take it back, now would you? Because you can't do that with things you buy at an auction—not when they let folks preview the stuff first."

"A card laid is a card played," I cried, eager to sweep the ethics issue under a rug, preferably a nice wool Heriz from Persia. After all, Homer was right. There was nothing to be done about the eighteenth-century breakfront now, except to sell it. I could always donate a portion of the profit to charity.

Hormer's grin exceeded the span of the Silas N. Pearlman Memorial Bridge. "Do I take it then you feel the same way about the Philadelphia highboy I bought last night, and sold not more than five minutes ago?"

"Homer, you didn't!" I am ashamed to say my voice resonated with pride.

I left the shop in Homer's capable, if somewhat stubby hands, and headed straight for the parking garage on King Street where I'd left my car. My real destination was The Market. While it was only three blocks from the garage on King Street to Percival Franklin's stall, they are long blocks, and the day was already hotter than the previous. I reasoned that the parking garage off Concord Street would get me a tad closer, and when both temperature and humidity are in the nineties, a tad becomes significant.

Just walking to the garage made me dew, so like any good Southern belle, the first thing I did when I got in the car was to check the rearview mirror. Sure enough, melting mascara had fused my eyelashes together, and damp hair clung to my face like kelp left behind by low tide. The most dispiriting thing I saw, however, were the trickles of lipstick that had managed to find otherwise invisible lines.

After turning on the AC, I raked my lashes with a miniature mascara comb, brushed my hair back from my face, and using a tissue and a dab of hand lotion, obliterated those nasty lines. Then I smiled at the reflection in the mirror.

"You wouldn't happen to have any perfume in your purse, would you, Mama?"

"Abby! How did you know I was back here?"

"I didn't. Not when I first got in. But when I checked myself out in the mirror—well, you're not invisible just because you want to be, you know."

"But I'm all scrunched down, Abby. I'm practically sitting on the floor."

The truth is, it was only after I smelled Mama's fragrance that I noticed the thatch of gray protruding above the back of my seat. Still, had my petite progenitress not pulled stunts like this before, I might have been truly scared. And just for the record, I *do* lock my car. Mama has her own set of keys.

But if she wanted to dance, Mama needed to pay the piper. "I wouldn't stay on the floor too long," I said, "because the last time I looked there was a huge spider crawling across the floor mat."

Perhaps that was mean of me, but it gave Mama a cardiovascular workout, one that she could use, now that she's retired and considers cookie baking a form of aerobic exercise. Who knows, I may even have prolonged her life a little.

"Abby, you're mean!"

I backed carefully out of my space. Towering SUVs on either side gave the impression that I'd parked in a gully.

"And hiding in someone's car isn't mean?"

"You're not just any someone, Abby. You're my daughter."

"What is it you want, Mama?"

"I thought we'd have ourselves a nice mother-daughter day," Mama said without missing a beat. "We could hit both the Citadel and Northwoods malls this morning, go to the Mustard Seed in Mount Pleasant for lunch, and then finish up our shopping at the Towne Center."

"What? And skip all the wonderful shops down-town?"

"Or we could do that instead. There's a sale on at Talbots'—"

"Mama, what is your *real* agenda?"

"Whatever do you mean?"

I stomped on the brakes and put my car into park. We were still in the garage and there was no one behind us, so it's not like I endangered our lives. True, Mama was not belted in—she refuses to wear one in the backseat—but all those layers of crinolines make an effective airbag.

"Get out now, Mama."

"Abby, I can't believe you're speaking to me this way, and after everything I've done for you. It's not every mother who would go through thirty-four hours of excruciating labor to bring an ungrateful child into this world."

"Mama, I keep telling you, it was thirty-*six* hours."

"Are you sure?"

"Yes, Mama, I was there, remember? Besides, you could have chosen the epidural. So either you tell me what you're really doing in my car, or you get to hoof it back to the house, or wherever it is you want to go."

"Abby, I'm scared."

"I beg your pardon?"

"I smell trouble." She meant that literally.

"Mama, I'm just trying to clear my name. And I'm not doing anything, except for gathering information. As soon as I have any concrete evidence as to who killed Amelia Shadbark—and maybe Evangeline La-Pointe—I'll go straight to the police. I promise."

A car with Ohio plates pulled up behind me, and rather than give its occupants a bad impression of Charlestonians (*they* didn't know I was from off) I put the car into gear and made a dignified exit from the garage. Mama must have smelled that there was a tourist vehicle behind us, because she turned and gave them an Elizabeth II wave. I'm sure it was her intention to pass me off as the chauffeur.

"Abby," she said when we were on the street, "if *I*

promise to keep my mouth shut—just be your silent shadow, so to speak—can't I tag along?"

"But Mama, it could be dangerous—"

"Aha! So you admit it then, you're digging up stuff that could get you in big trouble—the trouble I've been smelling."

"I admit no such thing, Mama. Besides, let's say that were the case, how could you tagging along do me a lick of good? Then I'd have to worry about your safety, which would only serve to distract me. The answer therefore is no. You cannot be my shadow."

"Try and stop me, missy," Mama hissed.

I knew mine was a lost cause. Like the War Between the States, it was over. I could accept defeat gracefully, and get on with the task at hand, or I could continue to fight a losing battle. Sometimes I think Mozella Wiggins is the female reincarnation of General Sherman.

"Okay, Mama, but I'm warning you—"

"Drive," Mama ordered. "Let's get on with the show."

I led Mama through The Market—rather, I dragged Mama through the place. She wanted to stop at every stall and examine the merchandise. Christmas was only five months away, she whined. Wouldn't it make sense to get a little shopping in ahead of the crowds?

"But I don't want an I Love Charleston T-shirt," I moaned. "Greg doesn't want one either, and neither do the children."

"Then how about a nice painting of Elvis and Jesus on a horse?"

I stared at the monstrosity. Jesus Christ and Elvis Presley were seated together on a golden palomino, riding off into a desert sunset. Elvis, who was in his pre-corpulence stage, rode in front, and Jesus, who had his arms around Elvis, rode in back. It was, of course, Jesus who held the reins. I suppose I could have seen the symbolism in that arrangement, had it not been for small figures of all Three Stooges and Marilyn Monroe in the background. They appeared to be chasing the horse; the Stooges with palm fronds in their hands, Marilyn waving a Confederate battle flag.

Connie Beth, the vendor, caught us staring. "That's brand new. My Elmer painted that last night."

"Your Elmer has quite an imagination," I said kindly. It was no worse a lie than saying to the parents of an ugly baby, "Oh my, what a baby!"

"Abby, I'm going to buy it," Mama cried. She seemed practically transfixed.

"Not for me, you're not. Or for Greg."

"Then I'll buy it for myself."

"If you do," I whispered, "you have to hang it in your room, and never leave the door open as long as it's there."

Connie Beth's ears were no larger than lima beans, but her hearing was apparently quite sharp. "Hey, what's that supposed to mean?"

"Nothing," I said. "Come on, Mama. A shadow has to keep up."

Mama spread her legs slightly, trying to dig her white pumps into the concrete floor. "Abby, I'm buying this lovely painting, and that's that."

"Suit yourself, Mama," I said, and started to walk away.

"Hey," Connie Beth barked, "is that any way to treat your mama?"

I turned. "Ex*cuse* me?"

"You heard me. My mama ain't alive anymore, and let me tell you this, lady. I'd give anything just to see her one more time. I sure as shooting wouldn't mouth off to her."

Mama smiled and patted her pearls. "I bet you and your mother were very close."

Connie Beth scowled. "I hated the woman—only that was then, and this is now. Believe me, if I could do it over again, I would. I'd be the best daughter I knew how."

"You hear that, Abby? This nice woman would treat her mama right, if she had a second chance."

"Oh brother," I groaned. I did my level best, I really did, not to roll my eyes.

Connie Beth's vision was as acute as her hearing. "I saw that look you gave me," she growled. "You think that painting ain't fancy enough for you, don't you? You want to waltz on down to the next building and buy one of them ugly statues from that young black man, don't you?"

"Well—"

"Then you ain't heard the news," she said triumphantly.

"News?"

Connie Beth's handful of teeth punctuated her grin. "That young man ain't there today. He was hit by a car."

25

I felt as if the concrete slab floor of The Market was going to well up and smack me in the face. I staggered back against Mama and leaned on her for support.

"Percival Franklin is dead!" I cried. "And it's probably all my fault."

Connie Beth glowered at me. "I didn't say he was dead. I said he was hit by a car. Happened right out there"—she pointed to the side of the shed—"last night, after closing time."

"But I don't understand. Surely we would have heard that on the news."

"Abby," Mama said gently, "we didn't watch the news last night, remember? You went to bed in a snit, so Greg, C.J., and I sat around and played dominoes until—"

"Did the police arrest the driver?"

Now that she'd made her point, Connie Beth was no longer smiling. "No, ma'am, it was a hit-and-run—driver got clean away—but Lord, it was the awfulest thing I've ever seen."

"You saw it happen?"

"I said it happened right out there, didn't I?"

"Yes, ma'am. Would you mind describing it to me?"

"Well—are y'all gonna buy something from me or not? 'Cause I got me a business to run, you know." Just for the record, although throngs of people were pushing past us all the time, not one person had stopped to give Elmer's original artwork a second glance.

"Yes," Mama said emphatically, "I want to buy this painting of Elvis and Jesus on the horse. The one titled *Two Kings*."

I looked closer at the bottom edge of the velvet monstrosity. Sure enough, that's what it was called.

"Why, that's just plain sacrilegious," I said. "Come on, Mama, we'll go ask someone else about the accident."

Connie Beth shrugged. "Suit yourselves, but there were only a couple of us still around then. I stayed late because business was so good, and Dharma—she's the one three stalls down who sells the alligator poop jewelry—she saw it, but she's off today. Dingo saw it—well, he heard it. Dingo's only got one eye; the other one's glass. Sometimes I think both of Dingo's eyes are glass. You should see some of the junk he sells."

"Like what?" Mama asked. "He's not the one who sells those cute little wallaby backpacks, is he? And the aprons with the kangaroo pouches for pockets?"

"They're made in China," Connie Beth said through gritted, albeit sparse, teeth. "My Elmer's paintings are one hundred percent American."

"Indeed they are," I said. Although I still had no intention of buying one of the hideous paintings, or even letting Mama buy one, I needed Connie Beth's cooperation. I smiled pleasantly. "I can see that your husband has quite an eye for detail. I assume that you do as well."

"Yes, ma'am. It was me them folks on the news interviewed. Did you know they don't pay you nothing for being on TV?"

Mama fingered her pearls. "Are you sure? I read someplace that Barbara Walters makes millions of dollars, and those young people on *Friends*—"

I poked Mama's cinched waist. "She means for being on the news," I hissed. I turned back to Connie Beth. "That's a real shame. I bet you were able to supply those news folks—and the police—with all kinds of information."

"Yes, ma'am."

I cut to the chase. "What did you say?"

Connie Beth took an angry step back. "Ma'am, I ain't telling you nothing unless you buy one of my paintings."

I looked around in desperation. "Don't you have anything smaller?"

She gave me the evil eye, but looked around as well. Finally she pulled a small painting, sporting a crude bamboo frame, out from behind a stack of velvet Elvises.

"Just got me this one. It's on sale for two hundred dollars."

I squinted at the thing, trying to keep an open mind. If she took down her poster of Gary Cooper, Mama might be able to hang this smaller painting on the back of her door. The subject matter wasn't too bad, either. There was no Jesus in this one, or Elvis either. Just the Stooges and Marilyn, *in a hot tub*. Curly had a beatific look on his face, as did Miss Monroe. The piece was inexplicably titled *An Ace Up Her Sleeve*.

"Okay." I fished out my debit card and handed it to Connie Beth. "Mama, I hope you like this one, because it's your early Christmas present."

Mama's eyes were glistening with tears of joy. "Oh, Abby, it's even prettier than the other one. I'll treasure it always."

I patted her arm affectionately and turned back to Connie Beth. "Now then, tell me about the accident."

"Whatcha want to know?"

"Everything. What color the car was, which direction it came from, where exactly Mr. Franklin was standing when it hit him. I want all the details."

Connie swiped my card through the machine and handed it back. "Well now, I didn't exactly see the car that hit the young man."

"But you said it was, and I quote, 'the awfulest thing I've ever seen.'"

Connie cranked up the evil eye a notch or two. "I didn't mean that liberally. I heard the accident. That's the same thing, ain't it? Anyway, I was the first one out there, and I called 911. That should count for something, shouldn't it?"

"Absolutely," Mama said. Even though it was my money being spent, she was vying for a discount. No doubt she hoped I'd buy her two of Elmer's masterpieces.

I took out my debit card again and fingered it seductively. "How bad were Mr. Franklin's injuries?" I asked. "Was he conscious?"

The evil eye was now all business. "Nope, he wasn't

conscious. And his leg was all twisted—kind of like a pretzel. You know, like them big ones you buy at the mall? I said to myself, you really are one lucky woman, Connie Beth, because just a few minutes later and that coulda been you."

"I'm so thankful it wasn't," Mama said. She graced Connie Beth with her best greeting company smile. "You sure you can't come down on the price of *Two Kings*? There's a spot in our living room—just above the fireplace—that needs a really good painting." She lowered her voice conspiratorially. "To replace that piece of horrible modern art my daughter has hanging there now."

"Mama, that so-called modern art is an original Cezanne! It was painted in 1894."

Sometimes Mama forgets that it is I who puts the bread and butter on her—make that *my*—William and Mary table. "Well," she said, "he could have at least stayed between the lines. Your brother Toy painted much better than that when he was in second grade. I still have one of your brother's paintings, if you want to put it up instead of that inspirational one." She pointed to the *Two Kings*.

I wouldn't say that Toy and I fight like cats and dogs, but there is definitely some rivalry going on between the two of us. For years I was happily married (at least I thought I was), busy raising two children, and involved in community affairs. Toy, who couldn't compete with that scenario, spent his days out in Hollywood, California, parking cars at celebrity-frequented restaurants. Then, when Buford dumped me and my world fell apart, Toy saw his chance to zoom ahead. He got accepted into an Episcopal seminary to study for the priesthood. You try competing with a brother called "Father."

As you may have guessed, I wasn't about to replace a Cezanne with something Toy painted. I'd sooner have the *Two Kings* hanging on my wall. On the other hand, I'd rather have an appendectomy—without the benefit of an anesthesia—than purchase another of Elmer's hideous creations. I certainly wouldn't, even on pain of death, hang it on my living room wall.

"Which hospital did they take Mr. Franklin to?" I asked, as I reached for the wrapped painting of Marilyn and the Stooges cavorting in the tub.

"MUSC, I think," Connie Beth grunted.

I grabbed the painting and Mama's hand simultaneously. Although she did her darnedest to resist me, by trying to dig the heels of her pumps into the concrete floor, Mama is no match for my strength. Not when I'm properly motivated.

Mama was still complaining when we found the surgical waiting room at the Medical University of South Carolina. The grandmotherly woman in admissions had informed us that Percival Franklin was undergoing his second round of surgery, this time to staunch internal bleeding.

"His sister's waiting up there," she'd said, "and I think she's alone. Maybe you could get her some coffee. And a Danish."

Well, I'd brought the coffee and two Danish pastries, but Mama brought her attitude. "Abby, we won't know what to say. We'll be intruding."

"Then we'll just sit quietly."

"But you don't know if she likes black coffee, or cream and sugar."

"That's why I brought the works."

"But Abby," Mama whined, "I read somewhere that hospitals are the number one source of infection. Your odds of getting sick shoot up the moment you walk in."

"Then don't touch anything."

We turned the corner. There were about a dozen people in the waiting room. Several of them were African American, but I had no trouble picking out Percival Franklin's sister; she looked exactly like him—well, a female version, of course. Same high cheekbones, same fine-textured skin. She could be a model if she wanted. Perhaps she was.

I approached the young woman. Her eyes were closed and her bowed head was resting on balled fists.

"Miss Franklin?" I asked.

"Shhh," Mama whispered loud enough to wake the dead downstairs in the morgue, "I think she's praying."

I touched Percival's sister lightly on the shoulder. "Miss Franklin, I brought you some coffee."

"And two kinds of Danish," Mama said. Her glance flitted around the room. I could tell she was afraid that at any second germs would leap at her from the chairs and magazine tables.

The girl looked up. "Sorry. Did you say something?"

"I brought you some coffee, dear," I said.

She looked confused. "I don't think I ordered any—never mind, how much do I owe you?"

"Not a thing. I'm a friend of your brother."

The large dark eyes focused on me for the first time. "Percy's? You're a friend of Percy's?"

Lying is, of course, wrong, but it's especially bad to lie in a surgical waiting room. Think of the karma. Next time that could be me—or Mama—behind those swinging doors.

"Well, he wasn't so much a friend as a business associate."

She took the coffee, black, but passed on the Danish. "The Market?"

Even fudging is pushing fate in a hospital. "Actually, I met him investigating the death of Mrs. Amelia Shadbark. Apparently he was her part-time gardener."

She tried to hand the coffee back, but I refused to take it. "You a cop?"

"No, ma'am."

"Then who the hell are you?"

"She's a busybody, that's who she is." Mama fluffed out her crinolines and patted her pearls. "I'm afraid my daughter just doesn't know when to mind her own business. Why, once—"

It undoubtedly generates bad karma to step on your mother's toes, but that's precisely what I did. It was the only way I could think of to shut her up.

"Why, Abby, I declare!"

"Sorry, Mama." I turned my attention back to the young lady. "I was one of the last people to see Mrs. Shadbark alive. I have a special interest in finding her killer in order to—well, prove that I had nothing to do with it."

"And you think Percy did?" Despite her hostile tone, she took a sip of the coffee I'd brought.

"No, ma'am. I got to know your brother a little bit— he gave me a beautiful carved camellia. He's extremely talented."

"You bet he is." Her eyes narrowed. "Now I know who you are. You're that lady who owns the antique business. The one who accused him of being a thief."

"I did no such thing! I was merely puzzled by seeing his name engraved on the back of a piece of Lalique. But then, as a friend pointed out to me, his name wasn't engraved after all, but part of the piece. I have to confess, that still throws me."

Her expression reminded me of the stray cat that showed up in my backyard one evening. It was obvious that the undernourished animal was nursing and had kittens stashed somewhere. I put out a bowl of Dmitri's food, and some water, but the poor thing—which bolted every time I opened the door—was too terrified to eat, even after I moved the food to the security of some bushes. You could see the cat's internal battle reflected in her eyes. Eventually hunger won out, and the stray cat ate from the bowl, but she had been right not to trust me. For her own good, and that of her kittens, I had to call animal control. Fortunately, they were able to track her to the crawlspace of an empty building two blocks away.

Percival Franklin's sister didn't have offspring stashed under a vacant house, but she did have a brother under the knife. I could feel her eyes appraise me.

"What is it you really want, Miss—"

"Mrs. Washburn," I said decisively. It was time for me to drop Timberlake and take up my new married name. Either that or revert back to Wiggins, my maiden name. Juggling two last names was getting confusing, even for me.

She set the coffee cup on a year-old copy of *Sports*

Illustrated. "Mrs. Washburn, then. So, what is it you want?"

"To tell you the truth, I don't know exactly. I just have this gut feeling that—"

"I smell trouble," Mama said.

I dismissed her with a wave of my hand. "My gut feeling is that what happened to your brother—the hit-and-run—was no accident."

The girl's eyes widened, but she didn't seem shocked by my statement. "What makes you say that?"

"Like I said, it's just a feeling. I feel that what happened to him was somehow connected with what happened to Mrs. Shadbark, and her neighbor, Miss LaPointe."

"What happened to her—this Miss LaPointe?"

Her reaction was encouraging. Evangeline La-Pointe's death had not been listed in the paper.

"She was murdered as well," I said.

She retrieved the coffee and sipped in silence for several minutes. When she spoke again, she looked at the cup, not at me.

"Just so you know, Mrs. Washburn, my brother was not into drugs. But ever—"

"I never said he was."

"Yeah, well, that's the conclusion some folks would jump to just because of the color of his skin. Anyway, what I was about to say is that ever since my brother quit his job at the glassworks, he's been looking over his shoulder."

The hair on the nape of my neck stood straight up. From the back I must have looked like a porcupine.

"Glassworks? Which glassworks is that?"

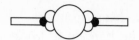

26

"Arcadian Designs," she said. "It's located on Savannah Highway down near Ravenel. Just across the road from Caw Caw County Park."

"Your brother made glass there?"

"He made lots of stuff there, but glass too. From what I understand, the company makes art reproductions. Percy didn't like to talk about his job there."

Now we were finally cooking with gas. "Do you know if that's where he made that fake Lalique?"

She frowned. "I don't know anything about Lalique, Mrs. Washburn. I don't know if the ones my brother made were fake or not. He made a lot of different glass pieces. He liked to show me his latest designs."

"René Lalique is a designer who's been dead a long time," I explained, trying not to sound superior. I mean, just because I was gaga over the man's creations, didn't mean the rest of the world necessarily knew about him. Lord knows, I know zilch about NASCAR racing.

Percy's sister was far more loyal than Toy would have been. Her eyes flashed with indignation.

"My brother had nothing to do with that woman's death, either!"

"I believe you. Miss Franklin," I said, guessing at her name. "Do you happen to know how many artists Arcadian Designs employs?"

"Ha! None now, that I know of. It was just Percy and the owner. Percy did all the creative work; the owner made all the money. That's why Percy quit."

"And when was that exactly."

"Last week."

"Who is the owner? Do you know his name?"

"Jackson, that's his last name. I don't remember his first. I only met him once. He came by my brother's apartment once when I was over there for dinner. I don't like to make snap judgments, Mrs. Washburn, but I didn't like this guy from the second I laid eyes on him."

"Would you describe him please."

"He was white." She blinked and looked away. "Bald and kind of heavy. And he had square glasses."

"That sounds like Homer Johnson!" Mama cried.

"Don't be silly, Mama. Homer is a retiree from Tennessee."

The young woman, whose name I still did not know, glanced at Mama. "I think this guy's name is Hubert, not Homer. Anyway, he came across to me as a con artist. Percy said ladies found him real attractive, but I didn't see it. He was always bragging to my brother about all the women he'd slept with, particularly coeds from the College of Charleston."

"Then it's definitely not Homer," I harrumphed. "They are not the same person. Homer Johnson is a happily married man. In fact, he has a daughter who's a professor at the C of C!"

Mama patted her pearls. "No, he doesn't."

"Yes, he does, Mama. He told me himself. Her name is Winter."

The pearls began a slow rotation. "There isn't anybody by that name on staff at the college."

"Mama, how on earth would you know that?"

The pearls picked up speed, but Mama's lips were as tightly sealed as an oyster at low tide.

"Mama, you didn't!"

The pearls became a blur.

"Mama, you checked on him, didn't you? You had the hots for a married man, so you checked him out!"

The pearls fell into resting mode with a faint clink. "He isn't married either. If he is—well, he wasn't married in Knoxville, Tennessee."

I staggered to a seat next to Percival Franklin's sister. I had yet to sort out the implications of this information deluge. But at best it meant I had hired a con man and a sleazebag to run my shop. At worst it meant—

"Oh my God," I moaned.

"Abby!" Mama cried, her voice shrill with alarm. "What happened? Did you just get sick? I knew it! I told you hospitals were unsafe, didn't I?"

"I'm fine," I wailed. "I can't believe I hired a murderer, that's all."

The Franklin girl rested a hand lightly on my shoulder. "You think this guy that my brother Percy worked for—making the glass and such—is the one who killed that rich old lady south of Broad?"

I nodded miserably. "Mrs. Shadbark."

"Why would he do that?"

"Because his scam was about to be exposed. Mrs. Shadbark had decided to sell her estate and move into the Bishop Gadsden Episcopal Retirement Community. She'd asked me to appraise her glass collection."

Mama has to find a "but" in everything. "But Abby," she said, "that doesn't make a lick of sense. Mrs. Shadbark was poisoned. How could Homer—or whatever his name is—find a way to do that?"

"Where there's a will, there's a way. Maybe he bribed Ingebord, the housekeeper."

"Well, whatever happened, I'm coming with you."

"With me where?"

Mama addressed her answer to the young woman seated next to me. "My daughter thinks she's some kind of James Bond. You wouldn't believe the tight spots she's gotten herself into. If she were a cat, she'd have used up all her lives by now. Well, this time she's not going to get in trouble all by herself. I'll be right there with her—wherever she goes."

Percival Franklin's sister smiled for the first time. "You remind me of my own mother, ma'am. She was real feisty, just like you."

Mama beamed. "You hear that, Abby?"

I hauled myself to my feet. "I'm not going to be getting into any trouble, Mama. I'm just going for a little ride."

Mama grabbed my right hand. "Like I said, dear, I'm coming with you."

I didn't have enough evidence to take to the police. It was that simple. But if I could find Arcadian Designs and take a picture of some counterfeit Lalique, well, that should give the Charleston police something to go on. Of course they'd have to involve the sheriff, since the area around Caw Caw was outside city limits, but

at least there would be proof that my so-called meddling had actually done some good.

Rather than waste precious time by returning to the
house for a camera, not to mention the time wasted
should we run into C.J., we swung up to the Citadel
Mall. There I bought one of those cheap, disposable
cameras, one with a flash, and Mama bought herself a
pretzel. Perhaps she did it out of sympathy for Percival
Franklin. I didn't bother to ask.

While Mama used the ladies' room, I called my shop
on a pay phone.

"Den of Antiquity," Homer said with his usual good
cheer.

"This is Abby. How are things going?"

"Fine as frog's hair, Mrs. Timberlake. I sold that
chest of drawers you have in the back room. You know,
the one with the veneer starting to peel off the front."

"Get out of town! To whom?"

"Aw, some woman wandered in who was just looking for a place to store her husbands' socks and under-
wear. She was right happy to take it off our hands."

"You go, boy! That piece of junk came with an estate. I was fixing to put it out on the street next garbage
day."

I know, it was a lame conversation, but all I really
needed to know was whether he was at work. It would
be foolish for Mama and me to attempt our reconnaissance mission with our prime suspect tailing us. I was
beginning to feel foolish anyway. Homer Johnson did
not sound like a maniacal killer to me, an overachiever
was more like it.

"Mrs. Timberlake?"

"Yes, Homer?"

"That friend of yours was just in here, wanting to know where you were."

"Which friend?"

"Big sort of gawky girl—a bit on the strange side."

Now that was rude! True, but rude. Homer had no business talking about my friends that way.

"Her name is Miss Cox. If she comes in again, or calls, tell her I took my mother shopping at the mall."

"Which mall would that be?" He was clever enough to make it sound like an innocent question. I wouldn't be surprised to learn he had experience acting in community theater.

"We're at the Northwoods Mall," I said, to throw him off track, just in case he heard mall sounds in the background. If we can't find what we want here, then we'll probably head over to the Towne Center in Mount Pleasant." This was, for your information, the opposite trajectory of our true destination. "If Miss Cox comes in again, Homer, you tell her we'll be home in plenty of time for supper."

"Will do. You have yourself a good day now, Mrs. Timberlake." Then he hung up. *He* hung up on *me*!

"Why, I never in all my born days!"

"Never what, dear?" Mama was back from the restroom, although she was still plumping up her crinolines.

"Seen a man as arrogant as Homer Johnson."

Mama sighed. "Or as cute. Too bad he's not who he said he was."

"He said he was married, for crying out loud."

"Married men can get divorced, dear."

I dragged Mama out of the mall. It behooved us to

shake a leg while Homer was still in the shop. There would be plenty of time on the way to Arcadian Designs to chide Mama for her wanton ways.

Willis Carrier, a Yankee, occupies the pinnacle of my personal pantheon of saints. Thanks to this native of Buffalo, New York, Mama and I were able to drive out toward Ravenel in search of Arcadian Designs in air-conditioned comfort. But just as Mama and I were crossing Tea Farm Creek Bridge, a car came barreling around us so fast that, at first, we didn't even know it was a vehicle. Mama, who claims to have met Judy Garland when they were both girls, was convinced we'd been passed by a tornado.

When I finally figured out what had happened, I shook so hard I was afraid my eyeballs would come loose, an event that might make further driving difficult. Fortunately, Greg and I had been out to Caw Caw County Park several times to hike, and that stretch of the road was familiar.

More folks should visit Caw Caw. The park is composed of what was once a rice and tea plantation, and is a walker's dream. The trails meander through woods and along the tops of old dikes that contained the rice fields. It's a great place to view migratory waterfowl, and from March through October alligators are visible and abundant.

The rice fields are set back from the highway, and the land along the highway is heavily wooded. I was vaguely aware that there were several small businesses tucked willy-nilly among the trees, but I had never paid close attention to them. Still, finding Arcadian Designs was surprisingly easy, thanks to Miss Franklin's excellent directions. It was located directly across from the park entrance.

Gaining access to the property was another matter. The whole shebang was surrounded by an eight-foot wire mesh fence, with a triple strand of barbed wire on top. It looked more like Stalag 13 than a glass factory.

We tramped along the perimeter in waist-high grass (knee-high to most other folks) looking for a breach in the fence. If anyone spotted us and challenged our right to be there, Mama would do the talking. She'd already concocted a story about a broken engagement and a ring tossed, foolishly, in the heat of the moment, into the tule weeds. We couldn't be stealthy about what we were doing, because we had to stamp our feet to scare away snakes and the odd rogue alligator.

Perhaps we should have split up—tramping in opposite directions—because it wasn't until we'd gotten three quarters of the way around that we found a spot where a fox, or some other animal, had dug a hole under the fence. We had nothing with which to dig to improve upon the hole, except for small pine branches, which are extremely soft. After the third branch broke in my hands, I sacrificed one of my sandals to use as a scoop. In no time at all, I'd managed to wiggle through the expanded hole.

Mama, however, got stuck. She was able to back out all right, but every time she tried going forward, she couldn't get her hips through the hole. True, her hips are slightly wider than mine, but the real problem was her voluminous underpinnings.

"Abby, I'll never make it through. Just go on without me."

"Nonsense, Mama. Lose the crinolines."

"I can't, Abby."

"Why not?"

"It wouldn't be decent. I always wear my slips."

"You don't wear them to bed."

"But this is different, Abby. We're out in public. What if we get caught?"

"Mama, we're on a reconnaissance mission, not a fashion show." There was no point to hurting her feelings by clueing her in to the fact that full circle skirts and crinolines went out of style in the sixties.

"But Abby, what if the wire rips my dress?"

"That wouldn't be the end of the world, Mama—not as long as you didn't get hurt. It's not like you're naked under there."

"But Abby," Mama wailed, "I'm afraid I am!"

"What?"

"I was in a hurry this morning, dear. I had to catch up with you after you sneaked out. I'm afraid I forgot to put on my unmentionables. You see, I only wear panties when I wear a nightgown, but last night was pajama night and—"

"TMI!"

"You, too, dear?"

"No! That stands for 'too much information.'" I took a couple of prolonged, calming breaths. "Okay, Mama, scoot on back—*carefully*—and fluff your slips up. I'll meet you back at the car in ten minutes. Fifteen, tops. And why the hell didn't you buy a pair at the mall?"

"Because I didn't think of it, that's why."

Perhaps because she had no knickers to knot, Mama was less obdurate than usual. She backed out carefully, and the last I saw her she was stomping down the tule weeds, warning the snakes to get out of her path.

Meanwhile I sprinted across the gravel, in one clean sandal and one that felt as if I'd used it to dig my way down to China. Halfway across the parking lot the strap broke and I literally ran out of my shoe. Since there was nothing to be done about the failed footwear, I kept on chugging until I reached the building.

Arcadian Designs consisted of a Quonset hut the size of an airplane hangar and a pair of smokestacks. The front door was padlocked, so I ignored that. But there was a small window on the side, about five yards down and about two and a half feet off the ground, that looked promising. It was the only window I could see.

Upon reaching it, however, I discovered that it was not a window after all, merely a small opening over which something, perhaps an air-conditioner, had once been fastened. A person of standard size could not have fit through a space that small. Mama, with or without her crinolines, wouldn't have made it. Even for me it was an extremely tight squeeze, and my bosoms may never be quite as full again, but I managed to wiggle through. Heck, I was so determined to get inside, I probably could have crawled through a dryer vent.

So determined was I, in fact, that I didn't notice how dark the interior was until I'd crawled inside. That's when I cursed myself for not thinking to bring a flashlight with me from the glove box of my car. I cursed again when I stepped on a piece of broken glass. What an idiot I was. An Abby with just half a brain would have bought hiking boots at mall. Mankind, beginning with the Egyptians, has been making glass for twenty-five hundred years. You can bet it's been breaking that long.

"Damn it!" I cried.

"You got that right," a voice behind me said.

27

Shards in one's sole are not nearly as distressing as a gun barrel pressed up against one's back. I took an involuntary step forward, thereby accumulating more glass splinters.

"Freeze, Mrs. Timberlake. You take another step and I swear I'll blow your frigging head off. Pardon my French."

"Why, Homer Johnson—if indeed that is your name. Fancy meeting you here."

The barrel, which was hard, but at the same time deliciously cool, pushed against my upper spine. "I'm going to be putting something over your head now, so that you can't see. You can resist if you want, but I advise against it. Unless, of course, you want to end up as a paraplegic."

"I won't move," I promised. "Will I at least be able to breathe?"

"Yeah, I don't see why not."

Homer slipped the "something" over my head. It was a paper bag! The same kind of bag your groceries get packed in. My indignation fought fear for dominance.

"What did you do? Pick this up at Food Lion?"

I felt the pressure of the barrel lift from my back, and a moment later lights came on in the room. Finally Homer answered me.

"I always keep a few bags in the trunk of my car. Never know when you're going to need them—like now." He chuckled. "In high school we used to joke about the ugly girls. Said we'd have to put paper bags over their heads in order to date them. That wouldn't have been the case with you, Mrs. Timberlake. You're one fine-looking woman, if you don't mind me saying so."

"Then maybe it's you who should be wearing the bag," I said. "Because frankly, Homer, you're not all that much to look at."

"And you're cheeky, too. I like that in a woman. Too bad we didn't meet under different circumstances. I wouldn't have minded dating you."

"It wouldn't have made a difference, Homer. I don't date palmetto bugs." I was referring to a species of giant cockroach that scuttle about the Lowcountry at night. Some of those critters are big enough to saddle and ride—at least for me.

Homer didn't have the decency to be offended. "Yeah, maybe we wouldn't have worked out as a couple, on account of you ain't smart enough for me."

"*Excuse* me?"

"Well, you crawled right into my trap didn't you? That hole under the fence—I dug it. And the hole in the wall, well, that ain't nothing but a bellow's vent. I took the grating off last night, kinda figuring you'd do something like this sooner or later. Figured if I made it too easy—like left the gates open—you'd see it as a trap. Hell, Mrs. Timberlake—pardon my French again—but you don't let a guy get a whole lot of sleep."

"No sleep for the wicked." Alack, the paper bag muted the peevish tone in my voice.

"And then there was the late-night visit I had to pay Mrs. Shadbark's neighbor. I swear, that woman has telescopes for eyes, and a mouth bigger than the Grand Canyon. Every time I sold the old lady a piece of my genuine faux Lalique, I knew she was watching. No telling what she would have said to the cops—or to you. Anyway, I really had to fight to keep awake the next day."

"I saw you yawning!"

"Mrs. Timberlake, I don't think you realize just how much trouble you've caused me. In order to beat you here, I had to drive so fast, I nearly drove off the road. Then, so you wouldn't suspect anything, I had to park across at the park, and run over here. Barely made it in time."

"So that was you driving a million miles an hour! How the hell did you know where I was going any-way?"

"Caller ID," he said with his smarmy chuckle. "It's a wonderful invention, ain't it? As soon as that phone rang I knew you *weren't* at Northwoods Mall. You were at the Citadel Mall, were headed west, over the Ashley. That could mean only one thing—you'd finally learned about this place. What happened, Percy regain consciousness?"

"His sister told me." Having said too much, I foolishly attempted to clamp a hand over my mouth, but hit paper bag instead.

The gun clicked ominously nearby. "Keep those

damn hands of yours by your sides—pardon my French."

"It wasn't French," I snapped. "And it's a stupid expression dating back over hundreds of years of Anglo-French animosity and has absolutely nothing to do with us Americans. Do you know that the French have a similar saying about the English?"

"Am I supposed to be impressed, Mrs. Timberlake? Like I said, you ain't all that smart. Otherwise you wouldn't be standing here in my glass factory with a paper bag over your head."

"You're right," I said calmly, "I'm not very smart, or I would have been able to figure out by now how you managed to poison Mrs. Shadbark."

"That was nothing, Mrs. Timberlake. Thanks to you, it was a piece of cake."

"Thanks to *me*?"

"Mrs. Shadbark called me to see if I could recommend someone to appraise her Lalique collection—the one I'd been helping her collect over the years. You know, Mrs. Timberlake, there wouldn't have been a problem if my apprentice, young Percy, hadn't gotten all vain about his work and signed a few pieces. Since you're not long for this world I don't mind telling you, I had me a nice little racket going. I've been supplying *genuine* antique Lalique to seven states."

"Bully for you, but what does that have to do with me?"

"Well, since there was no stopping her from selling off the collection, so she could go to that goddamn nursing home—pardon my French—"

"It's not French!"

"Yeah, well, anyway, I figured since you were new

to the Charleston antique community, and from the Upstate, you wouldn't know squat. I figured you'd buy them all up yourself, maybe get your Upstate butt in a peck of trouble. Anyway, so then when Mrs. Shadbark calls and tells me she's having you over to tea, I send her a cake." He laughed heartily. "A cake, get it? Killing her was a piece of cake."

"I still don't get it. Was the poison in the cake?"

"Arsenic. I have plenty of that on hand. You see, I use arsenic trioxide to make my glass. This time I used it to make icing."

"*You* baked the cake?"

He grinned. "I'm a man of many talents."

I shook my head and the paper bag rustled. "The police should have caught that. I'm surprised they didn't grill Brunhilde—I mean Ingebord—about the food."

He chuckled. "Shouldn't surprise you none. They ain't perfect, you know. Besides, I often baked cakes for the old lady. I'm sure that big foreign bitch didn't think a thing about it."

"Anyway, you could have killed me! And my friend, C.J.!"

"Not unless your taste buds were as deteriorated as Mrs. Shadbark's. And frankly, Mrs. Timberlake, I wouldn't have given a damn—pardon—oh, what the hell. Didn't either of you eat enough to get a stomachache, am I right?"

I seethed at having been deceived. To be honest, I was more angry at myself for having been such a sucker than at the murdering con man. I always thought I was a pretty good judge of character—Buford Timberlake aside.

"Don't think you're going to get away with this. My

husband hired a bodyguard. He could be here any minute."

"Yeah, right. If I know you, Mrs. Timberlake, you caught the guy following you and fired him on the spot. Either that or you've been dodging him like a cat between raindrops."

"How did you know? Have you been following me, too?"

He had a truncated laugh; just two snorts really. "Mrs. Timberlake, you give me too much credit. You've plumb worn me out the last couple of days. Hell—pardon my French—one time I had to be two places at once. Getting that flower back that Percival gave you, that wasn't easy, you know? I swear that boy wanted to be caught. Then, what with having to go to that auction at night, and that unpleasant business with Mrs. LaPointe, I never had a moment's peace. I think it's high time we both got a chance to rest, don't you?"

I'd heard someplace that the best way to keep an assailant from killing you is to engage him in a conversation, the more personal the better. If he thinks of you as a human being, rather than a target, he's less likely to do you bodily harm.

"I'm all for a nice nap—in my own bed," I said in my best conversational tone. "Although it would have to be a short nap. Twenty minutes at most. Anything longer and I'm liable to wake up crabby. How about you?"

"Long naps don't bother me, ma'am. But it wasn't a nap I had in mind for you. I was thinking more along the lines of eternal rest."

That didn't sound so good. Just the thought of it made me cranky. I grabbed at straws.

"Maybe we could discuss this over drinks. My treat, of course."

"I don't drink, ma'am. It's against my religion. No, what I had in mind was to feed you to them gators over there across the way."

"But I'm barely a mouthful! And I'm not nearly as tasty as I look."

"Yeah, there is always the chance the gators will only eat part of you, and the cops will find the rest. That's why I thought me up another idea. You want to hear it?"

"I'm all ears. And please, start at the very beginning."

"Like I keep telling you, Mrs. Timberlake, you ain't that smart. Stalling is not going to save your—well, you know."

"You mean my ass, pardon my English?"

"Yeah. But now this second idea I had, this will actually give you a chance at immorality."

"I think immorality is your bailiwick."

"Huh? I meant immortality. You see, Mrs. Timberlake, I plan to coat you in glass and turn you into one fine statue."

"You're joking!"

He didn't respond.

"*Aren't* you?"

"No, ma'am. I got me this client down in Miami. Rich woman—husband's in real estate. I've been selling her Lalique, Tiffany—you name it—for years. Of course it ain't the genuine thing, but she don't know that. Anyway, she got her a brand-new house now, with one of them great big entrance halls that's crying for a statue. She was thinking of marble, but I convinced her that everyone has marble statutes. But a life-size glass one—now, how often do you see that?"

I certainly never had. "I'm sure they're a dime a dozen if you know where to look."

He snorted once. "I know better than that, Mrs. Timberlake. Now where was I? Yeah, about this client of mine. She still wants something marble for the entrance, so I suggested putting you—only she don't know it will be you in there—on a marble pedestal." He snorted again. "You ever been put on a pedestal before?"

"My husband does it all the time."

"And she wants you—I mean the statue—to be blue to match her color scheme. No problem, I told her. Enough copper oxide, and I can get a bright peacock blue. And of course I'll have to go for frosted, to hide all the tape."

"Tape? What tape?"

"Oh, just some asbestos tape to keep you from combusting during the casting. Mrs. Timberlake, before I forget, how do you feel about opalescence?"

"*What?*"

"Because I can adjust the copper oxide so that in the right light you'll have a nice green shimmer, but then when seen from another angle, you'll be all blue again."

"Sounds rather pretty." I couldn't believe I'd said that.

"Oh, it will be. Trust me. Now what about the pose?"

"What about it?"

"Well, I can't decide if you should have your arms extended above your head, or not. I promised her a life-size statue, and frankly, Mrs. Timberlake, you're kind of short."

"Sorry about that. By all means, extend my arms."

"I was hoping you'd say that. Now, about the title. Even though my client lives in Miami, she's originally from Minnesota. On account of that—and all the shimmering you'll be doing—I was thinking of *Aurora Borealis*. Either that, or *Northern Nymph*. What do you think?"

"Definitely *Aurora Borealis*." What a lovely name for a shimmering statue.

"Mrs. Timberlake, if you don't mind my saying so, you're going to look right fine up there on that pedestal. This lady, I might add, entertains important folks from all over the world. Politicians, Hollywood celebrities—even royalty from time to time. You're going to be famous. I wouldn't be surprised if someday there's a picture of you—*Aurora Borealis*—in one of them fancy art books on glass."

I felt my heart race. Was it just fear, or was there a tinge of excitement as well? I mean, if my goose—make that pheasant—was going to be cooked anyway, why not have it under glass?

"Left is my best side," I said. "Make sure it's the side that faces the front door of the Miami mansion. And have me smiling. I never look good unless I'm smiling."

Instead of acknowledging my request, Homer Johnson grunted and fell on the floor somewhere near my feet. I could hear the gun he'd been holding skitter across the concrete.

28

"What happened next?"

This was the umpteenth time we'd been asked the question, but since Rob was paying for dinner at Magnolias restaurant on East Bay Street, Mama and I were both happy to answer. Their Mocha Crème Brulee is to die for, an expression I don't use lightly. But dessert tonight, in honor of Bob's fortieth birthday, was, and I quote from the menu: "American Classic Chocolate Cake, served with White Chocolate ice cream in a Benne Seed basket with White Chocolate and Raspberry sauces." That was a dessert worth killing for.

"Well," Mama said—it had somehow managed to become her story—"I flashed him."

I gasped. "Mama, you didn't!"

Mama turned the color of the aforementioned raspberry sauce. "I hit him over the head with a flashlight. The one Abby keeps in her glove box." She turned to me. "You knew good and well that's what I meant."

I winked. "Did I?"

"That's my Abby," Greg said, "always trying to stir up trouble."

At that point Mama, who really does try to stir up

trouble, explained yet again how she'd gotten tired of waiting for me, and thought to look for a flashlight before coming in after me. Although she'd had to abandon her crinolines and crawl under the fence, she hadn't had to use the vent hole. There was a back door to the Quonset hut factory, the same door Homer had used in his hurry to beat us inside, and it was unlocked. After knocking my captor cuckoo, Mama called the police and, of course, got all the credit. What else was new?

When she was quite through embellishing her tale, she sat back and asked for questions. Fortunately, I was able to glare everyone into silent submission—except for Bob, who hadn't been able to tear his eyes off his sister Wendy all evening. But Bob, bless his heart, addressed his remarks to me.

"We're just glad you're safe, Abby," he said. "That Homer Johnson fellow gave me the creeps the first time I met him."

"Then why didn't you say anything?"

"Would you have listened?"

"Well, anyway," I said, moving the show right along, "his name is really Hobart Jackson. Explain, Greg."

My hubby put his arm around me. "Most folks have a hard time giving up their names. More often than not, you'll find that the offender has picked an alias with the same initials."

Rob, who'd been basking in the happy knowledge that his surprise had gone over big with Bob, nodded vigorously. "If I had to pick an alias, it would be Richard Gere. People say I look like him, you know."

"They do not," I said. "You look like James Brolin."

He smiled. "I can live with that. And just so you

know, Abby, you would have made one hell of a good-looking statue."

Bob frowned. "I don't think that's really possible, is it? Making a glass statue out of a person, I mean."

C. J., who'd been mercifully quiet—thanks to the scrumptious food—swallowed her last bite of cake. "Ooh, but it is! At least for fish. Granny Ledbetter bought a glass fish at an auction up in Shelby, and on the way home she dropped it and—"

Mama came to my rescue by patting the big gal's arm. "Sweetie, this isn't going to be indelicate, is it? Because I was thinking of having another piece of cake."

C. J. nodded dolefully. "Actually, it was pretty gross. Granny said she couldn't eat seafood for two weeks."

"C. J!" we protested in unison.

She seemed surprised by our reaction. "Well, I didn't give you any details."

"Whatever are we going to do with you," I groaned.

"You could hire me, Abby."

"I beg your pardon?"

"Well, now that Mr. Johnson—I mean Mr. Jackson—is behind bars, what are you going to do for an assistant?"

"But C. J., dear, you already have a shop up in Charlotte."

"I know, but frankly, Abby, it hasn't done as well as I expected. I'd be more than happy to sell it and come work for you."

"As my *assistant*?"

"I could be your boss, if you insist. And anyway, I've always wanted to live in Charleston."

"You have?"

"Yes. Ooh, Abby, please say yes. Pretty please with sugar on top."

I sighed. "Okay. But C.J., you won't be able to live here."

"Ooh! Abby, you won't be sorry!" C.J. squealed again and gave me a painful hug. If she ever tired of the antique business, there was a career waiting for her in professional wrestling. "And don't worry, Abby, I wouldn't live here if you paid me. No offense, but this place is haunted."

The big galoot was right. Number 7 Squiggle Lane did seem to have its resident spirit. There was probably nothing I could do about that, but I could teach my friend proper etiquette.

"Use the term 'inhabited,'" I said. "Apparition Americans prefer we not use the H word. And good luck finding some place south of Broad that *isn't* inhabited."

"There's a house for sale practically across the street from us," Mama said, butting in as usual. "You could come over all the time."

"Maybe not *all* the time," Greg said, and squeezed my knee under the starched tablecloth. "Maybe you could visit her sometimes, Mozella."

"But—"

"Mama," I said gently, "there are times a married couple needs to be alone."

"TMI!" Mama cried. She was blushing.

C.J.'s joy warmed the cockles of my heart. "Just think, I'm going to be S.O.B. just like you all."

"It's not all it's cracked up to be." Mama sniffed.

"People are people," I said. "There are dysfunctional

families everywhere, even south of Broad."

"That may be true, dear, but even if you hadn't ruined our chances of being accepted into Charleston society—"

"I didn't kill Mrs. Shadbark! Hobart Jackson did!
And anyway, Mama, we never would have been totally
accepted. Not by the old guard."

"That's exactly the point I was trying to make. We
will always be—what is the expression, dear?"

" 'From off.' "

"That's it. But I was thinking, dear. We don't need
the old guard. We've got each other. We can be our
own little society. We can even have secret clubs, if
that's what you want."

C. J. nearly bounced off her seat. "Ooh, I love secret
clubs! Back home in Shelby . . ."

I looked at the faces around the table. Except for
Wendy, the newcomer, each one was precious to me.
With family and friends like these, I was home.

Coming in 2003

Tiles and Tribulations

by Tamar Myers

My best friend., C.J., is deathly afraid of Apparition Americans. Unfortunately, her not-so-new house on Rutledge Avenue has at least one very vocal semi-transparent resident. I told C.J. to expect spirit lingerers when buying a two-hundred-year-old Charleston mansion, but no, the big gal wouldn't listen.

Since I had warned her, I didn't feel it was my responsibility to attend the silly séance she had planned. It's not that I don't believe in Apparition Americans— I do. My own house is haunted, in fact. But mine is a benign presence who contents himself with jangling a bunch of keys and pacing up and down my long, narrow upstairs hallway. C.J.'s unwelcome tenant, on the other hand, wails like the banshee she might well be, and once she even touched C.J. with hands as cold as Popsicles.

So intimidating is C.J.'s spirit, that my friend has had a devil of a time getting a contractor to do some necessary remodeling. Three burly men have quit in the time it takes to change a light bulb, much less revamp a 1940's style kitchen. But really the strange thing is that, since the last workman ran off the job—leaving his tool belt behind—the ghost has taken on the remodeling job herself. I know this sounds bizarre, but C. J. swears it's true. She claims she comes home from work and finds wallboard replaced, paint scraped, tiles caulked, you name it. So far the repairs are remarkably like the ones C. J. wanted the contractor to do, although this has done nothing to ameliorate C. J.'s terror.

At any rate, my objection to the séance had to do with the fact that it was to be conducted, not by some proven expert in the field of the paranormal, but by Madame Woo-Woo. She was a self-styled psychic whose name C. J. had gotten from my mother, who found it advertised in the Yellow Pages. Madame Woo-Woo's ad claimed she was *the* expert in convincing confused Apparition Americans that their jobs on the earth were over, and it was time for them to return to the spirit realm. Madame Woo-Woo claimed a ninety-nine point nine percent success rate, and even offered a money back guarantee. At the prices she charged, she should have given her customers gold plaques certifying that their houses were hant-free, as politically incorrect locals might say.

I wouldn't even have been a part of the Madame Woo-Woo brouhaha, were it not for the fact that the medium had demanded that there be nine warm bodies at the séance, beside her own. She claimed it had something to do with numerology, but frankly, I suspected the woman was after more clients. Besides, it was the last night of *Survivor IV,* and I just had to see who won the million dollars. Yes, I know, I could have taped it, but it just isn't the same thing. Ask any sports enthusiast.

You can imagine my irritation then, when my mother called me at work to put the screws to me.

"Mama," I said, trying to keep in mind the thirty-six hours of agonizing labor she endured to produce me, "I am *not* going to the séance, and that's final."

"Are you afraid, Abby? Is that the problem, dear?"

"Of course I'm not afraid!"

"Abby, darling," Mama said, pouring on the sugar, "C. J. is your best friend. She needs you."

"Mama, the Woo-Woo woman says there has to be nine of us, besides her. Whether or not I show up is a moot point."

"What was that, dear? Did you say something about mooing?"

"Moot," I said as mutely as I could. I own The Den of Antiquity, a thriving antique business on King Street, in Charleston, South Carolina. The aforementioned C. J., besides being my best friend, is my employee. At the moment she was standing just a few yards away, closing a sale on an eighteenth-century highboy.

"Well, it might not be such a moot point after all, Abby, because I've found six others, besides you and I and C. J. We're good to go."

"What six others?"

"Well, for one, there is the real estate agent who sold C. J. the house. Since he didn't warn her about the ghost, he has a responsibility to be there, don't you think?"

"I'll buy that. Who are the remaining five?"

"The Heavenly Hustlers."

"What the hell is the Heavenly Hustlers?" I braced myself for Mama's answer. Last year she ran off to be a nun—they wouldn't accept her—*and* dated a gigolo named Stan. With her track record, I wouldn't be at all surprised if the Heavenly Hustlers turned out to be proselytizing prostitutes.

"Oh, Abby, don't you ever listen to a word I say?"

"Occasionally. But I don't remember anything about Heavenly Hustlers. Mama, you haven't gotten yourself tangled up with some kind of cult, have you?"

"The Hustlers," Mama huffed, "are a group of retired folk, like myself, who aren't content to sit on their duffs all day and twiddle their thumbs. Or do nothing but watch TV. We go to lectures, art exhibits, you name it. Last month we took a basket-weaving class from one of the Gullah women who sells those sweetgrass baskets at The Market. Next week we're driving up together to Brookgreen Gardens, near Myrtle Beach, to see the sculpture collection. In the meantime, we'd be glad to help C.J. out with her séance. Of course we can't all make it on such short notice—there are twelve in our group altogether—but the six of us can."

I sighed, both with relief and resignation. It was a relief that Mama had found a group of like-minded folks to hang out with, but attending C.J.'s séance was gong to be a major bummer. I would program the VCR to tape Survivor IV, but if my husband Greg did anything to screw that up—like substitute a sports video— there would be yet another Apparition American for Madame Woo-Woo to exorcise.

Don't get me wrong; I absolutely adore my new husband, Greg Washburn. A former police detective up in Charlotte, North Carolina, he is now a shrimp boat captain in Mount Pleasant, South Carolina, just outside of Charleston. Greg is both my lover and my best friend, and I am very lucky to have him in my life.

I know just how fortunate I am, because for over twenty years I was married to Buford Timberlake, who was more timber snake than man. That marriage produced two wonderful, but trouble-producing children, who are now both away at college. At any rate, Buford would never have put up with my mother living with us.

"Okay, Mama, I'll be there. What time is it again?"

"Eight, dear. But I was planning for us to get there a few minutes early and help C. J. put together some snacks. Maybe a nice dessert."

"I'm sure your Heavenly Hustlers would appreciate that."

"Oh, it's not for them, dear—although they're welcome to eat some too. It's for Madame Woo-Woo. C. J. says she's very temperamental."

I smiled to myself. C. J. isn't particularly temperamental herself, but she is a radish or two short of a relish tray.

"Yeah, well, getting there early is probably a good idea in any case. I want to check under the table to make sure Madame Woo-Woo hasn't wired it."

There was a pause, which meant Mama was thinking—always a dangerous situation. A wise Abby would have gotten off the line while the getting was good. Alack, I was too well-mannered to hang up on Mama.

"What will you being wearing tonight?" she finally asked.

"Clothes." Good manners did not preclude sarcasm.

Mama sighed dramatically. "I'm sure what you have on is fine, dear."

I wrinkled my nose at the phone receiver. I will always be inappropriately dressed to Mama. She is caught in a 1950s time warp and wears cinch-waist dresses with full-circle skirts puffed up by yards of starched crinolines. Standing at five feet even, sans patent leather pumps, she looks like a miniature, and very well-preserved, version of June Cleaver. Mama even wears a single strand of pearls, a gift my father gave her the year he died. That the beads outlasted even my first marriage is a wonder, given the fact that Mama never takes them off—not even to shower.

"I'm wearing jeans," I said. "If Madame Woo-Woo doesn't like it, she can lump it."

"It wasn't the psychic I was think about," Mama said. "It's C. J.'s ghost."

"What? Apparition Americans are into fashion?"

"C. J. has seen the ghost twice, Abby, and both times she was wearing antebellum clothes. So that's how the Heavenly Hustlers and I will be dressing. We want to make C. J.'s ghost feel comfortable."

"And C. J.?" I said the girl's name a mite too loud and she glanced my way.

"She's wearing a hoop skirt as well."

"Mama, where did y'all get clothes like that on such short notice?"

"From Ella Nolte. She's one of the Hustler's. She's also a mystery writer and has connections with the theater department at the College of Charleston."

"Ella Nolte? I've never heard of her."

"That's because you don't read mysteries, dear."

"I don't read fiction altogether, Mama. I mean,

what's the point? It's all made up." I was only pulling her leg, and Mama knew it.

"So how about it, Abby, are you game?"

"I'm game," I growled. Then I gasped. My worst nightmare had just walked through the door of my shop.

"Abby, what is it?"

"It's Buford!"

"Buford who?"

"*The* Buford, Mama. My ex."

"Hide!" Mama hung up her phone.

I glanced around my shop. There are plenty of places to hide in an antique store, especially given my size. I am four feet, nine inches in my stocking feet, and tip the scale at one hundred pounds the day after New Year's. I could easily fit into an armoire, even a dresser drawer.

Then it hit me. Buford lived all the way up in Charlotte. His presence down here in Charleston could mean only one thing.

"What happened!" I cried. I was on Buford like white on rice. He didn't even see me coming.

"Abby!"

"Is it Charlie? Is it Susan? Oh my God, there's been an accident, hasn't there? How bad is it?"

Buford took a step back. "Relax, Abby, it's not the kids."

"Then what *is* it?" I admit to living in perpetual fear that one, or both, of my two children will be involved in a horrible car wreck. As I've told them both a million times, it isn't their driving that worries me, but "others'."

Buford regarded me under hooded lids. His had

once been a handsome face, which in recent years had become fleshy.

"I'm on vacation, Abby."

"Right. And I'm Julia Roberts. Pleased to meet you."

Who was he trying to kid? Buford wouldn't know what vacation was if it sneaked up behind him and bit him on the butt. The man never quit moving; before he packed on the extra weight, he used to put his socks on while walking.

Our honeymoon was a three-day cruise to the Bahamas and Buford jumped ship at the end of the first day, so he could get back to work. And just in case you're wondering, *that* was quick was well. I didn't even warrant a "wham, bam, thank you, ma'am." Just a wham.

Buford smiled, his jowls retreating slowly. "I really am on vacation, Abby. After Tweetie died," he said, referring to his second wife, "I decided to take some time off and smell the roses."

"Un-hunh."

"I know you don't believe me, but it's true. The kids—particularly Susan—kind of pushed this trip on me. By the way, I saw both kids this morning, and they're doing fine."

So that was it! With their stepmother out of the picture, the kids figured they could maneuver their daddy and I into a reconciliation. I could understand their desire—even with Buford as one of the players—but it wasn't going to happen. Dr. Laura and John Ashcroft would dance naked together in Times Square before I hitched up with the timber snake. Heck, I'd hitch up

with Laura or John, before I got back together with Buford.

"It isn't going to happen," I said calmly.

"What's that?"

"The kids ploy. I'm not falling for it."

He frowned for a moment, then his florid face shone
with enlightenment. "Ah, so that's what you're thinking. No offense, Abby, but I'm not interested in a relationship either."

"You're not?"

"You sound disappointed, Abby."

"I am most certainly *not* disappointed! I'm merely
surprised." While I was telling the truth, I must admit
that one can be flattered even by unwanted attention.

"Well, here I am. I've got four days at my disposal.
Do you have any recommendations—as regards sight-
seeing, I mean."

"The Charleston Visitor's Center is at 375 Meeting
Street. They can tell you a lot more than I can."

A divorce lawyer by profession, Buford is not easily dismissed. "I was planning to make them my next
stop. I just thought you might have some personal favorites. In particular, I was wondering about restaurants. I was hoping we could do lunch. My treat, of
course."

Charleston is, without a doubt, the most charming
city in the country. The beauty of its architecture and
gardens is famous worldwide. Since the majority of
her visitors have discerning tastes, it is no surprise that
the city is home to some of the finest restaurants in
North America.

"Do I get to choose the restaurant?"

Buford chuckled. "Absolutely."

"How about lunch tomorrow, one o'clock, Magnolias Restaurant?" I was already planning my selections. For the first time I was going to have no compunctions about ordering anything I wanted on the menu. Maybe even everything. After all, when Buford dumped me in favor of Tweetie—a woman half my age and ninety percent silicone—he left me in a financial bind.

Actually, that's an understatement. Buford was not just plugged into the good old boy system, he had more connections than a box of Tinker Toys. He ended up with the house, the cars, custody of our seventeen-year-old son, and even the family dog. All I got to keep were my clothes—only because they didn't fit Tweetie—and three thousand dollars I'd managed to squirrel away into a personal account.

"Sounds good," Buford said.

Just wait until he saw the bill.

C. J. waltzed over to me the second the shop door closed on Buford's expanding bottom. "Ooh, Abby, I'm so proud of you!"

I smiled nonchalantly. "Thanks. I'm pretty proud of myself. The old Abby would have picked up that Civil War sword over there, and stuck it where the sun doesn't shine. Or better yet—"

"No, Abby. I meant I'm proud of you for agreeing to come to my séance tonight. I know how afraid you are of ghosts."

"*Me*? You're the one who—hey, wait a minute, how did you know I agreed to come?"

"I heard you talking to your mama. Besides, Madame Woo-Woo told me you'd resist coming at first, but that you'd finally give in."

"She did?"

"Well, she didn't say *you*—not exactly, at any rate. But she did say there would be skeptics whose minds would be changed."

"Frankly, dear, that sounds a little vague to me. I read somewhere that psychics and fortunetellers are often very skilled at giving answers that can be interpreted a variety of ways. The article also said they tend to ask leading questions. In other words, they've got great powers of observation, and good people skills, but they're not privy to any more information than the rest of us."

"Ooh, Abby, Madame Woo-Woo knows everything."

"C. J., dear, just how well did you research this Madame Woo-Woo? Did you check her references?"

She looked like a sheep that had been given the task of cloning a human. She scratched her head, and then looked at the door, as if longing for customers to walk through.

"Well?" I demanded. "Did you at least ask to speak to someone—anyone—who's hosted a séance for her before?"

C. J. hung her head. "No," she said in a tiny voice.

"And what about this group—the Heavenly Hustlers—that Mama rounded up. What do you know about them?"

"I love your Mama, Abby. Any friends of hers, are friends of mine."

"That's very generous of you," I said, feeling the

need to ease up. "But let's just both be careful, shall we? Mama has a tendency to hook up with some real characters. And as for Madame Woo-Woo, neither of us wants to be a seer's sucker, now do we?" I laughed pleasantly at my little joke.

C. J. shook her head vigorously. "Cousin Alvin's fiancée up in Shelby invented seersucker, and it hurt something awful."

I raised my right eyebrow.

"Please," I said. "Tell me all."

"Well, she was wearing a dress made out of regular material, you see. Something smooth like silk or nylon, but I forget which. Anyway, she was running late to church one Sunday and she noticed that her dress had a wrinkle in the skirt. So Brenda—that's Alvin's fiancee's name—took the steam iron and started ironing out the wrinkle. Only she didn't take the dress off first, see? And she had a whole lot of cellulite—" C. J. hung her head so low her chin rested against her chest. "Abby, I just made that up—about Cousin Alvin's wife inventing seersucker, I mean. But she really does have a lot of cellulite."

"So you don't know who invented seersucker?"

"I'm afraid not, Abby. But according to *Webster's* the word seersucker has been part of the English language since 1722. It comes originally from the Persian phrase *shir-o-shakar,* and literally means 'milk and sugar.'"

It didn't surprise me that my friend would know the dictionary definition of the word. After all, she'd memorized the book her senior year in high school, in preparation for college. The collegiate version, of course. It did surprise me, however, that C. J. backed out of one of her Shelby stories. That just wasn't like her.

"C. J., dear, is something wrong? Just a minute ago you came bounding over to me like a gazelle on speed, and now you seem to have lost your spunk."

"Abby, you remember how that voodoo priestess in Savannah said I had the second sight?"

"Diamond? C. J., she wasn't exactly a voodoo priestess. She was a retired school teacher who liked to entertain tourists."

"But she said I had the second sight, Abby, and you know I do."

"Then why the need to hire a psychic?" I asked gently.

"Ooh, Abby, you can be so silly sometimes. Just because I have the second sight doesn't mean I can talk to ghosts."

"You're quite right. But you still haven't answered my question. What's wrong?"

"I was getting to that, Abby. My second sight tells me that something horrible is going to happen at my house tonight."

The shiver that ran up my spine didn't stop there. It made it all the way up to my scalp where it danced a rousing polka.

"So why not cancel, C. J.?"

The big gal did her best to disguise her feelings, but there was no mistaking the pity in her eyes. "Because it's destiny, Abby. There's nothing I can do to stop what's going to happen."

"We'll just see about that," I said.